Palisades.
Pure Romance.

FICTION THAT FEATURES CREDIBLE CHARACTERS AND

ENTERTAINING PLOT LINES, WHILE CONTINUING TO UPHOLD

STRONG CHRISTIAN VALUES. FROM HIGH ADVENTURE

TO TENDER STORIES OF THE HEART, EACH PALISADES

ROMANCE IS AN UNDILUTED STORY OF LOVE,

FROM BEGINNING TO END!

A MOTHER'S LOVE

Lisa Tawn Bergren
Constance Colson
Amanda MacLean

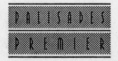

MULTNOMAH BOOKS
SISTERS, OREGON

A MOTHER'S LOVE
published by Palisades
a part of the Questar publishing family

© 1997 Sand Castles by Lisa Tawn Bergren
© 1997 A Mother's Miracle by Constance Colson
© 1997 Legacy of Love by Amanda MacLean

International Standard Book Number: 1-57673-106-5

Cover photo by Kathleen Francour
©1997 Kathleen Francour, Carefree, AZ All Rights Reserved
Cover design by Catherine Bergstrom
Edited by Jennifer Brooks and Shari MacDonald

Printed in the United States of America

For information:
QUESTAR PUBLISHERS, INC.
POST OFFICE BOX 1720
SISTERS, OREGON 97759

Library of Congress Cataloging--in--Publication Data
Bergren, Lisa Tawn. A mother's love/by Lisa Tawn Bergren, Constance Colson, Amanda MacLean. p.cm. Contents: A mother's miracle/Constance Colson--Legacy of love/Amanda MacLean--Sand castles/Lisa Tawn Bergren.
ISBN 1-57673-106-5 (alk. paper) 1. Mothers--Fiction. 2. American fiction--Women authors. 3. American fiction--20th century. 4. Christian fiction, American. 5. Domestic fiction, American. 6. Mother and child--Fiction. 7. Motherhood--Fiction. I. Colson, Constance. II. MacLean, Amanda. III. Title.
PS648.M59B47 1997 97-480 813'.540803520431'082--dc21 CIP

97 98 99 00 01 02 03 — 10 9 8 7 6 5 4 3 2 1

FROM LISA TAWN BERGREN:

To my mother Karen,
loving mom and faithful friend.

FROM CONSTANCE COLSON:

In loving memory of Jeff
and the other dear ones we miss so much.

I long for heaven more as those I love go on before.

And with countless thanks
to my husband, Mark,
whom I am so blessed to yet have and hold.

FROM AMANDA MACLEAN:

To my daughters, Melinda and Amy,
and to my mother, Elizabeth,
in celebration of "a mother's love,"
God's precious gift to each generation.

SAND CASTLES

by

Lisa Tawn Bergren

1

Matthew Morgan perused the menu and, for the second time, peeked over the top of it at his brooding five-year-old daughter, Hope. It was Mother's Day, and despite his best efforts to get around it, the precocious girl knew what she was missing. Or, more specifically, whom she was missing.

The waitress, the quintessential southern-California blonde, came and asked if they were ready to order.

"I'll have the special," Matt said.

"Good choice," the waitress said as she wrote. "I think it looks, like, *majorly* delicious."

"Great," Matt said, not truly caring what he ate today. Hope wasn't the only one who missed Beth. Mourning her death for almost two years had not filled in the gaping hole she had left in their lives. For him, the pain had lessened and to a great extent, the grief subsided. But he was at a loss in trying to be both mother and father to his little girl.

"What do you think, pumpkin?" he asked Hope. "What about the chicken picatta? You always like that."

Hope continued to peruse the menu as if she could read every word. "Umm. Okay."

The waitress gave the girl a sunny smile, obviously feeling bad for anyone not out with his or her mom that night. "Perfect. Do you two want our house special for the dressing on your salads?"

"Which is…?" Matt asked.

"Balsamic garlic. We also have a terrific orange vinaigrette."

"Do you have Thousand Island?" Hope asked.

"I don't know. I could try and, you know, rustle up some somewhere."

"And I'm afraid I'm pretty old-fashioned when it comes to dressings," Matt said apologetically. "Is there a bottle of ranch somewhere back there too?"

"Probably," the waitress said with a smile. Now he was feeling like the object of her pity. He studied her as she left them and then glanced around. Was he just imagining it? Or were all the other families looking at them and wondering where the mother in their family was? He told himself he was just being paranoid and watched as Hope picked out a sugar packet and popped it in her mouth.

"Now, Hope," he began, "I've told you not to do that."

"Whaa?" He managed to make out her grumbled challenge around a mouth full of sugar and paper.

"Because it's disgusting and rude. Now spit it out, please."

She frowned down at the table, then let the collapsed sugar packet fall off her tongue with all the grace of a cat ridding itself of a hairball.

Matt grimaced and glanced around to see if they had offended anyone. Fortunately, everybody else appeared to be otherwise involved. He sighed deeply. Fatherhood took more patience than he had ever expected. Especially on Mother's Day. He took a sip of his water and watched as his daughter reached for another sugar packet.

"Hope—"

"What? I'm not putting it in my mouth," she said saucily, tearing open the packet and pouring it into her water.

"Hope Emily—"

"What?" she repeated. "I can't help it. The water tastes bad here. I want to go home to the ranch."

Matt thought longingly of their beloved ranch in Montana and halfway considered the idea but then dismissed it. "We'll be back soon enough. Besides, this is supposed to be a vacation. Your idea, if I remember right. We'll be heading back on the plane before you know it."

"I want to go now."

Their discussion was interrupted by the waitress, who placed their salads in front of them with a "Here you go," then disappeared again. Matt bowed his head to say grace and peeked at Hope to make sure she had done the same. Thankfully, she had. "Father, thank you for this food and this day to remember Beth by. Thank you for the time we had with her, and we ask that you be with us as we continue on without her. Amen."

Hope did not join in with her customary "amen" but instead picked up a piece of arugula from her bed of European salad greens. "I hate this stuff. I wish I could just get a normal salad."

Matt hid a grin by taking a huge bite of salad. Beth had expanded his limited vegetable-eating repertoire during their brief years together, but in his opinion, what the population of southern California deemed edible was bordering on ridiculous. Still, he ate it. It didn't taste half bad most of the time, and at least he wasn't cooking.

"Would you please pass the butter?" Hope asked in her best adult imitation.

"Sure," he said, hiding another tiny smile. *Oh Beth, she's growing up so fast. And looking more like you all the time.* He watched as his daughter stabbed a tiny, hard butter floret and tried to spread it on her roll. Giving up, she popped the whole thing in her mouth and followed it with a French-roll chaser. This time Matt snorted, unable to conceal his amusement.

"What?" she asked.

"Nothing," he said with a smile. "I just always wrestle with those little butter doo-dads myself." He cleared his throat. This was as good a time as any to broach the subject. He felt it was his responsibility to check with her once in a while to see what was going on in her little head. If he could get that far.

"Honey?"

"Yeah?"

"Honey, how are you feeling about your mama today? Are you missing her?"

"I don't know," Hope said noncommittally. She reached for another butter floret.

"I bet you miss her more today than most, huh?"

"I don't know." She bit into her roll, avoiding his gaze.

"Well, I know I miss her. It just doesn't seem like there should even be a Mother's Day if your mom isn't around to enjoy it with you. If she were here, she'd be telling you to put that butter on your plate, break off a chunk, and then spread it on your roll."

Hope gave him her best pained expression, but he went on. "And you'd probably give her a handmade card, and she'd love it. She loved you so much. You remember, don't you?"

The little girl barely nodded. She was looking down at her plate, and her short brown hair covered most of her face. Staring at her chocolate-colored locks, Matt recognized for the first time that a slight wave like Beth's was emerging.

After a moment, she spoke. "I can barely remember what she looks like. I mean, I see her pictures and what she looks like on video, but I don't really remember myself."

Matt swallowed hard. He knew the feeling of an image that

was beginning to fade, the panic of losing the hard-edged facts of a person's being, as the three-dimensional faded into two. "That's okay, honey," he reassured her. He cast about for the right words. "Your heart kinda paints a picture of people you love, so that even though you can't remember what someone looks like on the *outside*, you remember how much you loved them on the *inside*. You remember that about your mama, don't you?"

"I guess," Hope said. She didn't look at him as the waitress removed their salad plates to make room for their entrees.

By the time they finished their dinner, Matt felt exhausted but relieved. As they topped off their meal with ice-cream sundaes, they actually laughed together, remembering how Beth had loved homemade ice cream and how when she first tried it, she put the rock salt inside the metal can instead of outside with the ice.

Hand in hand, they crossed the street to their eight-story condominium building, which faced busy Pacific Coast Highway on the east and the glorious Pacific Ocean on the west. He had chosen the spot because he was uncomfortable with the idea of Hope's living in a hotel for the entire length of their three-week stay. At least here, there was some semblance of hominess.

Matt was just thinking about relaxing with a good book and a cup of decaf on the deck when they entered the elevator foyer. There, in front of the one working lift, was a couple in the midst of a heated conversation. Feeling uncomfortable, Matt led Hope around the pair and pressed the button, mentally begging the sluggish elevator to speed its way down for once.

"Look," the woman said, her voice betraying her agitation. "For the last time, our date ends here. I'm sorry if you got a different impression."

Mercifully, the elevator dinged and the doors slid open. Matt quickly made his way in with Hope, then turned to hold the door for the woman. She obviously needed an escape. But when he looked up again, her much larger date had grasped her arm. He was flushed from collar to jaw line. The guy was obviously ticked.

"Ma'am?" Matt intervened gently. "Goin' up?"

"I am. Good night and good-bye, Jack. I think we've had our first and only date." She nodded down at his hand as if cueing him to let her go. Jack glanced furiously from her to Matt, who still patiently waited. Inside, Matt felt every nerve taut with unspent energy. As he stood there, forcing a disinterested look, he admitted to himself that pounding the guy would just be a convenient excuse to get rid of some frustration. *Help me out, Father. Give me control.*

Fortunately, Jack let the woman go, and she entered the elevator without another word. The doors slid shut with what seemed to the occupants a leisurely speed, finally cutting off their last view of Jack's sulking back as he turned and walked away.

Matt and Hope's elevator companion collapsed against the elevator wall. "Thank you. I appreciate it that you waited for me." She looked into Matt's eyes for a brief moment, her look telling him the story that she could not repeat in front of a child. It struck him that she was pretty, in an unconventional sort of way. The color of her eyes was a brilliant green, the exact color of birch leaves submerged under the Kootenai River, he mused. Uncommon.

"Was that your boyfriend?" Hope asked bluntly, staring up at her.

"No way."

"Did he take you out on a date?"

"Hope—"

"If you could call it that," the woman said, clearly amused. "Jack was my diversion for the night because my mom's on a cruise and I was missing her. It was a bad choice. I'm Ella O'Donnell," she said, introducing herself, "and I'm on the sixth floor."

"Hmm?" Matt asked, not connecting with her.

"Sixth floor. The button."

"Oh!" Matt said, embarrassed. *Smooth, Morgan. Way to go.* He quickly pushed numbers four and six. The elevator gave a little start and moved upward.

"You two new neighbors?" Ella asked.

"Temporary visitors," Matt said, nodding at the illuminated fourth floor sign as it dinged. "This is where we get off."

"Oh, well, thanks. It was nice meeting you. Should I just call you my knight in shining armor and his short attendant?"

Matt grinned as they exited, then looked back. She really was pretty. All eyes and a big, toothy grin that left a person with no choice but to join her in a smile. He found his voice as the door shut. "We're Matt and Hope."

"Nice to meet—" The door clamped shut, muffling the rest of her sentence.

The two paused for a second, then were silent as they walked to their condominium's door. "Did she look like Momma, Daddy?"

"Wha—no. You know that, Hope. Your mom had short brown hair and big brown eyes. That lady was much taller. I mean, her hair was longer. Different colored eyes." He fumbled with the key in the lock and then rushed on. "Not as pretty as your mom," he added lamely. The lock clicked, and the bolt slid open at last.

Matt recognized his last comment as a lie as his daughter walked behind him, directly into her room. Ella was every bit as pretty as Beth, just in a different way. And his comment had rushed out because for the first time in a long time, he felt guilty for looking at another woman. He pushed the guilt away. *Beth told me to look for love again.* But it seemed too soon, somehow. Like he was being unfaithful.

Moments later, Hope appeared in the kitchen doorway as he brewed himself a cup of decaf. "I wasn't talking about Ella's hair. I meant she looked like Mama. There was something about her…something about the way she looked at me that reminded me."

Matt managed to give her a nod, slightly sticking out his lower lip as he thought about what she said. Now that she had mentioned it, there *was* a familiar spark, something that reminded him of Beth. He pressed the Mr. Coffee "on" button and listened as the water started to percolate.

"You want to read with me out on the deck, pumpkin?"

"Yeah!" She ran off to her room to pick up the latest in her series of early-reader books about girls and their horses. Mostly, she just liked to look at the pictures.

"Look at this one, Dad," she said, pointing to her book beside him. "It looks just like the palomino we saw today up the beach."

Matthew nodded and smiled. "Do you want to go riding someday, sweetheart? I think the stable offices are just up the road."

"Maybe," she said with a shrug, moving away from him. "I'd rather just go home and ride Cookie." She settled into the lounge chair beside him on their tiny deck and looked over at him seriously. "Dad, this really wasn't a *bad* Mother's Day. Last year was worse."

"I'm glad, pumpkin," he said, reaching over to ruffle her hair, deciding to take her comment as a compliment. Maybe this whole California thing was not such a bad idea for an old Montana cowhand. At home it had seemed far-fetched—especially as things got busier at the ranch—but Hope had grabbed the idea of going to the beach and run with it. He'd almost said no to her, but then their friend Rachel had started in. "Matthew Morgan," she had said, pointing her finger and jabbing him in the chest. "You have a competent foreman, an able housekeeper and cook, and an able accountant. Go. It's the first time I've seen your kid so excited about something since her mom died. Do it for her. For yourself. You need some time to find that spark again."

"Spark?" he asked blankly.

"Yes. Spark. You're moping. Go away and find what God has in store for the rest of your life. Your daughter needs you. Not to mention a trip to Disneyland."

Rachel and Reyne, his deceased wife's best friends, had harassed him until he agreed. Matt had to admit that the extreme change of scenery *had* lifted his spirits, especially over Mother's Day.

"Hey, look at that," he said to his daughter. "The sun is going down for the night." And together they watched as the last tiny bit of the sun edged its way into the water and disappeared.

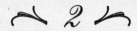

Two days later, Matt agreed to help his daughter build a long-promised sand castle. It was late morning, and the sun was just beginning to get hot when Ella approached and examined their work, obviously just coming in from a walk on the beach.

"My temporary neighbors!" she greeted them enthusiastically. "You call that a sand castle? Where are you from, Idaho?"

"Close," Matt said, looking apologetically at the castle and his daughter. "Montana. I'm afraid I haven't had much experience in castle architecture."

"I don't think it's so bad," Hope said defensively.

"Well, no. It isn't bad. You need more water. Hold on, I'll go get you my bucket. Hey, where's your mom? Mom's are usually great with castles. Much better than dads…sorry, Dad." She grinned at Matt, then frowned slightly at the look on his face.

"My mom died of cancer," Hope said, turning back to her digging.

"I—I'm sorry, honey. I never thought…. Hold on. I'll be right back."

Matt watched as she walked away, noting legs that were

tanned even this early in the season. Five minutes later, Ella was back. She briefly smiled into Matt's eyes as she handed him a trowel and Hope a bucket. "You can return them to me anytime. I'm in #642."

With that she started to back away. "Gotta run, neighbors," she said cheerfully. "My shift starts at noon." Ella pointed at Hope. "You watch out for sand elves."

"Sand elves?" Hope said doubtfully.

"You haven't heard of them? If you start a sand castle and leave it out overnight, they'll either level it or build on it, depending on how good they think it is."

Life as an oncology nurse was rarely easy, but some days were more horrific than others, Ella reflected. Like today. Sitting in the darkroom after reviewing X rays with the oncologist, Ella could not find the strength to move. It seemed impossible that yet another loving, otherwise healthy and happy woman of faith was about to die.

Cheryl Montane was not especially beautiful, but Ella had learned enough from their brief conversation to know that she was gorgeous from the inside out. She had arrived for a routine mammogram that had been put off for a few years—"Kids, a move, you know," she explained uneasily—and was immediately referred by her doctor to the oncologist on call. The staff had wasted no time, but they were already too late. Ella could see it like a death sentence was written across the X rays, spelling it out that this young mother had not long to live. Her children…her husband… Images of Cheryl holding tightly to her husband's hand flashed through Ella's mind. What would he do without her? *God, God, where are you? How can you let this happen over and over?*

"Can I have a minute? I don't know what's wrong," she

managed to say to Dr. Anders's back as he continued staring at the films. Ella felt strangled by sudden tears. She was expected to serve as moral support while Dr. Anders confirmed the Montanes' worst fears.

Dr. Anders searched her eyes for a brief moment before curtly nodding. "I need to make a phone call. I'll come back for you in a minute."

Ella nodded as she turned away, unable to stop the tears and not wanting to cry in front of a doctor. Even the most sentimental ones rarely cried. They saw too many tough cases to break down over each one. Usually she was right with them. Wasn't she the one patients relied upon to spread good cheer with an occasional doctor joke? The one who always had a smile at the ready and a word of hope to share? Not today. Today, suddenly, it was all too much.

She sank to a bench and stared bleakly at the X rays above her. Oh, why, why did it have to be this young mother? Why anyone? Why couldn't they find the cure? *Why, Father? Why?*

After several moments, the flood of tears was over, and Ella took a few deep breaths before rising and walking to the tiny sink to splash her face. She was just toweling off when Dr. Anders ducked his head back in. "Ella? Ready?" He averted his gaze, clearly uncomfortable with tears.

"Yes," she said, forcing a small smile. She pulled the films as she walked by, placing them in a large manila folder and handing them to the doctor as they walked down the hall to Cheryl's room.

She was resting as they entered, but she opened her eyes as soon as the door squeaked. Her husband set aside his book and stood to take her hand. Both looked like they knew what was coming. Ella moved to the bedside and took Cheryl's other hand as Dr. Anders spoke. She hoped her expression was encouraging.

"Cheryl, Gene," Dr. Anders said, nodding to the Montanes in greeting. "I'm afraid we have bad news." He moved to the mini light screen in the room and slid the films up against it as he told about the war going on inside Cheryl's body. Briskly, he noted where the cancer cells had metastasized deep inside her breast, pointing out the huge tumor, and dropped his tone a notch in explaining that there was no reason to operate. He clipped up the second set of films and pointed out the tumors in her lungs and evidence of bone cancer. There was no reason to try radiation therapy or any other. The cancer was too fast, too effective at its executionary mission. She had months, maybe weeks left to live.

The Montanes nodded numbly, taking each word Dr. Anders uttered as if bearing physical blows. Ella swallowed hard, trying to concentrate on the doctor's words so she could answer the Montanes' questions after he left. Patients always had questions a bit later, after the diagnosis had sunk in. But Ella could not concentrate. The doctor's well-meaning words were a monotone drone to her, and she was unable to make sense of them. All she could think of was one more motherless, wifeless family, robbed by cancer. The Big C, patients called it. Briefly, she thought of her neighbors on the beach. Had they gone through a similar moment?

Dr. Anders reached past Ella and gave Cheryl's forearm a gentle, perfunctory squeeze. "I'm sorry," he said lightly. "Let us know if we can do anything." With that, he walked out, leaving Ella to pick up the pieces as usual. Slowly, she dragged her eyes to meet Cheryl's, then Gene's. "I'm sorry," she said gently, sitting down on the bed beside Cheryl. Ella waited for a moment, and when neither one of them spoke, asked, "Do you have any questions for me? Or would you like me to give you some time?"

Gene nodded and glanced at his wife's face. "If you wouldn't mind—"

"Not at all," Ella said soberly. "I'll check back in with you in a bit, and we can go over your immediate plans." She swallowed against the knot in her throat and forced a small smile. "You won't be alone in this."

"Thanks, Ella," Cheryl said, looking as though in a fog.

Ella left the room and walked straight to the hospital chapel, ignoring the stack of paperwork and calls to be answered. She needed a break, a chance to breathe. Maybe a talk with the chaplain. In minutes she was sighing in relief as the heavy, soundproof wooden doors of the chapel thumped shut behind her. Cued by a bell in his office, Father Frank ducked his head in. "Ella!" he said, obviously glad to see her. "What can I do for you?"

"Maybe a prayer or two, Frank," she said quietly. Her friend sobered as he saw her expression and noted her tone. Ella sat down in a pew and stared up at the beautiful stained-glass window above the chapel altar. It depicted Jesus as a shepherd, tenderly holding his lost lamb and surrounded by others.

"Where is he?" she asked Frank in an accusatory voice, pointing her finger at the glass.

"Jesus? Why he's everywhere. Here, right now. You know that, Ella. You tell your patients every time they give you half a chance."

"I know that. I mean, where is he now? When a young mother of two down the hall is dying? Where are his miracles now?"

Frank sadly returned her look. "Hit a wall, Ella?"

"No," she said in irritation. "I'm just frustrated! I spend all this time, spreading the gospel, the Good News, and yet where is he? We need a miracle here. Make that *miracles*. Tonight. In about five different rooms on this ward."

Frank rose and paced, mulling over her words. She was aware that she had taken him by surprise. Ella had been voted "Most Eligible for Candy Striper" by her fellow nurses last Christmas because of her seemingly endless reserve of energy and smiles.

"You know God moves when he chooses to. There seems to

be no formula. It's a mystery that we have to accept and something we need to constantly pray will be done again. How about Josephine?"

Ella's mind raced as she remembered the sprite of a woman miraculously cured overnight of a cancer as widespread as Cheryl's. "Yeah, but she was one of a thousand women I can think of who prayed for healing."

"Still, Ella. Remember, we still have to pray that it will happen again. For each and every person in your ward. And others," he added softly, reminding her that she was not the only one who dealt with death, day in and day out.

Ella sighed. "I'm sorry, Frank. I'm just dumping. I know you're right. I'm just beat, you know? Even the happiest nurse in the cancer ward gets down once in a while."

Frank sat down beside her and took her hand in brotherly fashion. "It's understandable. I worry about you sometimes. Worry that you don't dump enough."

Ella smiled ruefully. "And who do you get to dump on? You have to get as tired as I do of seeing good people die."

"The Shepherd," Frank said, nodding at the window. "He probably hears more of it than he wants to. In fact, I know he does. But he understands. And venting keeps me in a place where I can serve others faithfully."

Ella glanced at the ground, understanding his point.

"Ella," he said gently, "you need to let go of some of the pressure. More often. Before you break. You're an excellent nurse. Your patients need you. But you need to be healthy in order to serve the sick."

She nodded and squeezed his hand. "Will you pray with me, my friend?" she asked.

"With pleasure."

⌒⌒⌒⌒⌒

That night another patient in Ella's ward died. Her name was Jana. Ella had known her for months. The woman left behind her grieving husband of twenty years and three children in their teens. Ella barely made it to the car before she gave way to the sobs that racked her body. She felt choked with grief and found it difficult to breathe. Then she thought again of her neighbors, Matt and Hope. They too had said good-bye to someone dear to them. How long ago? she wondered. It made her grieve all over again. *Help me understand, Father. Help me to be strong. To show people the hope of you. Help me, Father.*

Ella suddenly remembered the castle and her admonition to Hope to watch out for sand elves. This was one way she could bring a smile to someone's face. It would be like magic to the little girl when she discovered it the next morning.

She wiped her eyes and took a few deep breaths, then turned the key in the ignition. It never failed to amaze her when her old Honda Civic continued to start after three hundred thousand miles. "We oughtta be in a commercial, Jeffrey," she said, patting the cracked dashboard. "Now take me home. We have work to do."

It was after one in the morning when she reached the condo, but Ella was unfazed. Her most common shift was noon to midnight, so she had become accustomed to living as a night owl, often sleeping in until ten. She hurried to her bedroom and changed into sweats, then rummaged through her kitchen cupboards and recycling bin for castle-building supplies. She emerged minutes later with several cans of varying sizes, a pie server, a small knife and a larger one, loaf pans, and another bucket. At the last moment, she reached out for her plant sprinkler.

Ella could barely get the door closed and locked, her hands were so full. But she was all smiles for the first time that day. "Sand elfdom, here I come," she mumbled, wondering if Jana, her patient and friend, was looking down from heaven with a smile. The thought of it pulled the corners of her lips even higher. She was home. At peace. And whole again.

Dear Jesus, Ella prayed as the elevator sank toward the lobby. *Please be with Jana's family. And help others to reach out to them as I'm reaching out to Matt and Hope now.*

~ 3 ~

The next morning, Matt awoke to his five-year-old jumping on his bed. She was dressed in her customary jeans, boots, and western shirt, and judging from the sand all over her pant legs, had already been to the beach. "Now Hope, I told you not to go out alone—"

"Dad! You have to see it!" She was squealing and still jumping all around him, bouncing on the bed. "Wait 'til you see it! It's a...a miracle!"

Matt was feeling a bit cross with her disobeying him and then bouncing all around on the bed, but her words disrupted all sense of order in his head. A five-year-old using the word *miracle*. "What, pumpkin?" he asked her with a grin, sitting up and running his hands through his hair. "What's a miracle?"

"The castle! The castle! The castle!" she said gleefully, springing off the bed to the floor beside it. "Come on! Come see it!"

"The sand castle?"

"Yes, Dad! The sand castle! Wait'll you see it!"

He laughed and lowered his eyebrows at her as if she were crazy, but he obediently got up and began to dress. "Let me just get some coffee—"

"No, Dad! Now! Somebody might tear it down! You have to see it *now!*"

"All right, all right," he said in a fatherly tone. He laughed as he looked up and watched Hope bounce up and down like a personified Tigger to his morninglike Eeyore. "This really must be something."

"COME ON!" She was getting impatient as he pulled on his cowboy boots and tucked them under his jeans.

"I'm *coming.*"

She grabbed his hand and dragged him along, making him feel like a lumbering, reluctant elephant behind its trainer. He headed toward the elevator, but Hope insisted it would take too long. They took the stairs.

Minutes later, they reached the sand dunes slightly out of breath. Matt's eyes widened in astonishment. Their castle— what yesterday had been three feet-wide mounds with finger holes for windows—had been expanded into a six-feet-wide, three-feet-high deluxe castle, complete with parapets and towers and guard walls. There were even bricks drawn into the walls and a tiny drawbridge over the moat.

Gleefully, Hope asked, "Do you think it was really sand elves or just Ella?"

"Maybe both," Matt said with a smile. His eyes scanned the sixth floor for any sign of her, but he spotted nothing.

"What do you think this is for?" Hope asked, holding up a small red plastic spritzer. Just then a small corner of the wall gave way.

"I bet it's to keep it wet. It seems that as the sand dries out, it crumbles."

Hope immediately headed to the water's edge to fill the bottle, then came back and began spritzing. After she had given the castle a thorough once-over, she looked at Matt. "Let's build a surrounding village, okay?"

~ ~ ~ ~ ~

Later that night, when Hope was watching television, Matt walked to the front door. "I'm just going to run to Ella's and return this," he said, holding up the bucket. He looked at his little girl and smiled. She was exhausted after a full day on the beach. "Don't let anyone in who comes to the door unless it's me, okay? I'll be back in five minutes."

"Okay. Ask her if she did the castle or if there's really sand elves."

"Okay." Matt turned and closed the door, locking the dead bolt behind him. For the hundredth time, he wondered how Ella had done the whole castle herself, and even if she had been the one to do it. Even after several hours of work, his and Hope's surrounding village paled in comparison to the castle above it.

He whistled a little tune as the elevator whisked him up to the sixth floor, then he confidently walked to #642. Just as he was about to knock, he faltered. Maybe she wasn't alone. Matt didn't really know her. He cleared his throat and willed his confidence back, then knocked.

Matthew could hear her on the other side of the door. He hoped he looked okay. He knew people looked loony through a peephole, like a reflection in a Christmas ornament. In spite of that fact, she opened the door and smiled up at him.

"Sorry I'm dropping in unannounced," he said uncertainly. "I wasn't sure if you were working tonight or not...."

"Not today. Tomorrow." She leaned against the door. Matt thought she looked friendly. Better than friendly. Fetching, his mother would say.

"Well, um, I think a certain sand elf was missing her bucket."

"Ahh, I've been found out."

"I wanted to thank you. It made Hope's day."

"I'm glad," she said, smiling genuinely. Ella gently took the bucket from his hand, then looked at him as if waiting.

"Ella," he began, suddenly feeling like a teenager, "I'd like to ask you out for coffee or something, but Hope's in the condo alone. I need to get back," he said, nodding over his shoulder.

"Oh, sure," she said, nodding. "I understand."

"Would you mind having breakfast with the two of us?"

"That'd be great," she said, raising her eyebrows.

"And then maybe…sometime…you and I could go out."

"Maybe," she said with another big smile. "Let's start with breakfast."

Matthew nodded quickly and smiled back at her. "Well, good night, Ella. See you at the coffee shop across the road at eight?"

She groaned. "Too early for me. How about nine?"

"Nine it is. Incidentally, how did you get so good at sand castles?"

"Laguna's Sand Blast. Each year, I take part with my team from church. We've done pretty well. Third place two years ago, second last year."

"At that rate you should take the lead this year."

"One can only hope," she said, flashing him another grin. Matt looked into her green eyes and realized it was her spark that had reminded Hope of Beth. It was as if Ella carried a light inside that made her happy and whole, regardless of the circumstances around her. It was the flickering light of the faithful. His heart sped up a bit. He swallowed hard. "Well, I'll see you at nine in the morning."

"I hope you realize that nine is still a sacrifice for me."

"We appreciate it. Thanks again."

ᴧ ᴧ ᴧ ᴧ ᴧ

Hope and Matt had been waiting for five minutes when Ella showed up. "Sorry," she said, as she approached the booth. She slid in across from them. Matt noticed that she was dressed in slim jeans and a red cotton sweater that brought out the vivid green of her eyes. She wore very little makeup, and it pleased him. He wasn't a heavy-makeup kind of guy.

The waitress came up, and Hope immediately ordered a hot chocolate. "Double, tall skinny latte, hold the cinnamon," Ella said in a tired voice.

Matt snorted. "Californian," he said, ribbing her. "Just plain coffee, straight up, for me," he said to the waitress. She left immediately, fairly disinterested in her customers. Matt glanced down at his daughter and was brought up short by her look of concern. Clearly, she had noted the element of playfulness with Ella and did not approve. Matt swallowed hard, determined to ignore his daughter since his intentions were innocent. Hope would just have to get used to Matt's getting to know new people. Even if it was an attractive woman.

He looked over at Ella, but she seemed to be taking the whole scene in stride. "I heard the sand elves had a heyday with Pippin Palace," she said to Hope in a friendly manner.

"Pippin what?"

"Pippin Palace. Your sand castle. It must've been very special if they took on a project of that scope. It's not every castle attempt that gets the king's treatment. Or in this case, should I say queen's treatment?"

Hope shrugged her shoulders, and her eyebrows settled a little lower as she glanced over at Ella. "Why didn't they do anything to my village? Do they only work on castles?"

"Not always." Ella looked at her as if thinking over something quite serious. "Did you work very hard on your village?"

Hope nodded.

"Maybe you need to work on it a bit more. They don't come out for just anybody. Only for the people they think have done their share."

"Are you just saying all that? Have you ever seen sand elves?"

"Why, no," Ella said, meeting Hope's serious look. "Haven't caught a glimpse of one myself. But my dad told me all about them when I was about your age. Even had a close encounter." She leaned forward, as if she were about to share a secret. "One night, I was determined to see them, so my dad and I camped out on the beach near my castle. It was sad though." Ella shook her head dramatically and set her lips in a line of resignation. "I fell asleep sometime during the night, and that's when they appeared and did all their work."

"Why didn't you try again?" Hope's eyes grew narrower.

"Well, we woke up all wet from the sea spray. Our sleeping bags were sopping wet. I got a terrible cold, and my mother wouldn't let us do it again. I called it the Mom Block."

"I bet you thought your mother was terrible," Matt said, joining in.

"Horrible. I told her it was like being a fairy princess locked up in one of the castle parapets."

The waitress arrived with their drinks, and Hope immediately set to spooning the tower of whipped cream directly into her mouth.

"What'd your mom say?" Matt asked Ella.

"She said I'd just have to wait for my handsome prince to rescue me, because until then, I wasn't going out on the beach at night."

Matt and Ella shared a furtive, warm look that was interrupted by the clink of Hope's mug spilling on its side. "Whoops," the girl said dully. It was apparent that it was no accident, but Matt treated it as such, determined not to ruin their breakfast with a confrontation. He threw more paper napkins to Ella, who laughed and kept saying, "whoa" as she caught brown rivulet after rivulet from cascading into her lap.

It was Ella who caught the waitress's eye and ordered Hope another hot chocolate. "What do you say, Hope?" Matt asked.

"Thank you," she said, obviously not meaning it.

He ignored her and asked Ella another question. She launched into another animated story, and in watching her, he almost forgot the troublemaker beside him. As they continued to talk through breakfast, Matt found himself smiling more and more.

Ella was funny, spirited, amiable, and up-front about her spiritual life. Soon enough he knew that she was devout in her faith, very close to her parents—who lived a few miles away—and gentle in her touch with kids, judging from how she handled Hope, who seemed strangely testy this morning. Maybe she had not slept well last night.

One thing was clear as they parted after breakfast. Matt wanted to see Ella again.

All afternoon he battled the urge to call and talk with her. That night, he finally left a message, and she called him back the following afternoon while Hope was watching cartoons. Smiling after a half-hour conversation, Matt hung up the phone and almost tripped over his daughter as he turned to exit the kitchen.

"Are you going out on a date?" she asked in an accusatory voice.

"Not yet," he said, not wanting to hedge but also not wanting to blow things out of proportion. After all, what could come of it? He and Hope were in California only for another week and a half. He was just flexing his emotional muscles. Opening doors to see what God would do. It felt good to have a little female companionship, and he hadn't felt this alive in months.

"We might get together for dinner some night," he said, walking past Hope. "Don't worry about it," he added over his shoulder, shoving the image of her disapproving face from his mind. "Let's go work on your village. There might be a chance that the sand elves will approve and add their bit tonight."

~ 4 ~

By the time the Morgans went for their walk the next morning, the sun was swiftly rising toward its noon haven. Hope was still out of sorts, having slept until ten, and labored through her breakfast cereal as if eating it were a chore. If this was the way she was going to react to women in his life, Matt decided, he was going to have to sit her down for a talk or resolve to live alone. Feeling angry, he started to snap at her but stopped short, pausing and taking a deep breath.

Dear God, he prayed. *Give me strength for this. Give me patience. For my daughter's sake, give me the words to comfort her.* He looked at his daughter and sat backward in a chair beside her. "Do you want to talk about anything, pumpkin?"

"No," she said miserably, toying with the soggy squares in her bowl full of milk.

"Well, if you want to, we can. Want to check out your castle and village? It was pretty windy last night. If it's still intact, you should spray it down."

"Okay," she said, sliding off the chair and moving toward him. She slid her small hand into his and looked at him seriously. "I just really miss Mama."

He cradled her face with his free hand. "I know, sweetheart. So do I." He struggled to find the right words. "But, honey, Mama's gone. And she really didn't want us to be alone forever. There's nobody who could replace her. But let's give Ella and anyone else we meet the chance to be the special people God created them to be, and see how they fit into our lives. Okay?"

"Okay," she said softly, not meeting his eyes.

Hope left him and went to dress. When they stepped onto the sand minutes later, her spirits seemed to lift. And as they drew nearer the castle, they noted that several people were staring at it and pointing.

Much like the castle, the village had been transformed. There were tiny thatched roofs on what looked like adobe walls, and pebbles for fireplaces and chimneys. There were cobblestone streets and tiny fences around some of the homes. The castle was even bigger than before. Hope was astounded, her face transformed by delight as clearly as the castle had been transformed. Matt laughed out loud. How had Ella accomplished all this?

"This is the best vacation ever, Dad!" Hope hugged him fiercely around the thighs and fell to all fours to examine the village more closely. "Look at this chimney! There's a little white shell that looks like smoke! And look! This shell looks like a sheep in the front yard!"

Matt was amazed too. He looked on with Hope, examining all the details and changes, then settled down on the sand to look at the waves building, crashing, and sliding as he thought about his enchanting neighbor. Who else would get off a shift at midnight and come build sand castles to please a kid? It had been a long time since he had met someone like her. Since Beth, he admitted. Beth might've done something like this.

Hope spent a good hour playing in and around the castle with little plastic figurines. She was still at it when Matt spotted

Ella walking toward them. As soon as she was near, Matt rose and thanked her with a big smile.

She smiled back at him, flashing what he noted were very white teeth against the backdrop of a pretty, welcoming face. "Hey, neighbors," she said. "I see the sand elves were busy last night," she said to Hope.

"Yeah!" Hope said, momentarily unable to withhold the glee from her voice. "I'm going to play on the other side now," she said to her father.

"If you were a sand elf," Matt said to Ella with an insider's grin, "Where would you live in that castle?"

"That castle?" Ella asked, feigning offense. She adopted a highbrow accent. "Why that, dear sir, is none other than Pippin Palace! I need not see myself as a sand elf, with it being what it is to me."

Matt smiled, playing along. "I take it I should know the place? And your station in life?"

"Know of it?" she asked incredulously, her eyebrows raised. "It's famous throughout the land. *You've* heard of Pippin Palace and the righteous O'Donnells, right Hope?"

From across the castle, Hope reluctantly shook her head as if admitting defeat.

"Ahh. Foreigners, I take it?" She crossed her arms and looked over the Morgans.

"'Mericans," Hope confirmed sadly.

A hint of a smile crossed Ella's lips, but then she turned away. "I see I'll have to tell you the story of Pippin Palace."

"There's a story?" Hope asked.

"Ah, yes. You see, once I was small enough to live in this castle. We were a happy family and kingdom. But then my sister got married and moved away. I, unhappily, am the forgotten sister, sadly waiting in this parapet here for her knight." She pointed to a small, skinny tower to her right.

"Still kept under lock and key by your evil mother, eh?" Matt asked, intrigued with his companion and her creative, fanciful ways. They shared a brief look that told him Ella was just having fun. He glanced at Hope. She was as mesmerized as he.

"Oh, no," Ella said. "My mother has been imprisoned in the dungeon for years now, and my evil uncle has taken over the kingdom. My father is off in the Crusades, fighting for God. Someday he'll come back and chase away my evil uncle and set me and my mother free."

Matt paused a moment before risking an offer. "Well, I think anyone so into a magic kingdom should go with us to Disneyland. Do you think that you could escape your parapet tomorrow?"

"I could," she said with a smile.

"How?" asked Hope.

"I know secret passageways," Ella said with a wink.

"Can you get up by eight for breakfast?" Matt asked. "We want to be there when the gates open."

"Well, that's asking a lot," she said, pretending to really mull it over. "But I guess I could do it."

"Great! It's a date." The words were out before he could stop them, and he looked up quickly to see if Hope had noticed.

The little girl was standing stock-still, studying them both. She said not a word.

⌁ 5 ⌁

This is my favorite," Ella said, ducking under the chain fence to join Matt and Hope in the Matterhorn line. She distributed the other two chocolate frozen bananas. "It's just not a trip to Disneyland without one of these," she said. Matt smiled at her as he took his, and once again she wondered why it had taken so long for him to enter her life.

To her, Matthew Morgan was a prince, maybe the one she had been waiting for. It was as if she had known it as soon as she stepped into that elevator. No, before that. She'd known it when she looked over at his adorable, concerned, protective face as Jack grabbed her arm. It was a face a woman could trust. But how was she going to win Hope over? The little girl seemed not to like her. And Ella and Matt would have to get past that serious problem if they were to discover whether they were meant to be anything but friends.

The night before, Ella had called her mother. "Mom, I don't know what I'm thinking. They're *leaving* soon. To *Montana*. I can't just drop by there to see them. I think he's terrific, but he's only visiting! How can God do this to me? I finally meet a terrific guy, and he lives a million miles away!"

"Calm down, Ella," her mother had said sensibly. "Are you sure this isn't just a crush?"

"Mom, I'm thirty-four years old! I think I know when it's a crush. But…maybe. Oh, you're right. I've only known him… What am I talking about? What has gotten into me?"

Her mother had laughed at her. "Take a deep breath, Ella. It will all work out for the best."

"For the best? What if we fall in love? Get married? What about my job? I really feel like my work is a ministry, Mom."

"I know it, Ella. And you're great at it. But that doesn't mean that God can't use you in ways other than oncology nursing. Your skills are broad based. Don't limit your Father in what he can do for you."

Ella was struck silent at the thought. She loved her job, didn't she? Sure, she had been down and tired lately, but that didn't mean she wanted to quit. "I don't know if I could leave nursing, Mom."

"I didn't say leave nursing. Just don't look at your life as a long tunnel. Inevitably it will twist and turn. Look forward to those changes. They keep things interesting. As far as Matt's concerned… Well, maybe he's the one. Then again, if he's too dense to see the beautiful woman in front of him, maybe knowing him is just an experience that will help prepare you for someone else."

Ella snorted. "Or maybe I'm just getting all worked up for nothing. Maybe he and Hope will leave next week and it will all be over."

"Enjoy it for what it is," her mother urged. "Let God do the rest."

"Easy for you to say," Ella said. "When you've been married for over forty years, you think every relationship just happens. Dad's told me and Lynn what he had to do to win you over. Maybe I have to take drastic action here."

"Maybe. Maybe not."

"That's your sage advice? 'Maybe. Maybe not'?"

"Ella, I'm telling you to let God take the reins on this one. I know it's not your nature, but if you sit back and really let him lead you—and if he's truly in this—he'll give you your heart's desire."

"Yeah, I've heard that one before. I want to believe it, Mom, but I'm afraid. What if I risk my heart and he just flies off to Montana never to be seen again?"

"Then you'll pick yourself up off the floor, brush yourself off, and move on. If he's so thickheaded that he doesn't want your heart as badly as you want his, he's not worth it."

Her mother's words rang in Ella's ears as she watched Matt take a bite of banana and smile at her. He sure seemed interested. Her heart lurched with hope as he continued to stare at her warmly, speaking to her without words.

"I don't like this," Hope interrupted, handing her banana to her father. She turned away to hang on the chain as if it were a jungle-gym rope.

"Sorry," he said, looking at Ella. "I like mine. Hope," he said, "you can go throw this away. And you can thank Ms. O'Donnell anyway."

"Thank you," Hope said mechanically.

"You're welcome." She watched as the girl ducked under the chain and ran to the trash can. Just before she threw it away, she turned her back to the adults and sneaked another bite.

"She thinks she's so smart, hiding it from us," Matt said with a shake of his head. "It's tough, you know. My showing interest in other women. She's usually a great kid."

"I think she is great, Matt," Ella said, looking into his blue eyes. She longed to reach up and brush his light, sandy-colored hair from his forehead. It looked like he needed a haircut. Had Beth always reminded him? "I think she's just trying to adjust to me. Let me guess. Haven't been dating in Montana?"

Matt shrugged as Hope drew near again. "Not since Beth. Haven't ever been interested." His eyes penetrated hers with another meaningful look.

She smiled back at him, keeping her lips closed. Ella hated her big mouth. Was it a turnoff to Matthew? She hoped not. Altering her smile would be tough. *Just be yourself,* her mother had said. Matt turned to move forward with the line and gently, casually placed his hand at the small of her back. It was a small gesture, an idle gesture, Ella told herself. But his hand had lingered just a moment.

All morning, Hope had insisted that she go on the rides with her father, and Ella had agreed, anxious not to give the girl something else to hold against her. But when they got to the front of the line, a little redhead about Hope's age was looking around, obviously hoping to find a partner. She smiled over at Matt's daughter and miraculously, Hope smiled back.

"Why don't you ride with that little girl?" her father urged.

"Okay," Hope said amiably, momentarily forgetting her mission to keep her dad and Ella apart. She skipped over to the redhead and asked her a question. The redhead smiled and nodded.

"Whew," Matt said over Ella's shoulder, his breath warming her ear. "I thought I'd never get a chance to get close to you today," he said lowly.

Ella could not contain her grin this time. She let go until every pearly white was in view, and Matt smiled back at her, apparently not turned off in the least.

They kept going all day, stopping only for the occasional sugary drink or junk-food break. Ella could tell that Hope was impressed with her knowledge of the park, which enabled them to get to rides faster, but she remained distant. Finally, as the last float in the Main Street parade disappeared, Ella looked over to Matt—who sat beside her on the sidewalk—and the sleeping girl in his lap. The last lights of the float shone in his eyes, and he held his daughter so tenderly that it brought tears to Ella's own.

He looked over at her then, saying nothing, only staring back at her. To Ella, his eyes said it all. He wasn't thickheaded. He was interested. He was definitely interested.

～ 6 ～

The next day, Ella alternated between berating herself for falling for someone who lived so far away, and praying that he would show up. Countless times she paced to the patio window and past the telephone. *Come on. Pick up the phone, Matt.* She gave up trying to reach him with her experimental mental telepathy and sighed. *Please, Father. Please don't let me risk my heart for nothing.*

She called her mother, then her sister, Lynn. She even phoned friends she had been out of touch with for over a year, just to distract herself. As the period of silence between her and Matt grew, so did her doubts.

When she returned from a late afternoon matinee, she rushed immediately to her answering machine to check for messages and collapsed on her couch in despair when there were none. Just then, there was a knock at the door. She checked her watch. Seven. It took him this long?

"Hi, Ella," Matt said with a grin, leaning against her door-jamb with his arms crossed. "I got a baby-sitter for Hope. I know this is late notice, but would you like to go to dinner with me?"

She took a deep breath and squared her shoulders, willing herself to find the courage for her next words. She needed to get things straight. After all, she had thought about it all day! "Look, Matt, I think you're terrific," she said. "But let's be frank. Realistically, how far can this go?"

He looked surprised but, curiously, not offended. "Dessert?" he tried.

She laughed and looked down at the ground before meeting his look again. "I'm sorry. I just don't want to waste your time."

He tipped his head a bit toward her, and Ella's heart gave a little lurch. "If we're going to talk marriage plans, don't you think I should sit down at least?"

Ella felt the deep flush rise from her collarbone. "No...that's not what I...um...sure, come in." He didn't wait for another invitation. In seconds, he was sitting on her couch, an expectant look on his face.

"Look, Matt," she began, searching for words as she walked toward him. This was all much easier during her afternoon practice sessions. "I wasn't proposing—"

"I know, Ella. I was just giving you a hard time. But to be honest, I'm not one to mess around much myself. I can't risk heartbreak after Beth. For me or my daughter." He stood, then began to pace, wringing his hands as though he ached for a hat with which to occupy them. He looked at her, and it was as if he suddenly found inspiration.

Silently he stepped forward and gripped her shoulders, then slid his big hands down her arms to take hers. He looked deeply into her eyes. "But there's something about you that I think is irresistible. You're kind and fun and pretty. And something inside tells me that I should get to know you better. There. I said it. When God pushes me like this, I usually find it's in my best interest to follow through."

Ella sat down on the couch, hard. She had never expected

such a frank confession from him, even after her direct statements. Had she ever met a man so willing to discuss things up front? She could not recall.

His voice brought her back to the present. He knelt in front of her, still holding her slim hands in his own. She was still relishing the feeling of being held when his words brought her back around. "So Montana would never be an option?"

Now she was really stunned. They weren't talking about marriage, and yet they were. To Ella, there was a very thin veil between their conversation and poring over invitations with her sister. And they'd been around one another a total of what? Fifteen, sixteen hours?

He gently released her hands and went back to pacing, occasionally pausing to look meaningfully into her eyes. "I know this is fast, Ella. But I feel as if I know you. At least the main important stuff. I know that spark that lights a fire in your heart. I don't believe in coincidences, and I don't believe in playing games. I'm here with my hat in my hands—well, it'd be in my hands if I had one—because I'm interested in courting you. I'd like to try out for that prince position you talked about on the beach."

"Let's just start with dinner," she said, finding her voice at last.

Ella and Matt spent a good two hours over dinner, cherishing the time to learn about one another's lives. There was so much she wanted to know about him, and apparently, he felt the same. She liked what she heard about Matt and his life on the ranch. It was more conventional and old-fashioned than her own in some ways, but she found the differences refreshing. His life seemed like one that could meld with hers.

It was an uncommonly balmy night, full of the promise of

summer's heat. As they exited the restaurant, Matt took her hand. Ella cherished the feeling, wanting to memorize it so she could remember it when he left.

"I don't want this to end," he said.

"It doesn't have to," Ella told him.

"What do you mean?"

She smiled at the element of consternation in his voice and playfully pushed away from him. "I'm not coming on to you, you big lug. I'm asking you to join me in a bit of sand elfdom. I'm giving you the chance of a lifetime. A walk in Oz. The sprinkle of fairy dust. If you're man enough."

Matt grinned and crossed his arms, a habitual gesture, she noted. "Well, I usually keep a good distance between me and mythical creatures," he said, "but if it means spending a little more time with you, I'm game."

"Good," she said, linking her arm with his. "Let's go change and convince your baby-sitter to sleep a couple of hours on your couch. You have a lot to learn."

By the time they finished at two in the morning, Pippin Palace had been repaired where it failed, and expanded in other places. At first, Matt had resorted to old techniques, but Ella had set him straight.

"No, no," she said, as his wall crumbled almost from the get-go. "You need more water. Come here, I'll show you the consistency you're after." They went to the water's edge, bringing one of the battery-powered lamps with them. In a large tin bucket, Ella slowly added water to the sand until it was the right consistency, as liquid as possible while still holding its shape. "It's kind of like egg whites, when you get them to hold a peak."

He stared at her blankly, and she laughed. "Let me guess. You have a cook?"

Matt shrugged his shoulders and flashed her a guilty grin. "As charged. No way to take care of a ranch and a five-year-old *and* cook."

"That's okay," Ella said. *I could get used to having a cook.* She had just turned to walk back to the castle when she felt the cold spray of water seep through her shirt. She glanced over her shoulder with what she hoped was a superior look. "I hope you don't call that a water-fight challenge."

Matt's grin grew. Once again he crossed his arms. "I do. What do you intend to do about it?"

"Nothing now. I'm too smart to get all wet at one in the morning. I'm liable to wind up with pneumonia, and my mom will come down and forbid me to go out on the beach at night." She walked a few feet and glanced back to see that he was following. "Oh, but don't think it's over. Expect it when you least expect it."

She spent the next hour honing Matt's sand-castle-building skills, while trying to ignore his warm proximity and casual, glancing touches that sent shivers down her spine. Matt was warm and wonderful and seemed to be perfect for her. The thought of kissing him made her warm down to her toes.

They were finished with their work and packed up to go when she spied the half-full pail of water. Casually she picked it up and glanced over at Matthew. His arms were full of equipment and, smiling, she judged him incapacitated. Without hesitation, she let the salty water fly, giving him a satisfactory drenching. She laughed as he blinked and the water continued to run down his face. He looked down at his soaked shirt, then back at her, and gave a playful little growl.

Her heart skipped a beat, and she jumped into action, knowing she was on the defensive now. She turned and ran with every ounce of strength she had, but she could hear the pail and other metal equipment clanging as they dropped from

Matt's arms. Unencumbered, he would get her in seconds. She gave a little shriek and kept running, but suddenly his arms were around her and lifting her off the sand. Matt threw her over his shoulder with all the finesse of a miller with a sack of flour. Ella stifled a scream, reminding herself it was the middle of the night. But Matt was heading directly back down to the water.

"No! Matthew!" she laughed hysterically. "Please! I don't know what came over me!"

"Yeah! You sound very sorry! In you go." He pulled her off his shoulder and into his arms. She took the opportunity to grab fistfuls of shirt and hair, again begging him to stop.

"No way," he said with a grin, setting her down in front of him to pry her fingers from their holds. He held both her freed hands easily with one of his own and dragged her into the water. When the waves were swirling around their knees, he paused and pulled her to him. She giggled, half expecting him to kiss her, half expecting him to shove her into the next wave.

It was dark away from the lamps, and she could barely make out his face. He paused, as if vacillating on what to do, then finally turned her around so her back was to his chest, still managing to keep her hands in check. She felt helpless in more ways than one. Matt bent his head toward the side of her own and spoke lowly. "Look at that," he directed. She glanced up to see a waxing moon. "By the time it's full, in three days, I want to kiss you."

His words alternately thrilled and relieved Ella. He wanted to kiss her but was biding his time, letting the feelings between them grow naturally, not rushed by the physical. "And," he said, turning her around, "if I kissed you now, how could I throw you in?"

She laughed and shook her head. "You're not going to throw me in. You couldn't. You're too gallant."

"Like a prince?" he asked softly. He dropped her hands, and they stood together as several waves crested and swirled around their knees. "Possibly," she managed to say, breaking their lingering glance and moving toward shore. She spoke over her shoulder. "But don't think I owe you anything for not throwing me in. We're even now. Even-steven."

"Yeah, right," he said, following her uphill. "Think what you must to put your mind at rest. But someone wise once told me to expect it when you least expect it."

Together they collected the equipment where it had been strewn about, smiling all the way.

They stopped off at Matt's rental, laughing and shushing, trying not to wake Hope. As Matt awakened the baby-sitter and they set their sand castle equipment in the closet, Ella thought she heard a sound in the hallway. She looked up but saw nothing there. She checked her watch. "Two-thirty! Good grief, I better get going," she whispered. Hope was surely sound asleep, but *Ella* needed to get to bed.

"I had a great time, Ella. I can't wait to see you tomorrow." He looked down at her as if he wanted to say something really important.

"You mean today," Ella said, smiling up at him. After a moment, Ella stuck out her hand, and Matt shook it with a wry grin.

"I'll look forward to the next three days passing."

"As will I."

～ 7 ～

At 10:00 A.M., Matt trudged out to the kitchen in his bathrobe, exhausted after his short night's sleep. He had been in bed by three, but he had tossed and turned until six, unable to get Beth and Ella out of his mind. Was he being unfaithful to Beth by pursuing Ella? His wife had begged him to find love again, and he had to admit he loved every new chapter of Ella that unfolded. But he could not get rid of the niggling guilt. Finally, he had cried out to God to give him direction and peace, and fell asleep at last.

He poured himself a cup of coffee and looked through the kitchen doorway to the living room. Hope was sitting directly in front of the television set, entranced with cartoons. "Good morning," he said to his daughter and took a swig of coffee. Matt grimaced. The timer had obviously gone off at his customary 7:00 A.M. The coffee was cold and bitter by now. He was considering brewing a new pot when he noticed that Hope had not even looked up. "Hope? Are you okay?"

"Yeah," she said, not looking away from the TV.

"Whatcha watching?"

"Cartoons."

"I can see that. Which one?"

She refused to look at him. "I don't know."

"You don't know or don't want to tell me? Isn't that one that we decided wasn't good for you to watch?"

"I don't know."

"Well, I do. Either turn the channel or turn it off."

"Why?" she asked, her voice at once accusatory and whiny.

"Because I said so."

"So?"

Matt could feel one of his eyebrows go up in consternation and his pulse pick up. "Hope Emily, what has gotten into you today?"

She stood up and faced him, her hands balled up into fists. "I saw you two last night! You're going to marry Ella! I think that's just mean!" With that, she ran toward her bedroom, a blur of Winnie the Pooh pj's.

"Hope! Stop right there." Even to him, his voice sounded unnecessarily loud. He brought it down a bit, hoping to breathe some calm into the situation. "Come here."

His daughter trudged into the room as if unwillingly drawn by a huge magnet, resisting every step. Begrudgingly, she sat down. "And you guys are the sand elves. You lied to me," she said softly. "That wasn't nice."

Matt sighed and rubbed his forehead, suddenly battling a headache. He sat down next to Hope on the couch, casually putting his arm around her. "Okay, let's take this bit by bit. First off, it was not nice of you to spy on me and Ella. Please do not do that again. Second, we have not agreed to get married, just to get to know one another better. Sweetheart, I think you've been as lonely for your mama as I have. I'm hoping that someone nice will fit into our lives again—for both of us. I'm not trying to replace your mama. No one could do that. She was wonderful. But she knew we'd be lonely. And that someone else

51

might be able to be a part of our lives in a different way that would still make us happy. Do you understand that?"

"Maybe," Hope said miserably. She looked very small to him as she pulled her legs up to her chest and tucked them under her pajama shirt.

"Well, we'll probably have to talk about that some more. But I want you to give Ella a chance, okay?"

Hope said nothing.

"Look, you're right. Ella has been the sand elf, and last night I helped her work on Pippin Palace some. She did not do it to make you feel stupid. She did it to make you smile. Which she did," he said, reaching out to pinch his daughter's cheek. Hope pressed her lips together and averted her gaze, obviously determined not to grin back at him. "She never really lied to you. I would guess that if you had asked her a direct question, she would've told you the truth."

Hope sighed heavily, as if carrying the weight of the world on her shoulders.

"Come on. It's a beautiful day. Let's go for a walk. Or a race. You can see what Ella and I did to Pippin Palace last night." He rose and turned to make his way back to the Mr. Coffee machine.

Slowly, Hope slid off the couch and obediently made her way to her room.

When Ella showed up at their door that afternoon, Hope opened it.

"Hi, Hope," Ella said. "Is your dad at home?"

"Yeah. Did you make Pippin Palace yourself?" the girl asked, crossing her arms like a smaller version of her father.

Ella studied her for a moment and decided on the honesty track. There was something about the girl that told her she had better not try to pull the wool over her eyes any longer. "I was about your age when I figured out it had been my dad all along. Yes, it was me. Sand elves are just family folklore. Can I come in?"

Hope studied her for a moment, then stood aside to let her pass by. Just then they heard the shower turn off and Matt calling from the bathroom. "Hope? Did I hear someone at the door?"

"Yeah," she said in a low voice that her father was not likely to hear.

Ella studied her, and Hope looked right back.

"You don't want me to see your dad?" Ella asked softly.

Hope slowly shook her head.

"Oh," Ella said, nodding. "I'm really sorry you feel that way. Because I really like you both." She decided to ignore the girl's obvious slight. "What if all three of us went roller-skating this afternoon?"

When Hope did not immediately decline, Ella decided to push. "We could go to Balboa Island. You can skate on big, wide sidewalks. We could get cotton candy and ride on the Ferris wheel, and come dinnertime, we could talk your dad into a burger at Ruby's. Doesn't that sound like fun?"

Hope studied her, unsure of what to do.

"Hope? I asked if someone was at the door." Matt's voice was closer now. Ella guessed that he was in the bedroom dressing.

"Yeah," Hope said. "It's Ella." Her gaze did not leave their neighbor's. "She wants us to go skating."

Matt finally appeared in the doorway, looking handsome with wet hair and a freshly shaven face. His nose and cheeks were a bit sunburned, and the color made his blue eyes sparkle. "Oh, hi," he said to Ella, giving her a tender smile. "And you want to go, Hope?"

"I guess so," she said.

"Great. How soon?"

"About five?" Ella asked. "Let me just change out of my

uniform, and I'll be ready. I told Hope that we could eat dinner down there."

"Sounds good to me."

"To me too," Ella said, looking at both the Morgans with a warm gaze.

They spent the evening canvassing the island just off Newport's peninsula. An hour of laughing together at Matt's trying to stay upright was the best thing for Hope and Ella. Some of Hope's walls seemed to come down as the five-year-old warmed up to the woman.

They were on the boardwalk, skating side by side behind Matt, when Hope hit a crack in the cement and nearly went down. "Whoa!" Ella cried, grabbing her hand to try to save her. She failed, however, and they skidded to a stop on the ground instead, thankful for the long pants and polar fleece jackets that saved them from scratched knees and elbows. When Matt fell himself, after looking over his shoulder and trying to turn around, Hope and Ella dissolved into giggles. There was something hilarious about the big man on wheels. To Ella, there was something endearing about a Montana rancher willing to try skates at all.

After another hour, Ella and Matt pleaded with Hope to let them go back to street shoes, promising to follow her around for as long as she wanted. After that, unbeknownst to Hope, they walked hand in hand behind her, enjoying the sunset on the harbor as they passed tiny beach house after tiny beach house. Finally, even Hope grew tired of the skates, and they returned to the rental shop for her sneakers. "That was great!" she said as they emerged from the shop. "What's next?"

"How 'bout the Ferris wheel and a cotton candy *hors d'oeuvre*?" Ella asked.

"Yeah!" Hope yelled. The next second, she took Ella's hand to pull her along. Her eyes were wide, and she looked as surprised by her own action as Ella was. Ella looked over toward Matt and caught his grin, but when Hope spotted their pleased smiles, she dropped Ella's hand and grew quiet.

"Back to the sour dowager," Matt whispered in Ella's ear. "Can't get too excited about the new woman in Dad's life. It might actually encourage him."

Hope glanced over her shoulder to see them whispering and frowned. "Come on, you guys! Hurry up! We'll never get to the Ferris wheel!" she said grumpily.

"We'll get there," Matt said merrily, taking Ella's hand in his again. "Don't worry. Ella said it doesn't close 'til midnight."

They turned a corner, and Hope spotted the ride. She took off running. "And don't you worry," he said to Ella. "We'll teach Hope that it's okay to love again."

Ella's eyes widened. "Love?"

"Love," he said, smiling back at her. "I can smell it a mile away."

They had just purchased burgers and fries at Ruby's, a '50s-like diner at the end of a pier, and settled on a bench when Hope let her feelings be known.

"I like you, Ella," she declared, taking a big bite of hamburger.

Ella grinned at her and then at Hope's father. "I'm so glad, Hope. I like you too."

"Yeah," the little girl went on. "It's sad."

"What is?"

"That you can't have more dates like my dad."

Ella laughed out loud and met Matt's merry grin. "Yeah. I'd agree with that."

"When we go home, you'll just have men like Jack to date."

Ella sobered immediately. The girl was casual in her manner but was clearly making a statement. She saw her father's relationship with Ella as temporary.

"What if Ella came to visit us, honey?" Matt broke in.

"Oh, she won't do that. She works here. Besides, at home we can get back to normal. Just you and me and the hands on the ranch. I like it that way. I miss home, Dad. Can we go home soon?"

"Soon enough," Matt said, gently stroking Hope's hair. "Too soon," he said softly, meeting Ella's look.

∼ 8 ∼

Ella trudged off to work two days later, painfully aware that the Morgans' time in California was drawing short, and feeling the effects of her short nights. It seemed as if there should be some sort of temporary leave available at the hospital for someone in love, Ella thought. *Not sick leave, but... "Love leave," that's it.* She snorted under her breath at her train of thought and resolved to concentrate even harder on her work that day. Her patients deserved the very best, not a woman in a trance who watched the clock as each minute lumbered by.

Still, despite her best efforts, Ella had to berate herself for wanting to plead illness and head home. *What has come over me?* When she almost made a mistake in distributing medications, she sighed, turned directly toward the nurse's desk, and went to talk to the charge nurse, an older, large woman with graying hair and kind eyes.

"Eleanor," she said without preamble, "here's the scoop. I am falling head over heels in love with a man who is in California for only a short time. I'm trying to concentrate, but I am doing a poor job of it. I'd keep on going, but I just caught myself about to inject Mrs. Hanson's IV with six cc's more med

57

than was ordered. Can I take some personal leave?"

Miraculously, Eleanor laughed at Ella's excuse and told her to go. "I've been wondering what's been wrong with you these last few days," she said, still laughing. "It never occurred to me that you were in love! Get out of here. It's slow and I'll get John to cover your shifts the next few days. He's been wanting to pick up some extra money."

"Thank you! Thank you!" Ella said, squeezing Eleanor's hand in appreciation. "I'll make it up to you next month!" She was out the door in minutes. It wasn't until she was starting her old Civic that she remembered Matt had taken Hope down to San Diego for the day. "Well, let's get on home anyway," Ella said miserably to "Jeffrey." All the way home she fantasized about going down to San Diego and trying to find the Morgans at the Hotel del Coronado or SeaWorld but then acknowledged that the idea was crazy. "Okay, God," she said aloud. "I got out of work. Do you think you could arrange a little time with Matt even though he thinks I'm busy?"

Unfortunately, her prayer request went unanswered. Ella spent the afternoon watching time tick by, just as she had at work. "At least I'm not endangering anyone's life," she mumbled to herself as she cleaned the kitchen counter for the second time that afternoon. Needing to keep her hands busy, she dragged out her portable vacuum and edged the carpet throughout her condo, pulled down her living-room curtains to wash them, and cleaned out her refrigerator. She was in the middle of scouring her stove when there was a knock at the door.

Her heart skipped a beat as she glanced at the clock. Six. Was it Matt? He and Hope could be home! She hopped up off the kitchen floor and was practically running for the door when the sight of her image in the hallway mirror stopped her short. She looked terrible! Her hair was a mess, pulled back with an old handkerchief, and she had dirt all over her. Whoever was at her door knocked again.

Ella tiptoed to the door and peeked through. It was Matt and Hope. Even distorted by the keyhole, they looked better than she. She flinched as a big fist came up to knock again. "Ella?" Matt said, his voice muffled by the door. "Ella, are you home?"

"That was her car in the lot," Hope said with some authority.

"Are you sure, honey? She's supposed to be at work."

"I'm sure."

"Well, I thought I heard some noise in there. Maybe she's sick and can't hear me knock." The buzzer rang inside the condo.

Drat. I can't let him think I'm sick. She tiptoed back and stomped toward the door as if just arriving, then opened the door with as much confidence as she could muster. Matt and Hope blinked at her with some surprise.

"Hi there! Back from San Diego already?"

"Yeah," Hope said. "You shoulda seen Shamu and the baby penguins!" She marched into Ella's house uninvited, and Ella stood back to let Matt in too.

"I thought you had to work," Matt said. "Are you okay?"

"Yes. I might look like I've been run over by a Mack truck, but I'm fine. I got off early." *I'm on love leave.*

"Great! We just stopped by to change. We're going for fish and chips at Dana Point. Want to join us?"

"Sure," Ella said. "Can you wait fifteen minutes? I'll just hop in the shower and then be ready."

"We can wait," Matt said, smiling down at her. Seeing that Hope was distracted at the window, he whispered, "I don't think you need to change. You're kinda cute with smudges of dirt on your cheeks."

"Dad! You should see the view from up here! It's much better than our condo!"

"I'll be back in a few minutes," Ella said, grinning too. "Despite what you think, the world will be happier if I scrub up." She left them then, glad that she'd had the afternoon to clean her home. Hope had moved on to her picture table, and Matt was looking at her books. "There're drinks in the fridge," she called over her shoulder.

Twenty minutes later, she returned to her guests, dressed in jeans, turtleneck, and a slim wool sweater. "Fifteen minutes, hmm?" Matt asked with a smile.

"I'm always about five minutes off, it seems," she said.

"It was worth the wait," he whispered as they left her home.

They drove in the Morgans' rented sedan down the Pacific Coast Highway. Traffic was picking up as summer approached. "You should see it in July!" Ella exclaimed after Matt made a comment. "I avoid PCH at all costs when the tourists arrive."

"Maybe you should go away in July and avoid it all together."

"Where?" Ella said blankly.

"I don't know," Matt said, glancing in the rearview mirror at his daughter. She was absorbed in the view outside her window of busy shops, galleries, restaurants, and strollers. "Someplace north. Far north."

"Ahh," Ella said, understanding his meaning at last. "I'll have to think about that."

"I wish you would," he said, shooting her a look.

Ella just smiled.

They reached the harbor and walked among the docks, admiring huge cruisers with names like *What's Your Pleasure?* and old wooden sailboats called *Mary's Pride* and *Sweet Horizons*. Finally, they reached a favorite shop of Ella's, a fish market simply named Sam's. Huge fillets of freshly caught cod and salmon and halibut lay in the ice. The shop's specialty was fried fish and chips, which customers purchased and ate outside on the picnic benches. More extravagant meals like half a lobster or crab were also available. Ella thought to herself that it would be fun to pack a picnic with all the fixings and bring Matt back down for a romantic—and relatively inexpensive—dinner.

If only they had more time.

The Morgans were due to leave in just a few days, and the thought saddened her. They needed more time together! She needed more time to gain Hope's trust, to show her that loving another woman did not mean being unfaithful to her mother's memory. Each moment seemed to confirm that Ella and Matt were kindred souls, but how could they be sure? It was a whirlwind courtship, and Ella did not want to rush into anything. They had not even kissed! The thought brought her up short, and she searched the sky as Matt arrived with their food.

"There," she muttered in awe. There on the horizon was a huge, full, cream-colored moon.

Matt followed her gaze as he distributed their dinners, then smiled. "Let's say grace," he said smoothly. "Would you like to bless the food, Ella?"

"Sure," she said, her mouth suddenly dry. She took a quick swig of water and then said grace. By the time she said amen the moon seemed to be rising visibly into the sky.

Later, Matt tucked Hope into bed and closed the door behind him. A teenage neighbor had agreed to baby-sit, and Matt felt jubilant. He had left Ella earlier with a simple request. "Come out on your deck at ten o'clock. Dress warmly."

Now he had work to do. He checked his watch. Nine o'clock. He had just an hour. And despite what needed to be accomplished, he felt like it was sixty minutes too long. He smiled, thinking again of Ella's face as she spotted the full moon. She had looked excited, embarrassed at being caught. It was like sharing a wonderful secret. And tonight...tonight he would take her in his arms and meet her lips with his own.

Matt was pulling on a sweater when he heard Hope's first cry. Concerned, he went to her room. His daughter moaned again. She seemed to be half asleep. "Hope?" he said gently, shaking her shoulder. She came awake at once and cried out, more loudly this time. "What's wrong?" he asked.

"My tummy hurts."

"Where?"

"I don't know," she said, tears welling up in her eyes.

"Now Hope," he said sternly. "Are you just saying that so I won't go out with Ella?"

"No! Ouch! Daddy, it hurts! It hurts really bad!"

"Where, pumpkin? It's important that you tell me where."

"Over here," she said, motioning toward her lower right side.

Her appendix. "Do you feel sick to your stomach? Do you think you just ate something that didn't agree with you?"

"No!" she moaned in pain. Matt could see that she was not faking it. A burst appendix could be serious. Even fatal? He couldn't remember. All at once, the agony of losing Beth came rushing back. He couldn't do anything to risk Hope. The hospital! He needed to get her to the hospital! Debating about calling an ambulance, he decided he could not risk the extra time. He knew right where the emergency room was. They had passed it earlier on the highway. Gathering her up in his arms, he mumbled an explanation to the baby-sitter, threw some cash on the couch for her, and ran to the car.

Ella nervously paced the floor, well aware that it was almost ten. What did Matt have planned? How would it feel to finally have him take her in his arms and kiss her? Maybe she had built it up too much in her mind. Maybe it wouldn't be anything special. Or maybe it would.

She sat down hard on a dining-room chair, determined not to walk out on her porch until five minutes after ten. No use in his thinking she was desperate. It was good to let a man wait a bit. Besides, it was only fair after he made her wait all evening for whatever surprise he had planned.

Ella tapped the floor in time with the second hand. At four minutes past, she could not wait any longer. She opened the sliding glass door slowly and walked out on the porch with her head held high. She hoped she made a pretty picture for him. The moon was climbing in the sky, a brilliant milky white against a royal blue-black night. Ella swallowed hard and then searched the beach below for Matthew.

He was nowhere to be found. Disappointed, she stood at the railing for a good half-hour watching the foam on the waves swirl and surge, then paced the miniature deck. Had she misunderstood his directions? Was he waiting for her somewhere else? No, he had been pretty specific. Finally, she sat down in a lounge chair and somewhere around midnight dozed off. She awakened an hour later. Bitterly disappointed and genuinely concerned that something was wrong, she went to her telephone and dialed Matt's condominium. It rang and rang with no answer. "There has to be some reason he didn't show," she told herself. "There has to be." But inside her doubts grew.

Ella awoke to the doorbell buzzing and groggily looked at her clock. Ten o'clock, twelve hours after their promised date. If it was Matt at all. She ran her fingers through her disheveled hair and padded to the door, past the two empty pint cartons of ice cream and her shoes, which she had pulled off without untying them.

Her eyes widened with surprise as she looked through the peephole. Not Matthew. But flowers. She opened the door.

"Ms. O'Donnell?"

"Yes." Ella took the proffered pen, signed for the gorgeous bouquet, and reached for them. She pushed the door shut with her hip and walked to the coffee table, inhaling the sweet scent of Casablanca lilies. They were a favorite of hers. How did he know? And there were six, seven, *eight* stems of the incredibly, huge, picturesque white flowers fastened in the low, sleek vase, with a total of twenty-two blossoms or pods waiting to open. It was so big, it took up half the coffee table.

With trembling fingers she reached for the card. Had he changed his mind? Was this his version of a Dear Jane letter? Or some excuse? She opened the tiny envelope and pulled out the card.

Sorry doesn't begin to say what I feel about missing our date last night. Does an emergency appendectomy count as a good excuse? Hope we can take a rain check on that full moon. In the meantime, I thought these might help make amends. With love, Matthew

An appendectomy! Her heart soared as she deemed it as, yes, a good excuse. But was it him or Hope? Which hospital had they gone to? Who was their doctor? The protective nurse in her emerged as she ran around the house getting ready to check on the Morgans. She felt needed, useful, wanted again. And she was going to them just as soon as Jeffrey could get her there.

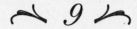

9

Ella found Matt in a hospital waiting room, dozing beside a cold cup of coffee in a Styrofoam cup. When she sat down beside him, he awakened and pulled her to him in a fierce embrace. After he released her, she said, "Whew! I guess you missed me."

"I did," he said with a smile. "I'm so sorry about missing our date. You got the flowers?"

"I did. They're beautiful. I take it Hope is the patient. How is she?"

"Good. She got out of surgery hours ago, and the doc said everything went well, but I felt uneasy leaving. Being in a hospital brings back some bad memories."

"I can imagine." She sat beside him in silence, doing just that. What had he gone through in saying good-bye to Beth? He had been largely silent about the whole experience. Ella took his hand and placed it in her lap, stroking it with the other. "You know that you'll have to tell me about her sometime."

He nodded wearily. "I guess. What do you want to know?"

"What she had, how she died. More important, what she was like and what it was like to say good-bye."

Matt sighed heavily. "It's tough, you know? Talking about it gets easier as the years pass, but it still is like reliving a bad dream when I go through it again."

"Let's start with the good stuff. What was she like? Where'd she come from?"

"Beth was this miraculous woman who walked into my life after I placed a personal ad in *Rancher's Journal.*"

"*You* placed a personal ad?"

"I did." There was no remorse in his voice. "I was a lonely bachelor in a place where there aren't a lot of eligible women. My ad brought me over three hundred interested parties."

"Of which Beth was the best?"

"Hers was the only one I answered. From the moment I read her letter, I knew she was special. She thought it was by God's design that she happened to receive a copy of the magazine at her job. Beth worked in some high-powered marketing firm in San Francisco. She got *Rancher's Journal* in one of a thousand media kits. But for some reason she paged through it that day. And wrote. The rest is history."

"Hmm," Ella said with a smile. She did not feel threatened by Matt's obvious love for the woman. His devotion encouraged her, made her feel more secure that he was indeed a man who could feel things deeply. Maybe he would have similar feelings for her some day. "Sounds romantic."

"Yeah," he said, pulling her hand to his lips and smiling at her tiredly. "Kinda like a chance meeting on an elevator, huh?"

"Kinda."

"Beth gave it all up for me. Left the city, her family, her friends. Except for her friend Rachel, that is. Beth got her to come visit one summer and Rach' fell for my buddy Dirk. They've been good friends."

"They should call the Elk Horn Valley 'The Hitching-Post Valley.'"

Matt chuckled. "They could do that. It's a romantic place. I hope you'll come see it."

Ella smiled at him, glad for the repeated invitation. She would call a travel agent as soon as she got home.

"Beth and I got married soon after meeting. After that we lost a baby in an accident, then Beth got pregnant with Hope. Having our daughter was like a miracle." His eyes shone as he traveled back in time. "I thought everything was back on track in life. I was wrong. A couple years later, we found a lump."

"What kind of cancer?"

"Lobular carcinoma."

Ella nodded.

"We didn't fool around. I loved her body, but I loved the woman more. She had a modified double mastectomy. Once again we thought we were back on track. She went a whole year, cancer free. Then we found out it was back."

"How many lymph nodes were involved?" Ella asked softly.

"By the time we found out, eighteen. It didn't take long for the cancer to spread. Everywhere." He swallowed hard, and his eyes glimmered with tears. Matt looked at Ella with a little shake of the head. "I really have dealt with this. I got counseling for me and Hope. Beth made sure we'd do it. Made us promise. So things are in order. I just don't know if I'll ever get over being sorry for losing her."

His words choked Ella. She stroked his face. "Oh, Matt. I don't know if you ever get over losing someone precious to you. The pain fades, the sorrow too. But people special to you leave little spaces in your life when they leave."

"I guess you've seen a lot of this."

"I have. Too many to count. Fortunately, most of the terminal patients I've known have gone on to a life without pain. A place where they can be whole and free again."

Matt grinned and nodded. "Beth did the whole death thing right, ya know? Made sure she told everyone what she needed to. Even left Hope a series of video tapes for important occasions in her life so she'd know her mother cared. That was the toughest thing for Beth. She knew I'd be okay. But she was so sorry that she wouldn't be around to mother Hope."

Ella smiled softly. "She sounds terrific. I think I would've liked her."

Matt looked at her meaningfully. "No doubt. I think you would've been friends."

Ella agreed to stay at the hospital in case Hope awakened so that Matt could grab some shut-eye. She sneaked him into a staff darkroom and left him snoozing on a cot practically as soon as he was horizontal. Then she went to talk with Hope's nurses. As Matt had reported, the girl had been fine throughout surgery and seemed to be doing well in recovery. She would be released in a few days.

Ella grabbed a cup of coffee and sat down to read an old issue of *Reader's Digest* in the waiting room. But her mind was not on the magazine articles. It was on Matthew and Hope. Was she really ready to be an instant mother? For years she had longed for a baby, agonizing over the time passing by and wondering if she would be able to have a child by the time she found a decent husband. But a five-year-old? Kindergarten. Brownie troops. Sunday school. Now *that* was instant motherhood. And the girl was clearly not convinced that Ella should be given the job at all.

To be fair, they had only met a couple of weeks before. And while Matt and Ella were able to recognize possible partners in one another, Hope obviously had not spent much time thinking about what it would be like to have a stepmom. Indeed, it sounded like Matthew had not dated at all. *Ella, you lucky dog, you're the one to break her in.* Was that all she was, really? A groundbreaker? Was it truly realistic to think that this relationship could go on once they parted? Sure, he had invited her to come see them. But was he thinking beyond the visit?

All the insecurities of being ditched the previous night resurfaced. It did not matter that Matt had had a more-than-adequate excuse for not appearing. Somehow, when he did not show, Ella lost some of her confidence. She felt every one of her thirty-four years and the twenty-plus years of fruitless dating. She wanted to be a wife and mother. Was Matt really ready to have someone step into Beth's shoes? Was he really ready for another relationship? Maybe Ella was just getting her hopes up for nothing.

She stood and paced, feeling her brow furrow as she concentrated. *Dear God,* she cried. *Please don't let all this be in vain. I'm too old to get all worked up just to be disappointed!* She paused and sat, leaning over to fold her hands and pray. *You know the desires of my heart. Please order it all as I trust you will—in the best interest for us all: me, Hope, Matt. Give me direction, Father. Confidence. Ease my doubts unless I really have something to be concerned about. Thank you for this, God. I'm falling in love, and it's great. But please, please don't let it all be for nothing. Amen.*

When she looked up, Matt was standing beside her, watching her. "Praying?"

She looked down and nodded. "Yes. You didn't sleep long."

"An hour. It was just enough to make me feel better than the walking dead. Thank you for standing guard."

"You're welcome. They say she should be released in a few days."

"Yes, I know. Ella, how 'bout—"

"Mr. Morgan?" a nurse interrupted.

"Yes?"

"You're daughter's awake. She's asking for you."

"Great!" He stood up quickly and then looked back at Ella. "You'll be here for a while?"

"As long as you want me here."

He smiled, then turned and made his way toward Hope's room.

By that afternoon, Matt was convinced that his daughter was out of the woods and comfortable in her room. Unlimited TV access was her kind of vacation, so she was not overly sorry to see him go for the day. He followed Ella home in his own car, and they parted for a few hours. Matt went home to sleep. Ella went home to pace.

At the appointed time, Ella was again out on her deck. The moon was still large and bright, with just a hint of the waning darkness claiming its left edge. Far below her, at exactly ten o'clock, Matthew galloped up on a white horse, towing a brown-colored mare behind him. He waved, dismounted, and bowed deeply. Then he motioned for Ella to come down.

He didn't have to ask twice. She turned and hurried out the door. Discarding the idea of waiting for an elevator, Ella scurried down the six flights of stairs. She arrived breathless on the central deck but immediately went to the last rock stairs that led to the beach. "My prince!" she quipped with a laugh.

Matt grinned as he caught sight of her. "Hey," he said, moving to join her and take her hand, "it's not a white stallion, but it'll have to do. The rental stables only have mares."

"Close enough," she said. "But I just want to point out that you give me a hard time about running five minutes late. You're twenty-four hours behind."

"Better late than never," he said, swinging up onto his horse.

"Come on. Let's ride. We're escaping, remember? The evil uncle and all. Now's your chance to leave the ivory tower behind. Not to mention get us back over to the private beach where these horses are allowed. You do know how to ride, don't you?"

"A little." She managed to place her sneaker-clad foot in the stirrup, grab the horn, and swing herself up and over. Sitting there in the saddle, her countless lessons at the equestrian center came back to her at once.

"It's a beautiful night," Matt said, pausing so she could draw alongside him.

"It is," she agreed, looking at the moonlight shimmering on the ocean waves. After they had settled into an easy pace for a while, Ella looked over her shoulder. "Oh no," she said worriedly.

"What?" Matt asked, following her gaze. Far, far down the beach, the lights of a lifeguard Jeep were making their way toward them.

"The castle guard! They're after us! Follow me!" She dug her heels into the horse's flanks and raced off on the hard dark sand where the water ebbed and flowed.

Laughing, Matt took off after her. It seems like years since his heart felt so light. Ella's expertise on the horse surprised him, as did the speed of the two horses, which had looked too old to move at more than the slowest walk. He was half disappointed, having visualized a lesson that might draw them closer together. But this was more fun. Matt dug his own heels into the white mare's flanks and soon matched Ella's stride. Carefully, he held back, so as not to get pelted with the sand her mare was kicking up. Where was Ella going, anyhow? The beach looked as if it were coming to an end.

Ella slowed and Matt could soon see why. The sand ended,

and the beach gave way to hard rocks. She let her mare pick her way through, then ducked as she entered what looked like a cave at the point. Matt followed, turning into the cave and spotting what she was after. Around the point, the passageway gave entrance to a quiet, idyllic cove.

In front of him, Ella left the cave and sat straight in the saddle, turning to see if he was coming. His breath caught, and he was glad his horse kept moving since he was not concentrating on the path. Ella was a vision, sitting straight on her mare, her long hair waving in a gentle breeze and shining in the moonlight. She grinned and her smile brought tears to his eyes. *How could I be so lucky, Lord? How could you give me two such women to love in one short life?* He knew. He knew she was the one. Did she?

Suddenly, he could not wait any longer. Free of the cave, he urged the mare toward Ella, gently herding her own docile mare toward the back of the cove. She backed up and laughed nervously. "What are you doing?"

But he did not answer. He just kept moving toward her, unable to think of anything else. Her mare, apparently sensing the approaching wall behind her and the other horse crowding her, stubbornly refused to move any farther. Matthew dismounted and was at Ella's side in less than two seconds, reaching up to pull her off her horse. In his arms, she looked up at him, well aware what he was after. But still he backed her up, up, up, until her own back was against a smooth boulder. He leaned close. "Is that a full moon?" he asked, nodding back toward the bright orb in the sky without looking away from her eyes.

"Close eno—" Before she could finish her sentence, Matthew leaned down to pull her close to him and kissed her soundly. Her mouth tasted sweet to him, and he could smell the sea air in her hair. After the kiss ended, he held her for a long time, not wanting ever to let her go. After Beth, he thought he would never desire another. He was wrong. This woman could drive him crazy. And it was more than her beauty. It was the way she had about her. The way she spoke. The way she looked at him. The way she dealt with his daughter.

"Ella," he said lowly.

"Yes?"

"I know we haven't been together long, but I feel like I had better tell you something."

"What's that?" she asked, leaning closer to rest her head on his chest.

"I'm in love, Ella. I'm in love with you."

His heart skipped a beat as she paused, as if not knowing what to say. Maybe she did not feel the same. Maybe he had misread—

"Oh, Matthew. I'm so glad," she said, apparently finding her voice. "I've been so afraid that my feelings were one-sided. That I was building it all up in my head."

"No, sweetheart," he said, cradling her cheek in his bearlike hand. "You are definitely not alone in this."

After a while, Matt pulled out a bundle of wood, a blanket, and a small bag of food and drink.

"What'd you bring?" Ella asked, looking over the crook of his arm into the bag. "Champagne and caviar?"

"Close. How 'bout hot chocolate and makings for s'mores?"

"Even better," she laughed. "I'll go look for roasting sticks while you build the fire."

Matt had a small, warm fire rolling in no time at all. He beckoned to Ella to join him under a blanket. Sitting side by side, they huddled together, staring into the fire.

Ella was the first to speak. "What are we going to do, Matt?"

"What do you mean?" he asked, knowing intuitively what she was after.

"I mean, we live a million miles apart from one another. How can we see if this is really what we think it is?"

He turned to her slowly, studying her in the firelight as if she were slightly crazy. "I know what this is. Don't you?"

Their remaining days together flew by, mostly because after three days of love leave, Ella's personal days were used up and, miserably, she had to trudge back to work. On their last night together, Ella hurried home to share a late night cup of tea in Matt's living room, and they talked about what was ahead of them. "We'll find a way, Ella," he promised her. "God didn't bring us together just to say good-bye."

She clung to those words after he was gone, mulled them over countless times as she waited a week to hear from him. Ella spent that time fighting the fear that it was all a farce, he really wasn't falling for her, and crying out to God to bring them back together. Sometimes she just cried. Was it really fair for this to happen to a thirty-four-year-old woman? After all, she wasn't just some teenager caught up in an infatuation. Or was she? How well did she know Matthew Morgan, anyway? Why didn't he call her? Didn't he know that she couldn't call him?

Finally, a letter arrived for her, carefully penned in awful, scrawling script that seemed choked with the emotion it tried to convey.

I miss you, Ella, terribly. Won't you please come to visit us? Enclosed is a ticket. You can stay with my friends. Come see us. See our valley. And decide for yourself if you could see yourself here for a year—ten years—maybe even a lifetime.

And once again Ella wept.

↰ 10 ↱

There it is," Matt said, pointing through the dirty wind-shield. "That's our home."

Ella smiled and looked through the drenching rain at the sprawling ranch about her and what she could make out of the big log house. "You say it like the Double M is a castle."

"Well, you know a man is king—"

"Don't say it."

Matt laughed and they pulled up in front of the house, which was bordered by a huge deck. Ella smiled as she spotted the porch swing and the big peeled logs that supported the roof above it. She would enjoy spending time out there with Matt, rain or shine.

Even now she could not believe she was here. The Elk Horn Valley was a long way from southern California, but something felt inherently right about it. It wasn't just being with Matt. It was the place itself. Matt had told her that when the clouds lifted, she would be able to see the towering Rockies on one side of the valley and the high hills to the west. The gorgeous green valley already made her feel safe, protected. How exciting it would be to see the gates around her!

"There's my girl!" Matt said, grabbing Ella's hard-sided suitcase from the back of the truck. Ella turned to where he was gazing but caught only a glimpse of Hope as she entered the house. "I guess she's not as excited to see me as you were," Ella said.

Matt paused to bend down and give her a quick kiss on the nose. "Take courage," he said. "That is just the court jester, determined to give us a run for our money."

They ran up the steps and shook off the rain as best they could before entering the house. "Oh, Matt," she said in awe, taking a sweeping glance of the huge, tastefully decorated home. "It's gorgeous."

"Well, thanks. I can't take all the credit. I built it. Beth decorated it."

"It's perfect. It could be in a Ralph Lauren ad."

"Ralph who?"

"Never mind." She moved to the gigantic picture window that started at the floor and soared high above her. Behind was a massive fireplace and big cushy chairs. "I could sit in here and read all day."

Matt came up behind her, enfolding Ella in his arms and kissing her on the cheek. "Or day after day after day."

She grinned and turned to face him. She was about to pull his head down for a solid kiss when she spotted Hope on the stairs beyond him. "Hope! There you are! It's good to see you!"

Ella no longer needed to wonder about being ignored. Hope kept moving up the steps, disregarding Ella's call.

"Hope Emily Morgan!" Matt thundered, obviously angered and amazed by his daughter's behavior.

"Matt—" Ella began. Forcing Hope wasn't going to win her over. Ella would end up like the countess in *The Sound of Music*.

"No, I can't let her be so rude," he muttered. "Hope, get down here right now!"

"No!" Hope cried, openly defying him by stomping her foot.

"I don't want her here! She doesn't belong here! She lives in California!" She turned and took off for her room.

"I'll be right back," Matt said, his face exposing his fury.

Ella reached out to grab his arm. "Wait. Matt, you can't force her to like me. This is a tough situation. Why don't you sit down here for a moment and calm down before you go and talk with her? If you go up there all angry, you'll accomplish very little. We need to make some progress with her if there are to be no barriers between us."

Matt sighed and ran his beefy fingers through his hair. "You're right. Okay, let's talk about something else for a bit, and then I'll go up. Tell me what you've been up to the last couple of weeks. I want to hear everything. I've missed you."

"Oh, Matt, I've missed you terribly."

"If only Beth had left a tape entitled *When Your Dad Gets a Girlfriend,*" Ella moaned as she slumped down on the couch two days later. "Things aren't getting better. Any suggestions?"

Matt shook his head and slumped down on the love seat beside her. The rain had continued nonstop, and it seemed to match his mood. He knew Hope was against his relationship with Ella, but he had thought that with time, she would be won over as he had been. How could his daughter not like the woman beside him? It made him feel furious at his daughter and torn between the two.

"Lunch was horrible," Ella said, voicing his thoughts exactly. "We can't keep on this way. She and I need to have it out. Would you trust me to take a chance with your daughter?" she asked.

He looked at her sharply. "Chance?"

She took his hand, and Matt noticed the spark of excitement in her eye. "I think it's the only way."

"Just what are you planning to do, Ms. O'Donnell?"

~ ~ ~ ~ ~

Ella knocked on Hope's door and entered without an invitation. Matt was right behind her. "Hope," Ella said, "you and I need to do something together. We can't go on like this, not speaking. Please get your rain slicker and boots on and meet me in the yard. I have the perfect project."

"I don't want to."

"I'm sorry you feel that way, but I still want you to come." She moved to the bed. "Will you dress yourself, or do I need to do it?"

Hope frowned and stuck out her lower lip. "I don't want to go. You can't make me." She turned to her father. "Daddy—"

"No way. You've been respectfully asked to do something by an adult. You know the rules, kiddo. Into your slicker and boots. It won't kill you."

"Daddy, I—"

"Now!"

Hope moved quickly off the bed at the sound of her father's tone, then more slowly dragged open the closet door and reached for her yellow slicker and galoshes. "Daddy, why—"

"No questions, sweetheart," he said. "You just have to do this. For all of us." She looked confused and glanced at Ella. "You are to respectfully mind Ella as you would any adult, got it?"

"Got it," she said miserably.

"Come on, Hope," Ella said, putting her arm around the girl and nudging her out of the room. "We're going to go have some fun if it kills us." But Hope shook off her hand and ran ahead of her, apparently determined to put as much distance between them as possible.

Once outside, Hope turned to her on the porch. "We can't go out there. It's raining."

78

"It's perfect," Ella said, picking up a couple of pails and trowels from the deck. "We're going to build another little village."

"How?" Hope pouted. "There's no sand here."

"No. There's something better. Mud."

Within two hours, they had built a river way underneath a canopy of bramble bushes, adding waterfalls and bridges and dams here and there. Hope got into it in spite of herself and fashioned small log homes out of sticks. She wasn't talking to Ella much, but as least she wasn't pouting.

Ella was digging more trench to lengthen the river, when her trowel caught on a root. She pulled, and a small clod of dirt went flying, spattering Hope's yellow jacket. "Hey!" Hope said. Seemingly without thinking, she reached for a handful of mud and with a grin, let it fly.

It spattered all over Ella. She did not waste a second. *These are the things that cement a friendship.* Ella scooped up her own handful of mud and with a shriek, threw it at the small girl. It hit Hope's neck and spattered up to her cheeks. The child giggled and threw another clod, hitting Ella on the back as she ducked. On and on went their mud fight—a release of pressure and anger and frustration—until finally, exhausted from laughing, Ella put her hands together to form a T. "Time-out," she gasped, smiling as she tried to wipe some of the dirt from her face.

Hope looked at her warily, but for the first time, there was a glint of happiness in her eyes. "I got you good with that last one."

"You did. I'll admit it," Ella said, smiling back. "But only after I nailed you on the rear end with *my* last one."

Hope smiled again and looked down. "Hey, look at this!" She knelt down on the ground, looking into the river way where she had been grabbing ammunition.

Ella joined her and knelt down beside the girl as she began to dig.

"Not too much, Hope. We'll need to cover them back up."

"Come on. Just a little more. So we can see them better."

"Okay."

Ella and Hope looked down into a small new nest made of earth, filled with what looked like tiny baby mice, pink and blind in the face of their suddenly opened home. "Aren't they cute?" Hope squealed.

"Yeah," Ella said with a grin. "If you like squirming rodents."

"They're not rodents! They're babies!" Hope cooed and laughed as they tumbled over one another in an effort to escape their invaders.

"We'd better cover them up, Hope, or they might get cold. Besides, we want their mother to come back to them, right?"

"Right."

"We better get out of here, then. We've probably scared her so bad, she's halfway to the Rockies by now." Ella turned and offered the girl her hand. She tried not to smile too broadly as Hope accepted it and they made their way out from under the brambles.

"Ella?" Hope asked, as they walked in the rain toward the house.

"Yes?"

"How come my mama couldn't stay with me?"

"Oh, sweetheart." Ella stopped and knelt in front of her. "She dearly wanted to. Your dad's told me how it was the saddest thing for her that she wouldn't be around to watch you grow up."

Hope looked down at the ground, then glanced at Ella. "Do you think my mama would be mad if I liked you?"

"I don't think so. From what I've heard about your mother,

she'd be very happy if we could be friends."

Hope bit her lower lip for a second, obviously deep in thought. "If you were to be my mother, would you go away too?"

Ella swallowed hard. This little girl had been through so much. But could she make such a promise? "If your dad and I ever get to that point, I promise you that I would try to stay with you for as long as possible."

"But she went to live with Jesus."

"That's right, honey."

"But you wouldn't, right?"

"I'd hope not, but you never know. Life is full of risks like that. When you love somebody, you're always risking that you might lose them. And that hurts. But if you never love anybody, then your life is pretty sad, don't you think?"

Hope nodded solemnly. She suddenly grinned. "Let's go tell Dad about our mud fight!"

Ella threw her head back and laughed. "Oh, I think he'll be able to guess, even though the rain has washed some of it off."

"Do you think he'll be mad?" Hope asked, looking up at Ella briefly as they walked again.

"I don't think so, Hope. I think that actually, he'll be delighted."

~ 11 ~

B y the time they saw their guests to the door, Ella's sides hurt from laughing.

"She's a keeper," Dirk said in a stage whisper as he exited, looking back to wink at Ella.

"No kidding," Logan said, bending to give Ella a quick kiss on the cheek. "She fits right in."

"You're just saying that because I'm crashing on your couch," Ella said with a smile. "You know, hospitality and all."

"No, he's not," said Logan's wife, Reyne. She paused by Ella's side, and Ella felt like she'd known Reyne forever. It was one of those rare, instant friendships that just started off right. Ella smiled at her and held her hand for a moment, hoping that Reyne sensed all the care she felt for her already.

"We are so glad to meet you," Rachel said, stopping beside the two women. "Dinner was excellent. I'm sorry you're leaving tomorrow. I'd like to come again."

Ella smiled with her, embarrassed now by Matthew's friends' lavish praise and attention. She was amazed at their seemingly genuine acceptance of her right from the start. "You all have been so nice. You've helped make my visit truly wonderful."

"Well, we hope you can come again soon," Rachel said, casting a meaningful glance over her shoulder at Matt. "You know there are several positions at the county hospital."

Ella's grin grew as she nodded. "Matt's told me."

"All right, all right," Matt broke in finally. "All of you out. I want some time alone with this woman before she leaves me." He put his arm around her as the party left the porch and hurried down the steps to their cars, dodging puddles and mud as they went. And suddenly, Ella felt as if she were home. It was like the Double M was her ranch, and Matt was her husband, Hope her child. Matt's friends were hers. Even Chad and Wellington were dogs she could get to love. She could see it all, feel it all. And it was wonderful. Oh, how she didn't want to leave!

"I can't believe it hasn't stopped raining! I wanted so much for you to see the whole valley."

"That's okay, Matthew," she said softly, smiling as his other arm went around her. "I'm already impressed. When I actually see the mountains, I'm sure I'll be in awe."

Matt turned her around to face him and after quickly scanning the room to make sure they had their privacy, kissed her softly. She hugged him fiercely, her hands just reaching around his huge torso. "I'm going to miss this place, Matt. I'm going to miss you."

He leaned back to intently study her face, and she met his gaze. It was as if they were silently communicating, and Ella loved every second of it. How long had she begged God for a man like this? How long had she cried out for a relationship with depth and desire? Tears sprang to her eyes as she thought about leaving him the next day. It was like a physical tearing inside. How could they part?

"What's wrong?" he asked in concern, lifting her chin when she dropped her eyes.

"Nothing," she said brightly, forcing a small smile.

"Ella—"

She shook her head. "Really. I'm fine. Just sad about leaving tomorrow."

"I know how you feel," he said, his face underscoring the pain in his voice. "Come with me, Ella." He took her hand and led her again to the front door and out to the porch swing. They sat down, and Matt cleared his throat. He looked so earnest it made Ella tear up all over again.

"Ella...I uh, I know how important your work is to you. How you feel called to it. I love that about you. But what Rachel said...what I said to you earlier... Have you had a chance to think more about a job up here?"

"I have."

Drawing strength from her expression, Matt practically jumped off the swing and knelt in front of her. He took her hand, paused, looked down as if praying and then back into her eyes. "Ella O'Donnell, I never thought I'd love again, but here I am, just crazy about you. Would you consider staying, for more than a job? For us? Ella, will you do me the honor of marrying me?"

Epilogue

The Friday Before Mother's Day, a year later

Ella smiled as the school bus stopped at the end of the road and Hope's small body hopped off it. She had gotten home just in time to welcome home her stepdaughter. Hope loved first grade, mostly because of learning to read and write. She ran up the lane and Ella sighed, trying to remember what it was like to have so much energy you wanted to run everywhere you went. She stroked her growing belly—straining her white maternity uniform's waistline—as Hope drew nearer. "Guess you're taking the extra juice out of me, eh, little one?" She directed her words toward her belly with a smile. "Ah, well, that's all right. I think you're worth it."

Ella opened the door and swung the screen door wide. "Welcome home, pumpkin."

"Mo-om," Hope whined. "I told you not to call me that."

"I thought it was just around other kids."

"No, all the time."

"Oh, okay," Ella said seriously. "How was school?" She helped Hope off with her backpack and jacket, glad that she and the child had become such close friends. When Hope had first called her Mom a month ago, she'd had to leave the room to weep. It still brought her heart to her throat when the girl used the term.

"Oh, yeah, I made you something," Hope said, going back to her backpack and unzipping the pocket. She brought out two brightly colored, construction-paper cards and handed one to Ella.

Ella eased into a chair to look at it. "Honey, it's beautiful. Did you make it yourself?"

The girl nodded earnestly, lifting her eyebrows.

"What a good job you did! 'Happy Mother's Day,'" she read aloud. "'You're a good mom, Ella. Thank you for coming to live with us. Love, Hope.'" Ella swallowed hard. Was it the hormones, or were things always incredibly gut-wrenching around here?

"Thank you, Hope. This is the greatest Mother's Day ever."

"It's your first Mother's Day," Matt said, coming into the kitchen. He looked over Hope's card and gathered the girl into his arms for a big kiss. "Next year, you'll have to teach your baby sister how to make a card. She's going to look up to you for that kind of thing."

Hope nodded gravely, thinking about the responsibility of being a sibling, and Ella spotted the other card in her hand.

"What's your other card, sweetie?"

"Oh," Hope said, looking a bit embarrassed. "It's for Mama. I mean my real mom."

"Oh," Ella said, hesitating for less than a second. "I know what we should do with that. Come with me. We're going for a ride." She reached up to peck her husband on the cheek, and Hope followed along behind her.

Matt came out onto the porch as Ella and Hope pulled up in the Subaru. Hope scampered out first and reached back to pull

86

a huge bouquet of white balloons out. He shook his head, wondering what they were up to.

"Balloons?" he called.

Ella shut the door and nodded with a smile.

"Yeah, Dad," Hope answered him as they climbed the steps. "They're Mama's Mother's Day gift," she said.

"Beth's gift," Ella said, as she panted up the stairs. "Let's go do it now, Hope."

"Okay. I'll go get the card."

"Punch a hole in the corner of it!"

"Okay!"

Ella turned to him and spoke softly. "She came home with that card for Beth. I felt like we needed to do something special. So we're going to airmail it to heaven."

Matt laughed and pulled his wife to him for a hug and kiss. "You're something special, you know it?"

"I do. Don't you forget it."

Matt leaned down to her tummy and talked to the baby. "You hear that, baby girl? Your mom's terrific! You're one lucky girl."

"Her dad's not bad, either," Ella said.

"That's what I hear."

Hope arrived, card in hand, and the trio walked out into the yard. Chad and Wellington ran around them, glad for the company, while Ella tied the card to the bunch of balloons. Then she asked Matt to say a few words. As he searched for words, she separated two of the balloons so she and Matt could each hold one. Hope had the honor of holding the rest.

When they were all standing there in a tight circle, Matt finally found his voice. "We choose this moment to remember what Beth was to us and always will be." He reached for Ella's hand, squeezed it, and then looked up in the sky. "Beth, honey, if you can hear me, we wanted to thank you for your time with us and let you know that we're moving on, never forgetting who you were to us. You were a great mom. So's Ella. I think you'd like my new bride. I think you would've been friends." He looked as if he wanted to go on but was too choked up to do so.

Ella spoke next. "It's my hope not to take your place, Beth, but to add something to your family's lives in different ways. Thank you for making a home, husband, and child that I feel so good about adopting."

"Do you want to say something, honey?" Matt looked at Hope, tears streaming down his face.

"No. I just told her I loved her in the card."

"She'll love getting it," Ella said. "Ready to send it?"

"Ready!"

Matt lifted the child, encircling her with his big arms. Together they and Ella raised their heads to the sky and watched as their balloons and a bright blue card raced upward, swirling and dancing around one another.

"Happy Mother's Day, Beth," Matt whispered, still looking up.

"Happy Mother's Day, Beth," Ella echoed.

"Happy Mother's Day, Mama," Hope said.

"Happy Mother's Day, sweetheart," Matt said to Ella, kissing her cheek.

"Yeah, Happy Mother's Day, Mom," Hope said, reaching out to hug her.

"Come on, Hope," Matt said, pulling her back to him and nuzzling his daughter's neck. "Let's go cook your new mom dinner. I think she deserves special treatment today, don't you?"

"Yeah!"

They turned to race back to the house, but Ella paused to walk just a bit behind them. She wanted always to remember this moment. For she felt truly beloved as a wife, mom, and mother-to-be. And there wasn't a house in the world that would feel more like her childhood vision of a castle than this place.

AUTHOR'S NOTE

Please respect the fine creation God has made in you. The American Cancer Society recommends that every woman get a baseline mammogram by age forty, and possibly earlier. Please ask your primary-care physician to help you decide when to receive your first mammogram.

After your initial exam, continue to seek mammograms every one to two years, as recommended by a doctor familiar with your family health history. Breast cancer is a highly treatable disease, but early detection is imperative.

For more information, call:

Susan G. Komen Breast Cancer Foundation 1-800-IM-AWARE

or the Y-ME National Breast Cancer Hotline at 1-800-221-2141.

ᴧᴧᴧᴧᴧ

Lisa Tawn Bergren is the author of *Refuge, Torchlight, Treasure, Chosen,* and *Firestorm.* She is also a contributing author to the Palisades Christmas novella, *Silver Bells,* available September 1997.

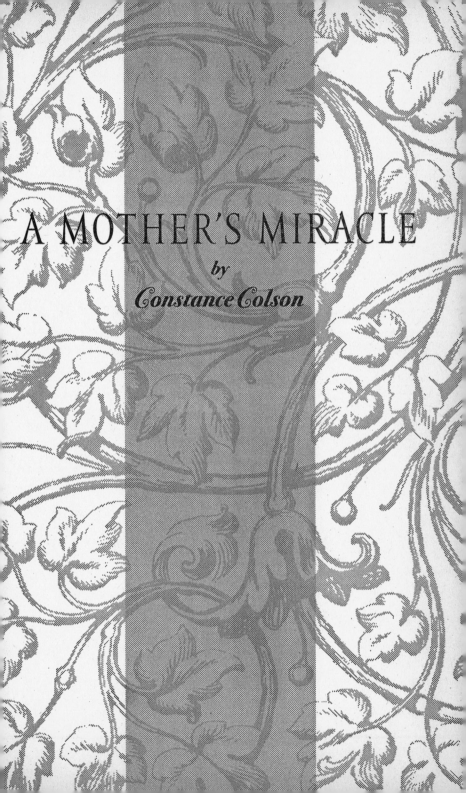

A MOTHER'S MIRACLE

by

Constance Colson

1

N ow what?"

For half a second, Bruce Foster wasn't sure if he had said the words or just thought them too loudly. Speech of any kind sounded strangely muffled under the burgundy canopy at his father's grave site. At least an hour had passed since anyone had spoken. The knot of people attending the interment had unraveled, leaving only him and Dabney.

"So, are you going to give it a shot or hightail it back east, Bruce?" his old friend said. Dabney had been solemn all morning, but now a lopsided grin angled down his face.

Bruce's blue eyes returned to the upturned earth and the polished wood and brass casket resting on the ground above it. "Am I going to give what a shot?"

"Your dad's business." Dabney exhaled an impatient puff of air. "What are you going to do with it?"

Bruce's hand tightened involuntarily, crushing his funeral program. He smoothed the paper out, folded it, and tucked it into the pocket of his twill pants. "Now's not the time, Dab."

"So when is?" Dabney laid his bony hand on Bruce's shoulder. "There hasn't been a good time to talk about it since you arrived, and you're going to have to make a decision right away. The property lease is expiring. With Conglomerate talking about closing, the village council is desperate for new blood. If you don't do something soon—"

"If I don't, you'll lose your job." Bruce shrugged off his friend's hand and regarded the flowers decorating his father's closed casket. There was a colorful mixture of the local and the exotic, lupines and wild daisies alongside antherium and birds-of-paradise. The arrangement was obviously Dab's work: flamboyant, with sharp edges and a bold design. Totally unlike Franklin Foster, although he would have liked the artistry. Bruce supposed that mattered.

"Come on, Brewster," Dabney said. "Unlike everybody else, I'm not worried about my job. Not even if you can't come up with the payroll for a while." His long neck jutted forward, gooselike. "Look, there's no good reason for you to go back to New York, right?"

"Dab—"

"What? I'm right, right? Why don't you stay in Copper Bluff? Maybe this is God's way of bringing you home—"

"I've heard enough greeting-card clichés today. And don't quote Bible to me, either. I'm not ready for it." Bruce shoved his fists deeper inside his pockets. "This happened too fast."

"The council's going to move faster. You know they're thinking about getting a casino in? Cassie Jenson's on the council now. Maybe you could talk to her. Bruce, are you listening?" Dabney pushed his hands forward like a bulldozer shovel. "Brrrm. Foster's Flowers. Flattened. Copper Bluff Casino where your dad's shop and greenhouse used to be. Are you ready for that?"

Bruce trained his eyes on Dabney but said nothing. *Cassie Jenson*. He hadn't heard the name on anyone's lips but his own for six years. Now it stirred emotions deepened by separation and time. The thought of her being so near added to his turmoil. He'd vowed to return to his hometown as a hero or not at all. Well, he was home. But no hero.

"You don't care about Foster's?" Dabney's voice grew louder with each word, filling the canopy. The breeze, which had been building since dawn's gentle rains, finally gathered enough strength to tug at the curtained walls, letting in the scent of moist earth and a wavering shaft of sunshine. It looked to Bruce like an invitation...or an escape.

He stepped outside. The wind moved through the sugar maples and aspens skirting the leaning fence, bringing the smell of new leaves and the sound of slapping leather. A strange memory hit him: he, Dab, and Cassie hiding behind a lilac hedge from what they thought was a ghost. He turned north, looking to the forest past the lilacs and crooked rows of gravestones. Lake Superior lay beyond the trees, unseen but exerting its influence. Like Cassie.

Bruce jammed his hands into his pockets and turned a slow circle. Of the number who had attended his father's funeral, only one person besides himself and Dab remained in the cemetery. Bruce could tell from the slight figure that it was a young woman. She stood in the shadow of a tall white pine, about a hundred yards away. Her dark hair moved with the wind, long and fluid. He couldn't see her downcast face, but something about her—

"Hey, there's Cassie," Dabney said, suddenly near. "Whoops, she saw us. She's leaving. We could catch up with her and ask about your dad's—"

"Let it go, Dabney." Bruce watched her hurry to her red Grand Am and drive away.

Cassie. He could not allow himself to think about her. He slipped his mind into neutral. Inside his pockets, his fingertips touched cool metal keys, reminding him of his rental. Thankful for the distraction, he struck out toward it.

"You're leaving?" Dabney followed him to the blue Mustang and climbed into the passenger seat. "Are you going to give the business a try?"

Bruce started the engine.

"Just tell me what else you've got going. Just tell me," Dabney said, snapping on his seat belt as Bruce drove down the rutted red earth, past hemlocks, lichened gravestones, and molding wooden markers. "You're never going to play ball anymore, and those garages of yours are wasting you. You've got nobody in New York...."

Dabney went on, but Bruce stopped listening. *Nobody in New York.* That was true enough. Nobody anywhere, now. But he still had ties in Copper Bluff. Memories, even if they were mingled with regrets. He'd weathered the worst part of returning: the snickers, sidelong stares, tongue-in-cheek comments about his "career" in the pros. Amazingly, it wasn't as bad as he'd expected. Sure, it hurt. But then so did a lot of things. Like coming home too late.

Dad, I'm sorry.

Pride, his old enemy, had again robbed him of what he loved best. It had alienated Cassie, ruined his career, and stolen time he should have spent with his father. Pride alone had kept him from coming home and going into partnership at Foster's. Now there was nothing to do but drive his rental back to Houghton, catch a plane, and fly back to New York.

Or he could stay and run Foster's.

Immediately he cast the thought aside. *Run Foster's? Without Dad?*

Why not? The seed Dab had planted grew roots that dug into the ground of his mind. Yes, why not? He'd been backpedaling careerwise since his accident. After getting cut from the Yankees two years ago, before he'd even pulled on a jersey, he invested his option money in his first fix-it garage. His plan had been to stay close to New York until he could heal and get back on the team. When it became apparent that his body would never again be pro-athlete material, he had thrown himself into his work instead. One garage had become two, then three, then four. If he kept up the pace, he'd soon be very rich. Very rich, very bored, and very unhappy.

Why not stay? Could there be a future for him in Copper Bluff?

It's crazy. Copper Bluff's going to be just another mining ghost town. Everyone else is talking about leaving. And I'm thinking about going into business?

Crazy. Just like something God would arrange.

For the first time since returning to his hometown, Bruce began to pray.

Cassandra Jenson turned on her Bunn coffeemaker and sat by the kitchen window to wait for it to brew. Nobody in Copper Bluff would have believed she didn't have it synchronized with the rest of her breakfast. Cassandra was known for making use of every second. Even her leisure hours did double duty as community work. As director of Copper Bluff's new tourism bureau and a member of the village council and chamber of commerce, Cassandra not only knew most of Copper Bluff's business, she helped create it.

But as she waited for hot coffee to trickle into the pot, Cassie often let her mind wander from business to dreams.

Today she gazed at the zinnias in her window planter. The rain-smeared view naturally led to soft thoughts, and before long, melancholy had draped itself over her heart like a thick lace veil.

Franklin Foster, gone. Cassie could almost see his New York

Yankees baseball cap, bowl haircut, clear blue eyes, carefully shaven face, green union-suit coveralls, and black work boots. Always the same. Dependable as the brown Ford pickup truck he had used to make deliveries.

The spot on Main Street occupied by Foster's Flowers and Greenhouse would have been better served by a business that attracted more tourism to Copper Bluff, but Cassie pushed Franklin's lease renewal through each year anyway. She said she did it because of her loyalty to established local businesses, but the truth was, she loved Franklin Foster. Better than her own father, who'd had little to do with her since the crisis that brought her home during her first year of college.

Cassie's hard work and dedication in the six years since had improved her reputation and increased her influence in the community, but it hadn't fulfilled her deepest needs. She'd found partial peace and healing since turning to Jesus, but saying good-bye to Franklin had renewed the sense of devastation she thought she'd overcome.

How long it seemed since she'd seen Franklin! Already, she was losing parts of him. His features had become shadowy in her memory; she couldn't remember the exact tone of his voice. *Just like Ian.* The thought jolted Cassie further, but it shouldn't have. In any loss or joy, she thought of Ian.

Cassie dashed away her tears and forced her mind to clear. She went for her coffee, drinking deeply and scalding her tongue and throat before she realized what she was doing. *Help me, Father. Let me forget.* She prayed and picked at her breakfast.

She'd almost drained her mug when she heard a knock on the kitchen door. Careful since her college days about whom she let into her house, Cassie looked out the peephole and was greeted by the face of her next-door neighbor.

"Rhoda, you can come in, but I was just leaving for work." Cassie pulled the door open wider, realizing how cold she sounded. "Would you…like a cup of coffee before I go? It's fresh."

"Thanks." Rhoda stepped in and handed her a ceramic pot. "I'm sorry to stop over without calling, but I was in my flower garden, and this geranium cried, 'Take me to Cassandra!'" Rhoda shrugged, smiled, and sat in the wooden chair Cassie pulled out for her. "What could I do? No flower's ever talked to me before."

Cassie felt a tiny smile on her face as she looked at the geranium, bursting with rocket red blooms. "You must have gotten it at Foster's."

"That I did. Thanks," Rhoda said as Cassie handed her a mug. "Tastes great, but I knew it would. I haven't had anything since six. No, I'm sorry, that's not a hint," Rhoda hurried to say as Cassie offered her one of the Danish pastries she'd had for breakfast. "I usually eat—and sleep—like Dabney's pet pig, but this morning, I was anxious to get outside."

"In the rain?" Feeling a tug of interest, Cassie sat in the chair across from Rhoda.

The woman nodded and put down her mug. "Best time for transplanting: early spring, first rain. Well, maybe this wasn't the first, but it does feel like spring has only now begun." Rhoda pulled her sweater closer around her. "Working the earth is good therapy. So is cooking, but I've made more than I can eat this week already. I need something to do so I won't spend my time worrying about not having a job next year if Conglomerate closes."

"So you plant flowers."

"Sure. Every plant is a living piece of hope. If it can survive, I can, too—even if I do have to go through a winter as harsh as this last one. That's one of the reasons I stopped by Foster's." Rhoda cocked her head. "You and Franklin were close, weren't you? I mean, closer than just friends—more like family."

"Why do you say that?" Cassie sidestepped Rhoda's question gracefully as she rose to get the coffeepot.

"Oh, no more for me, thanks. I mean, sometimes Franklin would talk about you. Over the past few years, I think I've heard him talk about you as much as he did his son. I'm sure Bruce is taking this hard, too, after being away for so many years. Did you see him at the funeral yesterday?"

Unwilling to speak, Cassie nodded.

"I heard he's taking over his dad's business."

"What?" Cassie stared at her neighbor. "Who said that?"

"Dabney. He was going to come over here and talk to you about it. Something about a lease, I think Dabney said, but his pig was trying to get at my moss roses, and I didn't catch it all. Ol' porky got a row of my marigolds before I could stop him. I'm sure he'll catch up with you before long. Don't worry, I mean Dabney, not the pig. It's funny, Bruce taking over Foster's right now, when everybody else is talking about jumping ship."

Cassie tried to lessen the shock of Rhoda's news by concentrating on her neighbor's rambling speech. Listening to Rhoda was like trying to track a hummingbird, Cassie thought crossly, but the thought did not keep her from puzzling over why Bruce would stay in Copper Bluff. She didn't want to question Rhoda about it. Her neighbor rarely landed on a topic; she'd touch down on one, then zoom off to another. This had been Rhoda's way for as long as Cassie had known her, which was since kindergarten. Rhoda hadn't changed a whole lot since then. For an instant, Cassie wondered whether Bruce had changed much in the six years since she'd seen him. "Rhoda, I—"

"You should be going." Rhoda sprang up and was at the door before Cassie could open it for her. "I'm sorry, Cassie. I've just been thinking about you, and…well, here." Rhoda pulled out a wrinkled, smudged envelope from her back pocket and held it out.

Cassie felt very small. "Thank you," she said stiffly.

Rhoda flung her arms around her in response. "God bless you, Cass," she whispered, then was gone.

Cassie stood dumbly, a dirty envelope in her hand and a dirty potted geranium on her glass tabletop near the fruit basket. She flipped the unopened envelope onto the table near the plant and peered out the window to watch Rhoda hop over the low shrub separating their yards. Then she reached for her coat and keys and headed in to work.

As she turned onto Main Street, Cassie conducted a mental tally of community improvements planned for the future: a small local art gallery in the vacant upstairs of the old Allouez Pharmacy; mining exhibits or, dare she hope, a modest museum in the historical society's building. Thoughts of Bruce slowly receded into the background, the furthest she ever succeeded in banishing them.

What can I do, Lord? How can I help this town? Cassie drove slower, praying and thinking, as was her habit each morning.

Copper Bluff had benefited from her devotion. Inexpensive but colorful banners waved from freshly painted streetlamps. Storefronts and window displays competed to attract the eye. Main Street's sidewalks were now shaded by young maple trees, with violets and petunias planted near their trunks. The purple flowers contrasted royally with the old red sandstone buildings.

Usually the sight pleased her, but as Cassie drove past Foster's Flowers and Greenhouse, she swallowed tears. For many reasons, she didn't want Foster's to close, but she definitely did not want Bruce Foster to be the one to keep it open. She calmed herself by recalling that the matter would almost certainly be decided tonight. If Bruce was contemplating taking over the lease, he was a bit late. A casino representative had been making overtures to the council for the past three years.

Foster's had a prime site along Main Street, close to the highway. The casino would almost certainly take its place.

Despite assurances from other community leaders that a gaming house would boost tourism and save the local economy, Cassie had preferred to pursue the tourism angle since learning that Conglomerate Mining and Refining Corporation might close shop. Conglomerate's shoes would eventually have to be filled, however, and the casino had the only feet big enough to do it.

Cassie pulled into the visitor center's lot and parked next to an unoccupied blue Mustang. She recalled seeing it before. Dabney's car? No, the plates showed it was a rental. The first tourists of the season, and already they'd disappeared. What a time to be late! She could only hope that when the car's passengers returned, they'd stop by the center.

Cassie quickly unlocked the center's doors and spread the counter with the new brochures. She scrutinized the room, trying to see it as a tourist would. Antiques from Copper Bluff's mining era and local country-style crafts decorated the walls and floor. Rhoda's homemade potpourri scented the air with cinnamon. The place looked and felt good. Cassie hoped it was good enough to trap the tourist now opening the center's doors.

"Welcome to Copper Blu—" Cassie's business smile faded as the man drew near.

"Thanks, but I've been here before."

Cassie said nothing. She looked at his thick, curly blond hair, pushed back from his forehead. That Foster smile. The angular features and slim athletic build that had made him Copper Bluff's star baseball player, homecoming king, and the recipient of every other honor the town could offer.

Bruce Foster had been Copper Bluff's favorite son. He was also one of the two men in the world Cassie never wanted to see again.

2

Bruce held out his hand, but the slim brunette made no move to take it. If anything, Cassie backed away slightly. Bruce took in the familiar contours of her almond-shaped face. Rounded ruddy cheeks, olive skin, dark brown eyes, black lashes, brows he'd often seen arched in question or irritation, and a slightly curved nose that completed the suggestion of a Middle-Eastern heritage. Her hair was longer and straighter than she had worn it in college, and her unpainted lips were set in a hard, closed line. Obviously the emotions he felt at seeing her again weren't reciprocated. They never had been, and he couldn't blame her. Bruce Foster, before Christ, had been an arrogant idiot. He hoped that Bruce Foster after Christ would be a better hit.

He shuffled through the pile of brochures on the counter in front of her. "These are nice," he said, trying to jump-start the conversation. "Somebody did a lot of work."

"Thank you," Cassie answered without a hint of warmth. "It took time to finish." Toned, shapely arms and neck indicated that she'd taken up aerobics once more, though Bruce doubted she was teaching classes in the small town.

"It's good to see you, Cassie. When you left the university, I didn't expect you to come back here. But then, I didn't expect you to leave the U, either," Bruce said, losing heart as she crossed her arms and made no effort to reply. He sensed that the barrier between them had grown bigger than ever.

"I guess there's no escaping Copper Bluff, is there?" Cassie finally answered. She gazed past him, as if remembering something. From the look on her face, the memory wasn't pleasant.

He ignored her gibe and surveyed the room in an attempt to find fuel to keep the conversation going until she thawed—if that ever happened. The room had a welcoming feel to it, a sense of place and history that intensified his feelings of rootlessness. "Decorate this yourself?"

Cassie nodded but still looked beyond him.

Bruce ran his hand over his jaw, felt stubble, and wondered if he'd remembered to rinse the conditioner out of his hair since he'd also forgotten to shave. Grief made even routine acts a challenge. *You're not here to impress her anyway,* he reminded himself. He gave up on small talk. "I...suppose Dabney's told you what I want."

"What?" Startled out of her thoughts, Cassie slowly focused on his face. Her brown eyes appeared large and dark.

Bruce jangled the car keys in his pocket. "I said, Dabney told me he'd be coming to see you this morning...but I guess he hasn't," he finished lamely. He wasn't up to one of their clashes. Losing his father had taken the fight out of him—and maybe out of Cassie, too, he suddenly realized, taking a second look at her. Though she looked trim and professional in her cream short-sleeved suit dress, she seemed to be fighting tears.

"Cass? You okay? We don't have to talk business today."

Her face relaxed; the tears receded. "This is about...Foster's, then?" She had difficulty saying the word, but no emotions showed. She was treating him like a stranger. He shrugged off his desire to press her further, willing to play by her rules.

"Yes, I'm considering keeping the shop open." *Local boy makes bad,* he thought, and watched for her reaction. "Dabney tells me the lease has to be renewed."

"It does." Her expression gave no sign of her feelings.

"Is there going to be a hitch? Dad…" Bruce choked, but kept going. "My father never seemed to have any trouble."

Cassie started to answer, then hesitated. When she spoke, her voice was all business. "You should be talking to the whole council about this, not just me. There's a meeting tonight at seven in the village hall." She began arranging her brochures. The conversation was unmistakably over.

What had he done to offend her now? "Cassie, what's the problem here?"

"I'm sorry about your father, Bruce."

It sounded like an accusation. Her eyes, too, were hard. There were no tears now. She had the inscrutable gaze of a pitcher: ready to act, thinking a thousand thoughts, yet letting none of them slip and betray the throw. Her gaze held, then released him. She gathered the brochures into a pile, her lashes lowered so her eyes revealed nothing.

Bruce continued to stare at her. The only sound in the room was his jingling car keys.

A minute passed.

"Cassie. Look at me." He could hear his own anger, but he didn't care. Maybe he had come down in the world, but he still deserved better treatment than this.

"I'm busy, Bruce." She moved to a desk behind the counter, sat down, and began sorting through a pile of papers.

Was this the Cassie Jenson his father mentioned so often in his letters? The Cassie Jenson, Bruce couldn't help thinking, who might've been a better daughter to Franklin Foster than Bruce had been a son? Bruce felt the ache in his throat sharpen.

Did she think he'd failed his father, too? Was that how everyone in Copper Bluff felt?

"Cassie," he began harshly, then faltered as he realized he was slipping into his old pride habit. *It's not her fault. I did fail Dad. And I can't take it out on anyone—not even myself.* Bruce reminded himself that he had found forgiveness, a forgiveness that covered all his sins. *Father, help me lose this attitude. Let me show Cassie how I've changed. How I'm changing.*

"Listen, Bruce." Cassie sat perfectly still, as if she'd come to a decision. "I'm busy. Unless you have something else to say, I'll see you at the meeting."

Something else to say? Nothing came to mind as he looked at her angry eyes, her rigid lips. She didn't want to see him; she didn't want to hear him. She only wanted him gone.

So why not make the lady happy?

"Good-bye, Cass." Bruce turned and left the building, not even feeling the pouring rain outside.

"It's all the pig's fault!"

Bruce stared at the crack in the greenhouse door.

"Brewster, come on; it's true!" Dabney laid a hand on his shoulder.

Bruce shook it off and opened the door just as a streak of brown pushed past his pant leg and into the greenhouse.

"There he goes again. *Sebastian!*" Dabney hollered, racing after the potbellied pig. "Come on, Bruce! If he gets into the perennials, it's all over!"

Shaking his head, Bruce turned his baseball cap backwards and broke into a sprint. The pig scrambled over a flat of marigolds and moved on to the second aisle, a rust-colored flower hanging from his snout. He was heading straight toward the perennials. Bruce streaked forward and cut him off.

"The door! Get the door!" Dabney cried as the pig tore back to the entrance.

Bruce reached the door an instant before the animal, then hesitated, stepped aside...and let the little porker escape.

"Oh, way to go!" Dabney scolded indignantly, hands on his hips. "Pig at large! Your fault, Bruce."

"My fault?" Bruce turned his baseball cap around the right way and went to see about the marigolds. "He was already at large when I entered the scene—or when *he* entered *my* scene. Why's he running around loose?"

"Copper Bluff's dogcatchers need something to chase. Thought I'd help out." Dabney snorted. "I told you already; I lost him this morning before I was supposed to see Cassie. I've been after him ever since, looking all over town. Believe me now?"

"Looks like he was after you." Bruce checked a smile as he recalled the way the marigold roots had dangled from the pig's snout like a scruffy beard.

Maybe the run had loosened Bruce up, sloughed off some tension; or maybe his lighter mood had something to do with being in this place his father had loved. Walking down the long aisles of seedlings and flowering plants, Bruce felt as though his father were near, just out of sight: hunched over a petunia, maybe, pruning it to bear more flowers; or watering the herbs at the east end; or up patching the window seams to ensure that sunlight, not rain, flowed through the building. Parts of Franklin Foster were still here, in this building, more crowded with memories than plants.

"This was the closest I've been to Sebastian all morning!" Dabney stewed. "I totally lost him for about an hour, and I was coming here to ask you for help. And you let him get away. No, you actually *helped* him get away!" Dabney sat on the concrete floor and wiped his rain-dampened forehead with one dripping purple sleeve. "I'm blaming you if he winds up a hit-and-run statistic."

Bruce turned assorted pots upright and assessed the damage done to the marigolds. Several stems were smashed into hoof-shaped indentations. "Are you kidding? Look what that pig did in twenty seconds. I wasn't going to see what he could accomplish in a minute. He ruined nearly half a flat as it is."

"So take it out of my pay." Dabney rose, then dusted his orange velour cutoffs and walked out of the greenhouse, pausing to shiver pathetically before he stepped out into the rain.

Bruce walked to the door and watched as Dabney searched the cedar hedges. "Dab," he called after a minute, "I bet if you stay here, Sebastian will come looking for you." *A pig named Sebastian. Leave it to Dab.*

Dabney straightened. "You really think so?" He rubbed his back and flicked a raindrop from his hooked nose.

"Maybe he thinks this is a game. You're the dog; he's the bone. Fetch." This time Bruce did crack a smile, but it vanished so quickly Dabney missed it.

"Pigs are pretty smart," Dabney conceded. "And he *has* come home on his own before. Without a scratch." Dabney rested his chin on his knuckle pensively, then wiped his face with his sleeve again and walked back toward Bruce. "I could use a break," he said, ducking into the greenhouse. "So it didn't go well with Cassie, huh?"

"I'd say if it's up to her, Foster's is finished." Bruce inhaled the rain-thickened air, then exhaled slowly, his breath visible.

"Sorry. I figured she might be an ally. The old alma-mater thing. Guess it backfired." Dabney tipped his head to the side in thought. "You were just bragging when you said you two were getting pretty close that first term at the U, huh? I should've figured."

"I never said that," Bruce protested. Had he?

"Oh no? I've got the letters to prove it, Brewster. Want to see 'em?"

"You kept them?" He *had* said it, then. More hot air coming back to haunt him.

"'Course I kept them. You only wrote me twice, big guy. For a while there, you got too famous to keep in touch with your old buddy." Dabney joined Bruce at the marigolds, picked up one mangled stem, and shrugged. "This could've been worse. You should see Rhoda's marigolds. Zippo. Sebastian wiped out a whole row in one grunt. That was your fault, too."

"No kidding?"

"No kidding at all. Rhoda and Cassie are neighbors. Sebastian escaped for a few minutes when I went to see Cassie at her place—as a favor to you, Brewster. Not that I succeeded. I probably shouldn't have taken him, but he looked at me with those eyes of his. Who could resist?"

"Not Rhoda's marigolds, I guess."

"Hey, you're coming out of it!" Dabney slapped Bruce on the back. "I almost think you were happy for a minute there. Sebastian has that effect on people. Want to go find him?" he asked cheerfully.

"We're waiting for him, remember?" Bruce and Dabney walked toward the door. "Besides, I think I just saw the hedge move."

"Sebastian!"

"Wait." Bruce grabbed Dabney's arm, then went back into the greenhouse and grabbed a ruined six-pack of marigolds. "Here. Bait."

"All right! We're in business." Dabney set the trap near the closest hedge. "You stand there. I'll wait by the greenhouse, in case he tries to make another raid."

"No way. *I* get the greenhouse," Bruce said, shaking raindrops from his cap. He took up his post while Dabney muttered, set the bait, then lay in wait. Before the rain had stopped, Sebastian was captive once more.

"So, I suppose you're going back to the Blighted Apple now," Dabney said as Bruce drove him and his pig home. "When are you leaving? This weekend?"

"I might stay awhile longer," Bruce said evenly. He checked his watch. "I think I'll go to the meeting tonight and see what happens." In the short time he had been home, he'd heard heated talk about the casino. If Foster's held onto its location, it would only be through community support.

And the Lord.

Bruce still felt ashamed to have returned to Copper Bluff just as the son of the late local florist and not as a big-shot Yankees left fielder. But his prayers assured him this was part of God's plan. Humility. That was one lesson he seemed doomed to learn over and over.

"Why, Brewster," Dabney said, grinning widely, "you've still got a little fight in you! That's what I've been praying for."

"A little," Bruce agreed. "But that's about all I've got. I'm open to seeing where God might be leading. I haven't felt good about being in New York. It was that way even before Dad died," he added regretfully. The heavy feeling settled inside him again.

"A little," Dabney echoed. "If your fight was faith, you'd be dangerous. A grain of that stuff can move mountains." Dabney patted the thick, mud-crusted skin of his pet, and Sebastian grunted contentedly. "That's all Cassie has, and look at her: from crisis pregnancy to career woman, standing this town on its ear and loving it. Sure, she's got some pretty deep battle scars, but she's pushing on. I wouldn't be surprised—"

"Crisis pregnancy?" Bruce mouthed the words before he said them.

"Hey, watch the road! You almost took out the new

'Welcome to Copper Bluff' billboard. Cassie'd get you for that."
Dabney gripped Sebastian protectively. "Slow down, will ya?"

Bruce did better than that. He stopped the car.

"Uh-uh. No-parking zone here, Brewster. You'd better keep moving."

Bruce shut off the engine. "Tell me about Cassie."

Dabney looked at him in surprise. "I did. Didn't you read any of my letters?"

"Tell me."

Dabney sighed. "Guess I shouldn't hold it against you. Fame." He sniffed. "I don't know a lot about it anyway. Cassie...doesn't let people get close, you know? Except for your dad. He didn't tell you anything about her getting pregnant?"

"Never said a word." That must have been when—and why—the senior Foster began taking her under his wing. "Was she raped?" Bruce felt burning, blinding fury. His fingers nearly sunk into the steering wheel as he gripped it.

"Smooth-talked is how I heard it—over a bunch of brews."

Not as bad as rape, but close. "Did she have the baby?"

"Yep. Right here in Copper Bluff. Named him Ian. She lived with her parents before she had the baby and afterward, too. Until he died."

Died. "How did it happen?" Bruce asked when he could speak.

"SIDS—sudden infant death syndrome. Happened at around six months. One morning, he just wasn't breathing." Dabney shook his head. "It crushed Cassie. She'd gotten over the shock, people were just getting used to the idea of her having the baby, and then he died." Dabney paused. "He really was a cute little guy. Big dark eyes. Always grinning. Cassie was a good mom," he reflected.

"Who was the father?"

"You probably know the answer to that, if you think about

it. She got pregnant at the U. That's why she never went back."

Bruce didn't respond.

"Well, you didn't think she flunked out, did you?"

"Who...was...it?" Each word was like a minor explosion.

"Some baseball player. I don't remember if she ever said the name. It was nobody anyone in Copper Bluff knew, so no one cared." Dabney looked at Bruce sharply. "You must have known him, though, if he was on the team."

Bruce sat, jangling his car keys, and putting the pieces together. Cassie no longer partying. Quitting her job at the aerobics club. Wearing all those shapeless, colorless outfits for the rest of the year until she left school.

Her recent behavior at the tourism bureau suddenly made sense. No doubt he had reminded her of another ballplayer...and the child she had lost.

3

Ian. Ian. Ian.

Cassie's baby was rarely far from her thoughts, but ever since Bruce entered the visitor center, her day had been a steady stream of memories. Even during the controversial council meeting that evening, Cassie had fought to listen through a fog of past events: learning that her nausea wasn't exam jitters; breaking the news of her pregnancy to her father; giving birth to her son; realizing that because of her choices, she surely had lost Bruce forever.

The memories had come in random order, as usual, each one touching off the next. Like wildfire hopping from treetop to treetop, faster and faster they burned until Cassie felt them consuming her oxygen. She couldn't catch a breath.

"So Alan was Ian's father and Bruce's teammate." Rhoda's voice brought her back to the present. "That I understand. But you're saying that Bruce just sat by after Alan took advantage of you? That he didn't care? I'm sorry, Cassie, but that doesn't sound like Bruce to me. He always had a big heart, even under that inflated ego."

Cassie looked at Rhoda through glazed eyes. When the tears

came, they would wash away her memories for another day. But she didn't want to cry in anyone's presence, including her neighbor's.

On the table in front of Cassie lay the card Rhoda had given her that morning. That card was the reason she'd invited her neighbor over. That and the ridiculous potted geranium that had come with it. After the long, crowded council meeting, Cassie had come home to an empty house. When she'd flipped on the light, there were the envelope and geranium: two points of color and, somehow, comfort. She'd sat down, torn open the card, and read it. She stared at the geranium, then across the yard to Rhoda's home. Rhoda's lights were still on, and yielding to an impulse, Cassie had picked up the phone and thanked her.

The next thing Cassie knew, she and Rhoda were sitting together in her kitchen, sharing coffee and the cinnamon rolls Rhoda brought over. Rhoda was an exasperating talker, but Cassie soon discovered that her old classmate was also an exceptional listener. How long had she been going on like a confessor to a priest? An hour, anyway. Cassie glanced at the clock above her fridge. Midnight! And tomorrow she had to give a speech at the community center's opening. She'd planned to finish and rehearse it after the council meeting tonight.

Rhoda caught her look. "You want to quit for the night, don't you, Cassie? Sounds like it's been a tough day for you, and tomorrow will probably be another." She rose and took their plates to the sink. "Especially if Bruce is staying around. How do you plan to avoid him? It's a very small town."

"I'm betting he won't be here long. You remember how much he used to put Copper Bluff down. Besides, his lease has only temporary approval. The casino's far from dead."

"I know. I heard," Rhoda said calmly.

Cassie focused on the woman's face. "Are you trying to say something?"

"Well, it sounds like you're leaning toward supporting the casino now. Do you know how it would change this town?"

"Do you?" Cassie shot back, glad for a chance to release some of her tension. "Does anyone? There are too many factors to predict." But the words didn't ring true in her ears.

"You're just thinking that if the casino is in, Bruce is out." Rhoda nodded. "That would be true."

"And unfair? Is that what you're implying? If anything, I'm biased *against* the casino. But despite Bruce's attack on it tonight, I don't see that there's any other way this town will survive."

"Isn't it a little soon to give up, Cass? The visitor center opened just last year."

"As Steve pointed out, we don't have the time or the capital to wait. Conglomerate may well close next spring, and if it does, Copper Bluff is done for."

"Who made Steve Milne mayor anyway? I know he's your boyfriend, but the guy's got no imagination. Now you, you've got nothing *but*. Look what you've done for the town in just a few years. If the council and the mayor would fall in line behind you, we could go places. What about other kinds of tourism? Skiing? Or promoting the lake or the fall colors, like you said."

"I think you were the only one who heard me tonight, Rhoda." Cassie rose and dumped her coffee down the drain with her ambitions. "Face it. The casino's coming."

"Well, I don't think it's right. If tourists will come for the casino, why won't they come for other reasons? Better ones? Bruce did have some good ideas on that score."

"He's just trying to protect his own interests."

"At the risk of your wrath, I have to disagree, Cassie."

"Really?" Cassie drew herself up. "If he's so interested in Copper Bluff, why didn't he come home a long time ago?"

"Some people take a long time," Rhoda answered softly.

Cassie ignored the statement. "Bruce broke his father's heart by not coming home. You know that, don't you?"

"Franklin's...and anyone else's?"

Cassie could feel the anger in her rising, anger she thought she'd expelled long ago. "What are you saying, Rhoda?" The words came through tightened lips.

"Listen, Cass." Rhoda stood and pushed in her chair, tucking the platter she'd brought under her arm. "This is a sore spot with you, and a place where I have no right to trespass. In the morning, you'll probably wish you hadn't told me any of this, although I want you to know that I can keep my mouth closed." She paused. "Whatever Bruce was or is, he loved you in high school. Everyone else knew it, even if you didn't. I don't think feelings like that ever go away completely. You might be overlooking something pretty wonderful."

"Rhoda—"

"I know, he drove you crazy." Rhoda winked. "So did I, remember? But if he really is planning to stay in Copper Bluff, you might want to keep an open mind. He may be more like his father than you know. And Franklin Foster wasn't a bad guy, was he?"

"No," Cassie agreed, the thought of Franklin warming her.

"I know you've been hurt a lot, but maybe it's time to give someone a chance to love you. The right way."

Before she could reply, Rhoda said quietly, "Before you get too serious with Steve, maybe you should look beneath the surface."

"Of Steve? Or of Bruce?" Cassie asked, icing over again.

"Both." Rhoda showed herself to the door and out of it.

Cassie sat at her kitchen table until dawn, staring at the red geranium and thinking about subjects she'd avoided for many years.

"Cassie."

Deep in the cloudy vestiges of her morning soulsearch, she hadn't heard Bruce enter the visitor center. Numbly she watched him walk to the counter, feeling as shaky as she had the last time he'd come in. Again she forced herself to appear unmoved. "Once more, you're our first visitor of the day." Her voice sounded much lighter than she felt.

His face mirrored her true emotions. "I'm no visitor," he said, frowning. He stood a few feet before the counter, his hands resting in the pockets of azure-colored shorts just the shade of his eyes.

The logical thing would have been to ask him what he had come for, but Cassie refrained. If it was something other than the lease, she wasn't quite ready to know.

"I'd like to talk with you, Cass."

Cassie sat at her desk, pushed aside the advertising copy she'd been drafting, and folded her arms against the cleared space. "Go ahead." She smiled, bright and false.

Bruce continued to look at her, a slow, steady search that deflated her smile. "I'd like to take you out for lunch," he said, as if struggling for words. "Saturdays must get pretty long." He forced a grin.

"Long, but not busy," Cassie replied, thankful to be talking shop. "We are seeing a trickle of visitors, but not enough."

"Not enough to take the place of Conglomerate." Bruce nodded. "I think you're heading in the right direction with your tourism angle. Would you like to talk about it over lunch?"

His gaze was less intense, less threatening than it used to be, but she didn't feel equal to being alone with him, not even for lunch. "I think we both said what we needed to at the meeting."

"I told myself that, too." He grew sober again. "But it's not true. At least not for me. You just admitted you're not busy, and I promise I won't take much of your time. Please have lunch with me."

Please? This wasn't the Bruce she remembered: loud, proud, and oh-so-sure of himself. The change was refreshing but startling. What was he up to?

"You do eat, don't you, Cassie?" A genuine smile spread over his face, bringing with it a trace of the boy she remembered, the boy who hadn't yet discovered he could do magic with a bat and mitt. He had been a true friend then. Sometimes she still missed those days.

"I eat," she replied, shaking off memories.

"Good. I'll be back around noon." He turned.

"Bruce!" Her exclamation caught him just as he was opening the doors. "I didn't say yes."

"You have other plans?"

"I...might," she hedged.

He almost looked amused. "But you don't, or you'd say so. I'll see you at noon. Still like pasties?"

He remembered? She loved the ethnic food, but she wouldn't admit it. "I was planning to pick up something at the Cozy Café and spend lunch working. Just because no one's coming in doesn't mean there's nothing to do." She waved a hand toward the advertising copy on the desk.

"The Cozy's still open? Great. We'll go there to get the pasties."

"I'm not having lunch with you." As she spoke, she upbraided herself. What else had she thought about all morning except the past and his part in it? *Go, Cass.* Still, she wouldn't budge. She couldn't.

"Cassie." His face was drawn. "I'm not going to beg. I'm not going to annoy you until you say yes. But I found out something yesterday that makes it impossible for me not to talk to you."

Found out something? In spite of herself, Cassie felt her interest kindle.

"I've got some things I have to say," Bruce continued, apparently unaware that he'd already hooked her. "I could say them here. But I'd rather do it at the ridge. If you and the rest of the council are going to run me out of town, I want to spend some time there before I go. How about coming with me? We'll have a picnic. It'll only take an hour."

A picnic. How many hundreds of such outings had they had atop the ridge or in the mine beneath it? The activity didn't scare her; it was the things he had to say. She had things to say too, but it would be so difficult.

Just get it over with, she told herself. *This might be your only opportunity.* "All right, Bruce. One hour."

"Thanks, Cass."

As he left, she had the frightening feeling that their relationship was headed not to an end but to a beginning.

4

"Cass, I'm really sorry. I would've killed Alan if I'd known."

Cassie looked at Bruce over their lunch of pasties, then beyond the ridge to Lake Superior, blue and smeared with humidity. A flock of twenty-three migrating Canada geese flew parallel to the horizon, but wind and distance didn't allow Cassie to hear their honking. She counted each one before she answered Bruce. "It's probably good you didn't know then; though it's hard for me to believe you didn't. You and Alan were friends. You were the one who introduced me to him."

The look of violence on his face was her answer. She took a bite of pasty, giving herself an excuse for silence. The past few days had brought too much soulbaring, but it was necessary, she reminded herself. Bruce wouldn't be in Copper Bluff for long. For a moment she came close to regretting that fact—if what he said was true.

She studied the bobbing golden flowers that had taken root in the hill of old mining tailings around her. Sometimes she'd speculated that perhaps he hadn't known, but it seemed too incredible. The whole world knew. She corrected herself; Copper Bluff knew. But that was her world, not the surreal

University of Michigan campus. An experiment: that's all her time there had been. Partying had been a temporary lifestyle that brought with it eternal consequences: a life had been created. And despite the pain, Ian had been worth it. If only she still had him. If only—

"Cass." Bruce's half-eaten vegetable pasty sat in the napkin on his lap. Crumbs scattered before the ridge's winds. "I'm...so sorry you had to go through it alone."

His tenderness unsettled her. Where was the blustering Bruce she'd known so well? "I wasn't alone, exactly," she said, as if she'd rehearsed it, which she had. This was the reason she'd accepted his invitation. She had once loved him, and it was her duty to tell him about the Lord who had saved her. "I—learned a lot from going through it." A tremor of fear shot through her, and she stopped following her memorized script. Why was sharing her faith always so difficult? And why did it suddenly matter so much if he rejected it? Nervously, she smoothed the white lace that held her ponytail.

He was looking at her, obviously wanting to ask how her pregnancy had happened, what she'd learned. She braced herself, but the questions never came. Instead, he looked over the vermilion ridge toward the hole where Copper Bluff's fortune had begun and ended. "Still there," he mused.

Grateful for the reprieve, Cassie nodded. "But no one uses it. I don't know if anyone even remembers." The hole had once been an outcropping of copper. It was first discovered by the Chippewa. Later it drew the Jesuits, French, and British explorers. Eventually, the outcropping had given way to a mine shaft for the Americans. The shaft led to ten levels, many of which had remained underwater for decades, none of which Conglomerate had used. Copper Bluff itself sat on many such excavations; each had been exploited and abandoned as the rich copper deposits that gave rise to the rush of 1843 petered out.

"Dabney said he never goes in anymore, either." Bruce finished his pasty, then crumpled the wrapper and his napkin and cup into the trash bag he'd produced from his Mustang. "Want to?"

"Go into the mine? The last time I did, we were kids."

"I don't feel any older, do you?"

Cassie turned away. She did feel older. Ages older. She folded her trash and placed it in the bag. "I have to get back."

"Not dressed for a hike?" he asked, looking at her peach linen jumper and white slings. "Or not interested? All right. I'll take you back." He stood and reached a hand toward her. "Thanks for listening, Cass."

Again, his words took her by surprise. She stared at him suspiciously as Rhoda's words came back to her: "Look beneath the surface." *Sounds like a mining cliché.* Cassie dusted off her clothing, picked off a bit of blue fuzz from the blanket Bruce had spread for their picnic, and took his hand to stand.

It was the first time they had touched.

Not the first, she tried to reason with herself as the warmth of his hand spread through her. With a jerk, she broke free— and her heels skittered on the black tailings.

"You used to wear tennis shoes." Bruce chuckled as he reached for her. "A better choice, up here. But you didn't know you'd be coming to the ridge this morning, did you?"

He steadied her, at least physically. But his arms around her did nothing to quiet her heartbeat. It was as erratic as it had been at the university when she discovered too late that somewhere along the line, she had come to love him. Realizing that she still did was just as much of a shock.

It's physical attraction, she argued with herself, *not love.* So that strange electrical energy still sparked between them. So what? He didn't even seem aware of it. He chattered amiably, asking whether or not she thought the childhood treasures they

122

had hidden in the mine were still there. Still, he hadn't let go of her arm, and they were very nearly at his Mustang.

As he opened the door for her, she leaned against the vehicle's metal frame. "I can take it from here."

Slowly, Bruce withdrew. "You always could."

He walked around to his side of the car, glancing at her before he ducked inside.

She could feel every imprint of his touch.

Green floral tape wrapped around the wire, then the rose stem, bonding the two together. Bruce pulled and twisted the tape, molding it and the greens into a finished boutonniere. He held it up for Dabney to see.

"Not bad." Using the flower cutter, Dabney severed the stem of another carnation and stuck it into damp Oasis foam. "Now all we've got left is one groomsman's boutonniere, three bridesmaids' arm bouquets, the table arrangement, and the flower girl's basket." Dabney didn't miss a beat as he worked on the unity-candle arrangement. He tucked in another sweetheart rose, then nestled the white tulle netting low so the flame wouldn't torch it and turn the wedding into a four-alarm fire.

"I did the basket when I got back from lunch," Bruce said, starting on the last boutonniere. "When do you think we'll be done?"

"Got plans?"

"I was thinking of running up to the ridge and going for a climb," Bruce said, feeling a mix of pleasure and shame as his boutonniere took shape. From the big leagues to boutonnieres. Despite his natural interest in floral design, he'd avoided working in the flower shop even during high school. Jocks didn't do flowers. He'd missed out on a lot by keeping his image, he now realized. An unspeakable amount.

He quenched a wave of sadness by completing the boutonniere and moving on to finish the last touches of the table arrangement. If his father could see him now....If Cassie could understand....

"Done!" Dabney threw up his hands. "What a masterpiece! And did you see the bridal bouquet? Beautiful. I love it when they give me free rein. My reputation must be spreading."

Bruce grunted. "So when do you think we'll be done?"

"Here? Not long. There's only the church setup to do after this. That'll be a breeze. It's all arranged—we'll store the flowers over there until the candlelight ceremony." Dabney began fashioning an arm bouquet. "If you're planning to check out the mine, be careful, Brewster. There's a lot more water in those shafts than when we used to go exploring.

"That's what Cassie told me."

"When? Did you see her again?" Dabney looked up, a pink-tipped carnation wobbling in his hand.

"We had lunch today," Bruce said tersely, concentrating on his design.

"Hey, is something going on with you and Cassie? Are you meeting her at the mine? You can take off anytime, you know."

"No, I'm not meeting Cassie at the mine—or anywhere else." Bruce frowned. Lunch had obviously been uneventful for Cassie, but he couldn't forget how he'd trembled when their hands had met. No wonder she'd broken away and nearly wiped out on the tailings. After she pulled back, he had laughed and babbled like a dolt to cover his confusion. She could still short out his system without even trying. Pitiful. The way he'd acted was pitiful.

A stomachache had plagued him the rest of the day, *the result of forcing down his pasty at the ridge.* His churning insides had nothing to do with his emotions, he told himself. Nothing. It was just the stress of doing his first wedding order without his father.

Right.

"Bruce!"

"What!" He nearly jumped.

"I said, are you ditching me and heading up to the mine? It's no big deal. I can finish up," Dabney offered.

"No, I'll help." Bruce managed a weak smile.

"Hey, it's no problem. I like flying solo. It's almost closing anyway. I'll remember to give myself time and a half. You go ahead. Enjoy yourself."

"Time and a half? I'll stay. There should always be at least two in the shop when there's an order to do, anyway," Bruce recited, hearing his father's voice in his head before he realized whose words he was repeating.

The electronic doorbell rang behind the front desk, warning them that a customer had entered the shop. Bruce wiped his hands together and prepared to wait on whomever had come in.

"Ah, about the two-in-the-shop thing," Dabney said, reaching for Bruce's arm. "I, uh, asked Rhoda Billinger to come over. You know, to help out. For free," he added quickly, his hand falling awkwardly to his side. "She's good. She helped with Mother's Day last year as a favor, and she loved it. She's been...she's been wanting to know more about floral design, and I've been teaching her...and....Well, I didn't think you'd mind!" Dabney stormed out to the front desk, leaving Bruce to stare after him.

When he saw the shy hug Dabney gave Rhoda, Bruce understood why his friend had been trying to get rid of him all afternoon. Dabney. In love. Bruce shrugged. Well, it was spring, after all.

He left them alone in the front of the store while he finished his arrangement, and interrupted only before leaving the flower shop.

He'd always enjoyed the ride up to the ridge. Above, a living arch of maple, ash, and aspen leaves turned the sunlight green over the highway. Besides being the most beautiful route to the mine, it was also the most direct. The road had been resurfaced, but was as winding as it had been a decade earlier. Coming out of a curve, Bruce slowed as he glimpsed a bundle of black emerging from the roadside hemlocks ahead. As he watched, a bear cub wandered onto the highway and paused to sit and scratch its stomach with a back paw.

"Hey, buddy, better move off." Bruce rolled down his window and laid on the horn. He looked for the mother bear, then turned back to the cub. It had a green ear tag with a black number, the work of some benevolent ranger. The cub was a foundling, maybe. Or an orphan of roadkill.

Bruce watched the cub rake its claws against ragged brown-tipped fur, lightened by the sun. The cub scratched rhythmically and gazed at Bruce with soulful eyes.

"Come on, little guy, get moving." Bruce honked again, then started to open his car door. With a reproachful look, the cub let his hind leg drop, leaned back on his haunches, then pushed himself forward and ambled into the forest ferns.

As his father's brown pickup followed the final switchback up the ridge, Bruce was still thinking of the cub. He realized that he himself was an orphan now, too.

His mother had died when he was seven. He could remember her through snatches of memories, such as the day she took him to visit the "trolls," the name Upper-Peninsula inhabitants called those living in lower Michigan. Leah Foster had a loving heart and fiery spirit. His father had told many stories to illustrate that fact. Bruce recognized the same qualities in Cassie as he grew older. Probably that was why she attracted him so much.

Get her out of your system, Bruce. His obsession with Cassie had to end. Time and distance hadn't squelched it. Maybe he needed a direct confrontation. *But wasn't that what lunch was all about?*

Bruce sighed wearily. *Why, Lord? Am I supposed to lead her to you? Is that why I can't shake her?* Shortly after receiving Jesus' forgiveness, Bruce had asked his new Savior to touch Cassie's heart also. Two years had passed since then, and the prayers linking him to her had caused his love to grow as deep and solid as an undiscovered vein of copper.

As he reached the ridge, Bruce pulled off the rocky road and shut off the Ford's engine. *Show me, Father. Let me know what I'm supposed to do.* He opened his eyes and slipped his keys into his pocket, grabbed the knapsack he'd packed earlier, and stepped outside.

It was then he realized he wasn't alone.

Parked behind and opposite him, under a brushy overhang that hid it from a view of the road, was a red Grand Am.

ᐰ 5 ᐱ

Moist, red conglomerate rock walls absorbed the beam of Cassie's flashlight as she struggled down the steep opening of the mine shaft. Following old skip rails, she inched her way ahead. Her boots slipped on the wet, rusty metal, and she felt as though each step might plunge her into darkness, but she kept going.

Sixty feet down, she glanced behind her. Daylight had receded to a high, ragged hole above the shaft. Darkness crowded her beam, and Cassie fought a growing sense of claustrophobia. The impromptu climb wasn't the adventure she remembered. Of course, she'd never climbed alone. There had always been Bruce.

Gritting her teeth as she knocked her knee against the jagged rock wall, Cassie pressed on. The water dripping from the low, sloped ceiling lessened as she proceeded, though the eerie sound of its echo continued on behind her. She spied a piece of candle, a relic of years past that reminded her she had no extra batteries. The thought of becoming stranded in blackness set off a chain reaction of panic inside her, but she forced herself to breathe steadily and continued her climb.

When she reached level, though rocky, ground, Cassie rested at the base of the rails. On the ground beside her stood a rusty lantern, its handle worn thin by time and moisture. The lantern and a battered skip car near it had last been used by the miners who abandoned the shaft in 1887. It was impossible not to feel transported to the previous century, impossible not to feel as if she were breathing the same air that had been brought to the miners by adits that reached the surface. She was smelling the same dankness, seeing the moist vapor of each breath. She nearly expected to hear the dull impact of picks, the stutter of air-powered drills. How much sweat had been shed in these narrow rock halls? How much life burned away and discarded like candle stubs?

The shaft was humid and cold, around forty degrees. Cassie's body remained warm in her down jacket, hiking boots, and blue jeans; but her face and bare hands felt chilled. She rubbed her hands together, then moved forward, exploring the idea that had taken hold of her that afternoon. Sweeping her beam up the angled stope to her left, Cassie illuminated the raised ceiling. The stope was thirty feet higher than the shaft walkway. Red rubble from dust to boulder lay in its twenty-four-degree incline, matching the rock's natural angle. Huge timbers supported the man-made cavern, and Cassie couldn't help wondering how much weight bore down on the old, possibly rotted, wood. She quickened her steps.

After another fifty yards, she played her light into a miner's crawl hole which led to the second level. She faced it, sensing rather than seeing the two-hundred-foot drop.

A blast of air erupted from the hole, pitching her sideways. Arms flailing, she smacked the pock-marked wall with one hand and gripped it, hugging the rock and pulling her rubbery limbs away from the opening as she thanked God she had not tumbled. The mysterious blasts were capable of toppling a -

man. She'd never experienced one before, and she lacked the rope that would make it safe to climb to the next level. She'd need to make another trip to determine how many levels of the mine were above water.

Air blasts were a problem, Cassie acknowledged as she neared the shaft's end, though they might be manageable with new timbers, safe steps, and guardrails. Breathing air was abundant; she could feel its slow circulation. The mine's lowest level had been flooded since the pumps quit running a hundred years earlier. How fast was the water rising? In case of a torrent, were the upper levels safe? Many strikes against her plan already existed. Maybe the whole idea was a bust.

She reached the end of the shaft and directed her beam to a domed rise. Descending from the top right corner, in green and white, was a small copper vein as thick as her leg and several feet long. Cassie studied it.

"Ha-lohhhhhhh."

She pivoted and faced the length of the tunnel.

"Ha-lohhh! Hal-loh!" Was it really someone shouting? The underground chambers distorted noises. To the imaginative mind, a falling boulder could sound like rushing water, a dynamite blast, even a shout. She'd been fooled before. She stood still and listened.

"Hehh-lowwww." No question remained. A man's long, insistent call grew closer, though the sound was blurred by the shaft walls. Cassie hit the button of her flashlight and waited in blackness.

A glow lurched toward her, first as weak as a lit cigarette, then brighter and bigger. Crunching footsteps halted, then resumed. The man had stopped calling but kept coming, pausing only to search a stope or drift with his sweeping light.

Who was the shadowy form behind the beam? Someone who'd seen her Grand Am, or he wouldn't be hollering down an abandoned mine shaft. It had to be a stranger. A local would recognize her car and call her name. Cassie fought the urge to jump headlong into the crawl hole. Instead, she grasped a loose rock, judged how far her light would reach, weighed the heavy stone in her hand, and prepared to let fly as she punched her flashlight's on button.

Bruce's startled face lit up a split second before Cassie's missile launched.

"You're trying to kill me now?" Shaken, Bruce flashed his beam at the large rock that had almost smashed his temple. Even on the rebound off the shaft walls, the thing had nearly nailed him. Angrily he trained his light on Cassie, who had grabbed a second rock and was now releasing it to the shaft floor.

"Sorry," she said curtly. She dusted her hand on her jeans.

Bruce stared at her, openmouthed. "Sorry? That's it? Cassie, you shined your light on me, and *then* you threw! Why?"

"I couldn't stop," she muttered, turning toward the crawl hole.

Bruce strode forward, and barely refrained from pinning down her hands to save himself the trouble of another near concussion. "What about the second rock?" he demanded. "Why'd you grab another?"

She shrugged, tracing the crawl hole's descent until her flashlight's beam could reach no farther. "Do you have a rope?"

Bruce shook his head in disbelief. It probably wasn't Christian of him to want to strangle her. "A rope." He shook his head again and thought back to the contents of his knapsack. His breathing slowed; the adrenaline flow tapered off. "Yes, I have a rope, Cassie." He sounded almost calm. Amazing.

"Good. May I use it? I am sorry, Bruce."

"You haven't explained what the second rock was for."

131

"To finish you off," she replied evenly. "I panicked, all right?" She turned away, her voice betraying fear. "I was going on instinct. I saw it was you, but I couldn't stop in time."

Cassie afraid? Her face was impassive, but her actions had been those of someone scared silly. "Okay," he finally answered. He wanted to ask why she'd been so frightened. The mine never held any terror for her before. Nothing on earth had. It didn't figure.

"I—I'm glad it was you, Bruce." She faced him solemnly.

He lowered his flashlight and gave her a grudging smile. As articulate as Cassie could be, sometimes he just couldn't figure out what she was saying. She probably hadn't meant to imply he was a satisfying target. *Probably.*

With his rope, they lowered themselves to the second level, which was above water. A check of the next level proved it was relatively dry as well. They made a quick descent to the fifth shaft and the alcove that had been their clubhouse. In the farthest recess, Bruce knelt, pushed aside a large rock and three smaller ones under it, then reached his hand into the exposed hole.

Cassie's flashlight revealed his find: shreds of what had been their club rules—dictated by Cassie; five soggy, curled scraps of baseball cards; several pieces of copper; various artifacts, including the stone bowl of a native pipe; a hunk of iron pyrite they'd believed worth millions; and a corroded green band.

Bruce rubbed the metal with his thumb. "Our bracelet." The three-dollar jewelry had cost him his savings for a mitt and served as the ring that sealed their secret marriage, which had been officiated by Dabney. He held it out to her.

"No, thank you. That thing should stay buried. Let's go."

Bruce replaced the rocks but slipped the bracelet into his pocket. Climbing up the shafts was harder than climbing down, and when they reached the second level, he persuaded Cassie to take a break.

Amid the darkness of the mine, sitting on the red clay, they shared a flashlight dinner of more pasties, this time with strawberries and water. Less romantic than a candlelight dinner, perhaps to some, but not to Bruce. In their old childhood haunt he felt at ease; self-consciousness and past mistakes were left behind.

"Another?" he asked, holding a Ziploc bag full of berries.

"I can't even finish my pasty. You planned on eating all this yourself?" She pointed to the heap of food left untouched.

"Lunch didn't sit too well with me," he said. As he repacked the food, he felt a wave of sadness. She'd want to leave now, and when he saw her next, it would be a whole new ball game. That was their way: pockets of intimacy, then walls that had to be scaled anew.

"Bruce, before we leave, I want to say something," Cassie began. "Maybe my life doesn't show it, but I've changed. Eternally. Ian was a priceless gift, despite the circumstances of his conception. If I hadn't become pregnant, I wouldn't have been forced to realize my dependence on Jesus. Ian's life was the miracle of creation that led me to the miracle of salvation." She bent her head, evidently embarrassed. "What I mean is…"

"You're a Christian." His voice disclosed none of the swirling emotions inside him. Two years of prayers had been answered. That face and soul he loved so dearly was saved. He ached with thankfulness and had to labor hard not to sweep her up and rock the mine with shouts of joy. *Thank you! Thank you, Father.*

Cassie went on, unaware of his reaction. "Everything changed when I got pregnant: my life, my future, my present, my body. Especially my body. I knew the incredible changes I was going through weren't the result of random evolution. A God was in control, molding me into a mother. When I felt Ian move, when I held him in my arms, when I lost him…I had to know who that God was. And I found out. I found out he became a man and died for me. I know that sounds strange, but it's the greatest miracle of all." She looked as if she was going to speak more, but took a bite of pasty instead. Her fingers twisted the torn fabric at the elbow of her jacket.

"Cassie, I understand. I'm a Christian, too," Bruce said, reaching for her hand.

"You?" She pulled back and started choking on her pasty. Covering her mouth, she leaned forward, sputtering.

He handed her the canteen. "Happened two years ago," he said when she finally stopped coughing. "My trip to the major leagues ended at the hospital after a car accident, as I'm sure you know. But I came face-to-face with God then. When you're flat on your back, you have to look up." He told her of his regrets concerning his relationship with his father, and with her, and somehow wound up asking for her forgiveness. She gave it, wide-eyed.

"I can hardly believe it. I'm—glad, Bruce."

He was well aware that she'd said his name and "glad" in the same sentence. Twice.

They hiked back to the head of the mine shaft, talking excitedly about the changes that had occurred in their lives since college, laughing over their tangles through the years, and sharing the ways in which the Lord had worked.

As they emerged into the sunshine, Cassie tried to wipe clay from her clothes, hair, and face. She grinned at her reflection in her car's rearview mirror.

"I'm a wreck," she declared, fishing a bandanna from her glove compartment. The interior of her Grand Am was strewn with papers, clothing, and assorted containers, which she kicked aside or tossed into the backseat to make room for him. "Sorry. I never seem to have enough time to get this clean. There's space for you now."

"Thanks," he said, sitting down and opening his knapsack.

"Thank you—for coming." She refused the canteen of water he offered. "No, I got enough in the mine. It's a good thing I didn't stone you after all." She actually smiled, causing Bruce to fumble with his canteen cap. Sister in the Lord or not, she could still make his senses spin. "I'll repay you for those batteries. And for the pasties, too."

"Are you going to tell me what brought you down there? I know you must be planning something," he said abruptly, trying not to focus on his feelings. He and Cassie had no future together, he reminded himself. The lease was only temporary. And in less than two days, he was going back to New York. Thank the Lord that he could leave Cassie to the Father's care.

She laid her jacket in her lap. "It feels wonderful to be rid of a few layers." She leaned back in her seat and stretched her arms above her head, then turned her attention back to her jacket and examined a long red tear with down oozing from it. "This is totaled. Just like when we were kids. You'd think I'd learn. It'll have to be my exclusive mining outfit from now on."

"Mining outfit? What's going on, Cass? Are you plotting to get the mine going?"

"I can't; it's Conglomerate's. And they haven't pulled out yet," she said, flashing him a smile and reaching for his canteen. "Perhaps I *am* thirsty."

She was stalling, but Bruce didn't mind. He'd store up every moment of the day as lifetime memories. Cassie didn't hate him. Didn't blame him. And she was saved! He'd been bursting with that knowledge since she'd told him. It could have made him sing if he'd had any kind of voice.

Instead, as she moved closer, he found himself leaning over to kiss her. Drawn by the dark eyes in that dear, familiar face, he acted without forethought. For six years, he'd seen her only in his dreams. But now she was near. So near. Close enough to

135

touch if he wanted to. And suddenly, he wanted to. Their lips met for the briefest of moments.

"Bruce—"

They stared at one another. Had he really done it? Cassie looked as shocked as he felt.

"Cassie, I—" He reached out to apologize, touched the silken hair at her neck, and...kissed her again.

"Bruce!" She pushed him firmly away. Or had she trembled, just a little? In his own state, Bruce couldn't judge. He withdrew to his side of the seat and faced the windshield, waiting for her to lash out at him. He deserved everything she had to say.

There was dead silence.

He glanced at her. She was grasping the steering wheel, facing front.

"What...what did you do that for?" she finally asked.

For the life of him, Bruce didn't know.

He sat, tongue-tied, watching Cassie's forehead sink toward her wrists on the steering wheel.

Suddenly, her head whipped up. "Hey!" With a quick swipe, she cleared a streak of clay from her watch. "Oh, no, it's almost seven! I've been gone two hours! I can't believe..." She glanced in the rearview mirror, grabbed a hank of her muddy hair in one hand, and moaned. "Bruce, get out! I've got to go."

"Where—"

"The community center!"

Sensing her urgency, Bruce did as he was told. As he closed the door, Cassie's tires spun in the tailings. In seconds she had disappeared, though he could still hear her Grand Am bottoming out on the rocks.

Shaking his head, Bruce went to his father's brown pickup and plopped into the front seat. His elbow hung out the window. In the side mirror he spied a long rip that had sliced his sleeve so that it dangled open, revealing a scratch that ran the length of his forearm. His face sported red smears along his forehead and jaw, but it was on the reflection of his lips that his eyes rested. Lips that had kissed Cassie.

Unbelievable.

He untied the bandanna at his neck and emptied his canteen onto it, then washed his face and dabbed at his hair as his thoughts formed. Then he changed into an extra union suit his father kept folded on the floor.

"The community center it is," he said, reaching for his father's Yankees cap on the dash and hesitating only a moment before pulling it on. With a final glance into the mirror, he started the pickup and headed down the ridge after Cassie.

6

And I think that with the kind of partnership I'm talking about, Copper Bluff and Keweenaw County will not only maintain the present job force but expand—greatly. We may never reach the forty thousand workers of the late 1800s, but together we could draw that many annual tourists." Cassie paused and eyed the friends and neighbors who listened to her in the packed community center. She found it astonishing that they never heckled, as they did in her nightmares. God had given her a gift of speech, Steve said. So far, he seemed right.

She tried to gauge the crowd's mood, and saw both frowns and nods. Steve sat beside the podium, facing the audience. His smile had grown thin since she'd begun speaking, and his thick arms rested heavily over the front of his gray Brooks Brothers suit. In the back of the room, looking as scruffy as a prospector and sporting a large grin, stood Bruce. Cassie took a steadying breath and forged on to the finish.

"Community is the heart of Copper Bluff. May this community center serve and strengthen us as we face a future that is uncertain, yes, but with another potential boom in sight. Think big, everyone. The future depends on us."

Cassie stepped down to both applause and hoots; the crowd surged forward.

"Great speech, Cassie!"

"Bigger gamble than the casino, I'm thinkin'."

Fielding hugs and questions, Cassie kept selling her idea until a large, strong hand took her elbow.

"Cassandra, what do you think you're doing?" Steve asked quietly. "You were supposed to dedicate this community center, not start a public debate." He drew her aside, waving off the crowd with an assuring smile. "I'll bring her back," he promised in a raised voice as he propelled her to a screened-in porch occupied only by children.

"Hello, Steve." She plucked his hand from her sleeve. "Good to see you, too."

"You're upset. I apologize for dragging you off, Cassie. But a national park?" His eyes narrowed, lighting with shrewd amusement. "Are you working for Conglomerate?"

Cassie's brows flicked upward in warning. "The park can happen, Steve. I know it. I realize it will take a lot of work; paperwork in particular. I was counting on you for that."

He chuckled. "Cassie, Cassie—it's not possible. Not even with you at the helm."

"But I only pitched the idea; you haven't heard all—"

"It can work, Steve," a voice broke in.

Both Cassie and Steve turned at the interruption. Bruce stood in the doorway, hands buried in the pocket of his union suit and blue eyes peering out from under the bill of his base-ball cap. He looked for all the world like his father. Cassie shivered as she stared at him, a reaction that had nothing to do with the cool evening air coursing through the porch and against the thin gown she wore.

Bruce stepped forward. "If you'd told me what you were after today, I could've been more help, Cassie. And had more to say to Steve here." He reached for Steve's hand and shook it. "She's onto something. I was in the mine today; it's got potential."

An irritated smile twisted Steve's mouth. "And who are you to say anything? A failed ballplayer. Or are you a florist now?"

Bruce's face remained placid, though his tone grew brisk. "My degree in marketing and minor in business tell me she's right, Steve. But I'd bet on Cassie anyway. Always."

Cassie hoped the porch's dim lights would camouflage her blush, which she suspected was doubly deep from his compliment and the memory of something else he'd given her this evening. Two somethings. She felt her breathing quicken and concentrated on slowing it before she spoke. "Thanks, Bruce," she said lightly. "Steve, we can talk about this later. And we will. Listen." She nodded in the direction of the crowd.

Inside the community center, excited conversation was punctuated with exclamations as people chose sides. Folks were taking the idea and running with it. The sound encouraged Cassie. She hooked her forefinger on the necklace at her throat, zipping over the pearls. "I would have spoken to you and the council first, Steve, but I only got the idea this afternoon, and after I investigated the mine, I hardly had time to make myself presentable before my speech. I couldn't wait for a council meeting. Most of the town is here tonight, and we need to begin immediately. The park could take Conglomerate's place!"

"You got the idea this afternoon?" Steve's mouth hung open, then snapped shut. "And you announce it before beginning inquiries, getting contacts, checking out the legalities? Do you know how much red tape a national park—"

"As I said, Mr. Lawyer," she answered, resisting an impulse to tweak his flushed cheeks, "I'm counting on you for that."

Turning toward Bruce, she lost her playfulness. "We've got

unfinished business, too." As her thoughts and emotions raced, she looked away. She'd be hanged if she betrayed her feelings before she knew his. "We'll start negotiations tomorrow," she said coolly. "Give me a call after church."

Without waiting for an answer, Cassie slipped out of the porch and into the crowd, losing herself amid the lovely chaos of Copper Bluff in an uproar.

Bruce waited impatiently until the last agitated citizen left Cassie alone in the community center. He had watched all evening as she breezed through the crowd in her black silk dress, handling question after question with the same infectious enthusiasm. Bruce chided himself for his earlier behavior. Cassie was a beautiful, capable woman, and he'd behaved like a starry-eyed adolescent. Stealing a kiss—make that kisses. He'd be better off leaving for New York pronto.

And yet, he could still feel the tingle of her touch on his skin. It was a sensation he could compare only to the rush of stealing home base or accomplishing a grand slam; even those moments fell pitifully short. And this wasn't a game. Not to him.

As he observed her working the crowd, he tried to guess her feelings. Was she annoyed at him? Offended? Or just humoring him? Her reaction to the kiss had seemed to match his, but the way she'd treated him on the porch...so cold. Was it all for Steve's benefit? What was Steve to her anyway?

"You're still here?"

Bruce raised his head to find her approaching, neither smiling nor completely straight lipped.

"Still," he said, unsure how to proceed.

She stopped by the wall next to him and idly reached for a drooping yellow streamer. The colorful decorations hung halfway down from the ceiling now, and skins of burst balloons littered the white tiled floor. "I apologize for Steve. When he gets steamed, he fires at everybody—except his public." She jerked the streamer loose and crumpled it as she spoke. "Steve prefers to run things his way. But he is a Christian. He realizes he's got some growing to do, and he's working on it."

Her apology took Bruce off guard. "I'm glad to hear Steve's a Christian," he said. He really was, but he also had to be honest. "I'm not as glad about what I think you're telling me. Are you and Steve seeing each other?"

"Steadily. For a while now." Her face was unreadable.

Bruce braced himself. As long as the topic was broached, he might as well ask. "Do you have any plans? Marriage? family?" He took a deep breath. "Breaking up?"

She didn't answer immediately. "That's a little abrupt, don't you think?"

"Depends." He watched her reaction. "What's important to you, Cass? Settling down? Having children? Or are you more into a career?"

She quit crunching up the streamer and tossed it into a trash can without answering.

He waited, but still she said nothing. "A career and children?"

No response.

"A career, then children? Are you open to adoption?"

Maybe her silence should have cautioned him, but he was determined to finish the inning. "How do you feel about me, Cass?" He took her hand, marveling at how wonderful the simple action felt.

She pulled back and leaned against the wall. "Bruce, I don't want to discuss this now. I've got to go home and get some sleep. I'm on my church's serving and activity committees for our May festival tomorrow. It's going to be a busy day—all day."

She didn't need to add how big a day she'd had already, but Bruce couldn't let her walk. Not yet. "Cass, I thought I was meeting you after church tomorrow. Negotiations, remember?" He tried coaxing a smile from her and only lost his own. She wouldn't even look at him.

"Negotiations, yes." She studied her black pumps, ran a weary hand down the seamless waist of her dress, as if to push the exhaustion from her frame. "I'll be worn out tomorrow night and overworked on Monday. Perhaps all week. I can deal on a local and state level, but federal...." He could see her ticking off a mental list. "How would it be if I called you when I get a break?"

"Maybe you don't want to talk with me at all," Bruce suggested, keeping his feelings in check until she answered.

"It's not that. I just—I'm extremely busy." Strain pinched her face. "I'm not playing games with you, Bruce. Though perhaps you deserve it." Her brows raised as she met his eyes.

Savoring the contact, he took his cue. "Look, Cass. I apologize for kissing you, and I hope it doesn't ruin what I considered a great afternoon. I'm sorry for how I did it. It was impulsive, way too early. But I'm not sorry that I did it."

She raised her chin as if for a fight, then lowered it again, and he was amazed to see a smile playing at the corners of her lips. "I can't say I'm sorry, either. I think." Her smile vanished as she sobered. "I'm taking a chance here, Bruce, but considering how long I've known you and what you've told me about yourself today, I feel...a measure of trust toward you."

A *measure* of trust? Was it so hard to come by? Bruce felt himself growing irritated as he anticipated where she was leading. A strike was about to sizzle over the plate. He could feel it. Might as well speed up the delivery. "But?"

"But I want to know if you're going to be around, Bruce. If you're leaving, I think we should forget what happened."

Concern replaced the self-centered tension in his shoulders. *Is that what you do when things get tricky, Cass? Just forget?* There was so much about her he didn't know. Two days wasn't enough time to learn it—or to tell her what she needed to know if their relationship was to move onto serious turf. "Is forgetting what you want to do, Cass?"

"If you're leaving, yes." She refused the hand he held out to her.

"I know long-distance relationships are tough, but can't we take this slow? Write letters? Call? Visit when we can? Regardless of how I acted today, I'm in no rush. I want to take the time to get to know you right. I...care about you, Cass." *Care about you,* he was careful to say. Not *love you.* Honest or not, he wasn't going to leave himself completely vulnerable. "If you're worried about me seeing someone else while we're apart, don't be. There's never been anyone else."

"So you're leaving."

"Monday," he answered.

She nodded, tight lipped. "I hope you have a good trip, Bruce." She said each word with careful deliberation, then turned on her heel and walked away.

"Cassie, you know my situation with the lease better than anyone," he protested, but she was already opening the door and stepping outside. "Cassie!" He slammed his palm on the door frame before following her into the parking lot. She went straight for her car and got inside.

For the third time in three days he watched her Grand Am pulling away. Three times. Three strikes. Or was it his final out?

∼ 7 ∽

The May festival led to another late night for Cassie, then a week filled with council meetings, village meetings, and negotiations with Conglomerate regarding the mine. Steve was buried up to his bolo tie in paperwork, but Cassie's idea had gained considerable public support. She was riding the crest of a wave that might continue to build for years to come.

Why, then, was she so miserable?

It couldn't have been what she received from New York: a Mother's Day card, signed simply, "Love, Bruce." And a wicker basket of daffodils, hyacinths, and tulips from Foster's.

It was thoughtful of him to remember; more than that, to legitimize her. For she *was* a mother, down to the marrow of her bones. Ian lived in her memory. But no one spoke of him, not even Steve, who again claimed he wanted to marry her, although she had yet to see a ring.

As much as she wanted to experience again the miracle of pregnancy and birth, to see her own features in a tiny baby face, she had little time to think of it. Volunteering to serve on the new park advisory commission to promote the proposed

Copper Bluff National Historic Park, juggling village duties, and manning the visitor center took all her energy. Rhoda quit Conglomerate to help with the flux of tourists, phone calls, and faxes caused by the national media attention; but after two weeks, Cassie and Steve decided to hire another full-time worker, hoping that the state monies pledged to set up a full commission staff would come through.

"I'll write up the job description, Cassie," Steve told her when they found a few minutes together. He made her sit in his chair while he leaned against his desk and waited for the lunch he'd ordered for them. "Just tell me what you need."

"Someone we can use for both the center and the park, with an education and background in management, good PR skills, a thorough knowledge of the region...." Cassie's voice stumbled as she fought to speak through her exhaustion.

"You're joking."

"I realize it'll be difficult."

"Impossible, if you insist on someone with local knowledge. You were incredibly lucky to get Rhoda."

Cassie sank into the smooth black leather of his chair. Her burning eyes shifted to the window, and she looked over Main Street, then past it, east, toward the highway—toward New York, she realized dully.

"I don't see how we'll find anyone with those credentials before Conglomerate closes—or even after." Steve broke the long silence and stood, as his secretary brought in two bags. "Thank you, Edna. Give us a half-hour before the next meeting, will you?"

"That long?" Cassie joked after Edna left, trying to get into better humor. "I'm accustomed to eating in ten minutes or less." She lost her appetite altogether when she saw their lunch.

"Bad choice? I know we haven't had pasties in a long time, but I thought you liked them."

"I do." She attempted a smile. "Please ask the blessing, Steve."

"Will do. Father God, thank you for this meal."

Cassie waited for the amen. Steve rarely made long prayers.

"And, please," he added finally, "help us. Amen."

"Feeling a bit overwhelmed?" she asked, picking at her pasty's crust.

"A bit?" He laughed. "I'm out of my class. I spoke with the governor this morning. She says we can present our proposal to the secretary of the interior this fall."

"Perfect." Cassie tried to sound more pleased than she felt.

"*If* the proposal is approved, it's perfect," Steve corrected her. "And if we get support in Congress."

If. If the proposal was approved, *if* Congress supported the bill, *if* Bruce hadn't gone... Cassie shook her head. The thoughts were invading her working time now.

"...do the interviews, hiring, paperwork, etc.," Steve was saying. "That's fine with you, isn't it?"

"I missed that last part. What?"

"I said, I'll have to do some reaching, but I'll try to spare you the details. For the new staff." He eyed her. "Are you with me, Cassie?"

"I'm following you, yes. All right," Cassie agreed. "Thanks." She wiped her hands on a napkin and stood to leave. "I'll...see you later, Steve."

"The commission meeting at seven tonight?"

"I guess so," she answered wearily.

"And, Cassie," Steve added, showing her to the door, "you're doing a fantastic job, but you're working too hard. Eat something before the meeting. And try to get some sleep." He gave her a peck on the cheek. "I know the excitement makes it hard. After all, this will probably be the biggest success of your life."

She smiled wanly, knowing the true reason for her poor

appetite and insomnia. "Good-bye, Steve."

Cassie walked back to the visitor center, engrossed in her thoughts. *Biggest success of my life? Hardly. Ian was my greatest. And I hope not my last. I want another son. I want a family. And I don't think it's ever going to happen with Steve.* Taking a deep breath, she opened the doors and faced the crowd of tourists. *Bruce, I wish you had stayed....*

In the outskirts of New York, lying on his back and staring into the guts of a Plymouth Voyager, Bruce tried not to think about how he should have stayed in Copper Bluff. He didn't ordinarily fix the vehicles that came into his shop. Since he'd returned, though, he'd had to keep busy. So, as he struggled with a tight fit on the starter he was installing, he mentally ran through the monthly figures just in from his other three garages.

But other thoughts hounded him.

He told himself that if Cassie cared, she would have done something to help him stay, like championing a long-term lease for Foster's. But he didn't believe it. Besides, he'd never relied on other people's influence before, though being in the big leagues—or almost being in them—had given him powerful contacts. Contacts that would come in handy where a proposed national park was concerned. That was one reason to call Cassie.

Foster's was another. Bruce's business sense told him the casino would never risk building with talk of a national park in the air. Foster's lease would get approval now. He could return to Copper Bluff.

Could he, really?

His game plan might include moving back and running Foster's. But dating—maybe marrying—Cassie? That would never make the playbook. His greatest boyhood fear had been realized: He was less than a man, and not because he liked working with flowers. His car accident had fractured his pelvis, torn ligaments, and inflicted numerous internal injuries. Sure, he was sound now—outwardly. But the accident had stolen more than his ability to play pro ball. It had robbed him of his ability to have children.

And that punch still winded him.

He exhaled, releasing sorrow with air as he shifted his shoulder blades to ease the tension. *Give me peace, Lord. Help me to trust you for my past. For my future.*

Cassie had had a son of her own. Could she be satisfied with adoption? Could she give up her right to be a biological mother?

Bruce didn't feel that was fair to ask of any woman, which was another reason he'd never seriously dated since his accident. These were issues that ultimately had to be faced, but they weren't the kind to be addressed at the beginning of a relationship. On the other hand, waiting to discuss it after the relationship was under way seemed too late, too unjust all the way around.

But knowing and loving someone first and finding out that she felt the same…for a moment, as he had sat in his father's Ford, looking at his clay-smeared reflection in the side mirror, Bruce had felt hope. It seemed right to follow Cassie. But when she wouldn't even give their relationship a shot because of distance—

"Bruce, call for you."

Bruce gave one last shove on the starter and slid out from under the van. "Thanks, Wade. Finish this?"

"Sure." Wade took Bruce's place on the greasy dolly and rolled underneath the Voyager.

Wiping black stains from his hands, Bruce made his way to the office and picked up the phone lying on his desk. "Hello, Bruce here."

"Hello, Bruce," answered a male voice Bruce couldn't identify. "Steve Milne. This might be a crazy idea, but I've got a proposition for you."

"Enough," Rhoda said, bending over Cassie's shoulder to view the document she'd worked on all day. "It's closing time."

Cassie sighed. "I'll have to continue working at home then." She grimaced at one phrase she hadn't been able to get right. "I can't let Steve see this yet." She made another mark with her pencil, then stuffed the papers into her briefcase. "Ready to lock up? How many today?"

"Tourists? About seventy."

"Down from yesterday." Cassie's frown deepened.

"And up from a week ago. Cassie, you're invited over for supper," Rhoda announced, holding open the doors of the visitor center for her friend before locking them. "You skipped lunch again. You've got to be hungry."

"Thanks for the invitation, but even I am capable of whipping up a Ramen noodle special, Rhoda. I should stay home tonight. I'll eat, finish the proposal, then clean my house. It's nearly as bad as my car." Cassie paused next to her Grand Am.

"Tacos," Rhoda said quietly, opening the door of her army jeep.

Cassie turned as Rhoda's words sank in. "Did you say tacos?"

Rhoda was looking at her and grinning. "I did."

"Is an hour too soon to come?"

"Should be about right," Rhoda answered, and did a quick reverse out of the parking lot.

Cassie was able to get in some cleaning before she crossed the hedge to Rhoda's yard. In the homey, country-style atmosphere of Rhoda's dining room, she ate five tacos, which Rhoda

150

seemed to consider a triumph. During the meal they chatted, but the pauses were long, and by the time they cleared the table all conversation had ceased.

"Since we're so serious tonight, I should tell you that Dabney and I are talking about getting engaged." Rhoda picked at the clean dusky rose tablecloth, a blush on her full cheeks. "I know you think he's goofy, but he is committed to the Lord. He's even got me memorizing Scripture. He's reliable, fun to be with. And I love him."

Cassie leaned across the table to touch Rhoda's arm. "Congratulations. Dabney's very fortunate, and so are you. You don't have to sell him to me."

"Well, most people think Dab's cracked—even after they get to know him. I never thought I'd fall in love when we started dating. It was Sebastian I fell for first, that blessed potbellied pig."

Cassie folded her arms. "So you'll get married, have kids, live happily?"

"Ever after, yes. Only I don't know about the kids part."

"You don't want children?"

"Of course, but children are a gift—one I'm not sure I'll receive. My sister found out she can't have them, and her problem is genetic. I may be the same."

"Oh, Rhoda!"

"You don't have to look so heartbroken. We can adopt, I hope."

"Yes, but…"

"Dabney's adopted. It's a wonderful thing."

"I know, but to have your own; there's no feeling on earth like holding your own child. I think of Ian so often. I couldn't bear knowing for certain that I'd never have another child." Cassie stopped and traced the scrolling of her chair's wooden arm. "I'm sorry, Rhoda. I shouldn't say this to you."

"Then let's change the subject. How are you and Steve doing?"

"I respect Steve…" Cassie began, squirming on the soft cushion underneath her. She wasn't nearly as comfortable as she'd been when she had first come.

"But no sparks? It was the same with Dabney and me for a long time. Not to worry. Doesn't mean a thing. Sparks come with love, not the other way around."

"You sound as if you've changed your mind about Steve."

"Not at all; I'm just clarifying a point. Often chemistry doesn't amount to a hill of beans."

Cassie frowned, thinking of her reaction to Bruce. Chemistry? More like nuclear fission. But Rhoda was correct; it had come *with* love, not before it. With Alan, the sparks had spontaneously burst into flame—scorching, searing heat that rapidly burned itself out and left only cold, dead ashes.

"Cass?"

"Hmm?"

"You don't want to talk about you and Steve? Okay by me."

"No." Cassie cleared her mind. "It's all right. With Steve and me, there are sparks. And he says he wants to marry me."

"But you keep thinking about someone else."

"I'd hoped it wasn't apparent." Cassie rubbed the crease between her brows. "Bruce is thousands of miles away. That's probably for the best. How could we be right for each other? I'm fairly certain he's never been with anyone else, Rhoda. And look at me."

"I'm looking." Rhoda smiled gently. "Don't you think he can forgive you, Cass?"

"It's not that," Cassie responded hurriedly.

"Um…health problems?"

"No, thank God. Alan wasn't carrying anything—that I got, at least. But Bruce is a reminder. He was friends with Alan.

Teammates. And they resemble each other—both slim, athletic, blond, blue eyed. Bruce doesn't mean to, but he brings back so many things I want to forget. When I look at him…"

"You remember Alan. And Ian?"

"I always remember Ian."

After a heavy silence, Cassie got to her feet. "Thanks for the meal. Someday I'd like you to teach me how to cook, but now I've got to go home."

"More cleaning? I'll help."

Though they argued about it all the way to Cassie's, Rhoda insisted on staying long enough to give the house a partial face-lift. Afterward, they rested in the kitchen over grape juice, Colby cheese, crackers, and talk, ending with the topic of daily quiet times with the Lord.

"I don't see how I can squeeze it in, but I'll pray on it, Rhoda."

Rhoda grinned. "That's the whole idea."

"All right." Cassie reached for her friend's hand. "Let's pray. Now. Let's thank God for our friendship, for the way he's blessing you and Dabney."

"Any prayer requests for you?"

"For me?" Cassie sobered. "I want a family, a husband and children, Rhoda. Let's ask God if Bruce and I could live happily ever after, too."

~ 8 ~

Before he could come up with another excuse, Bruce picked up the phone on his nightstand and punched in Cassie's number. He fingered a button on his pajamas, glancing at the clock. Nine already? She'd probably be on her way to the visitor center. What would he say to her answering machine? Hello, this is Bruce; I'm planning to move back to Copper Bluff on the off chance that you and I—

"Hello?"

Cassie. Live. "Ah, hi, Cass. This is Bruce," he gargled. He cleared his throat, wishing he felt better prepared.

"Hello." Her voice was gravelly with sleep.

"Did I wake you?"

"Usually I'm at the center by now." She still sounded groggy.

"Sorry." Time for a quick exit. "Should I call back later?"

"This is fine." Bruce heard her yawn. "You were one of the reasons I was up so late last night, actually. You deserve an apology. I shouldn't have given you an ultimatum, but I felt overwhelmed."

He could relate. "I didn't mean to dump so much on you."

"It wasn't just you."

He waited, but she didn't go on. "Well, thanks, Cass. You've made it easier to say this. I've almost decided to take the job, although I haven't called Steve back yet—"

"Steve?" He could hear an edge to her voice and imagined her eyebrows shooting up. She was awake now.

"He called me last week and said you were looking for someone to pinch-hit as commission staff. He also said Foster's lease would be renewed. Indefinitely."

The line sounded dead.

"Cassie? Weren't you in on this?"

"Not exactly." She sounded irritated.

His hope plummeted. "And you don't like it?"

A long pause. "I don't like the pressure. You and I would be working closely. If things didn't pan out between us..."

"Cass." He tried to keep resentment from his voice. "If things didn't work out between us, I wouldn't blame you...and I could still do my job. I want to move back to Copper Bluff, and I'm committed to the park idea. It was one of the options I mentioned in the village meeting when I first came, remember? I'd like to come now. If you want me to."

She didn't respond.

"Cass, do you want me to come?" There was no reason to hold the pitch any longer. He had to know. Would she swing or sacrifice? He could hear her inhaling deeply as she considered. He held his own breath.

"Yes."

"Yes?" he repeated, stunned.

"Yes! Listen, Bruce, I apologize for cutting this short, but I do have to go to work."

"Okay, see you Friday. Maybe after work we can take a walk in the pine grove, have another picnic or something. We'll talk about it when I get in. 'Bye, Cass."

He was about to plunge the receiver to the cradle and do a

155

victory dance when he heard a small, panicky voice ask, "You're coming Friday? So soon?"

"Steve said you needed someone right away." What was troubling her now?

"We do need someone as quickly as possible," she answered, her reluctance evident.

We? So that was the trouble's source—Steve again. "Cassie, can I ask you something?"

"I suppose."

"Are you and Steve...still seeing each other steadily?"

Another long pause. "We are...."

Bruce's heart dropped into his slippers.

"But I'm reconsidering that, too. I haven't mentioned anything to Steve, but I was planning to talk with him today."

Relief and hope momentarily robbed him of speech, but she spoke through his silence.

"I'll see you Friday, then. And, Bruce? Welcome home."

Several times that day Cassie thought of calling Bruce back and telling him to postpone his arrival, but she didn't have his number and didn't want to ask Steve. There were three area codes for New York, including the one for cellular lines, and directory assistance gave her twelve listings for Bruce Foster in the Bronx alone. Besides, he'd probably be at work, and she didn't know the name of his garage.

The hours ticked by, each one bringing him closer.

Why should it scare her so much?

It seemed such a large commitment, not that commitment scared her. She'd been committed before. Many times. To...well, her job, for one. And Ian. And God.

True, she'd told Rhoda that she'd quit work in a heartbeat if she had to choose between it and having a family, but there were levels of commitment. Like the levels of her commitment to God.

Actually, that was almost as touchy a subject as was Bruce.

She was committed to the Lord, but at present her job demanded her time. When things slowed down, her spiritual life would be better.

Think it through, Cass. If family is so important that you'd quit your job for it, and if your job is so important that it takes priority over God, then… Any way she cut it, God was left in the tailings. Dead last.

Dead was a good way to describe her walk with him lately. But only lately. It would improve. He understood. He'd given her work to do. She had to do it well, didn't she? Her job was a ministry. She was saving Copper Bluff.

She was saving? Wasn't that Jesus' prerogative?

Cassie rubbed her throbbing temples and stared at the document on her desk, scored with slashes, arrows, addenda. Her mind felt like the confused text. Too much—she'd been through too much, and there was too much going on for her to start a serious relationship now. She'd been insane to tell Bruce to come. Crazy. The whole thing was crazy.

Just like something God would arrange. The thought came gently, but it remained even after she pushed aside her papers and leaned forward, resting her elbows on the empty desktop space.

Are you hinting that I need a quiet time, like Rhoda said? All right, Lord. Cassie held her face in her hands and prayed, shutting out the sounds of the fax machine, the telephone, the conversation between Rhoda and the tourists at the counter. Slowly the imaginary weight on her shoulders and the real tension in her forehead lessened. How good it felt to leave several of her burdens on the Lord's broad shoulders! Someday she'd have to learn how to do it more often. Someday—the day that never came.

157

The rest of the week was frenzied. By Wednesday night, Cassie had to stop herself from calling Bruce and asking him to come sooner. Despite her frenetic schedule, she doggedly started each day with a quiet time, choosing Psalm 46, verse 10 for memorization and meditation: "Be still, and know that I am God." The verse sustained her through eighteen-hour days, three-hour meetings, and hour-long phone calls as she and Steve and Rhoda battled red tape.

On Thursday morning, she opened her eyes to fog.

Fog? Either her brain was melting or the sunny day forecasted had not yet begun. She rubbed her grainy eyelids and pulled back the window shade even farther. Milky white banks of fog lay across her yard. She couldn't see Rhoda's house or even the hedge divider. Fog. Gloriously heavy. Just the kind she had loved as a child.

Cassie vaulted from her bed, undaunted by the time. Six o'clock only meant she had three hours before she had to be at the visitor center. The prospect pushed back the weariness she carried around like a backpack of iron pyrite. Today she'd have her devotions outside. In the mist. Today, if only for a while, she would be still and know.

After wolfing down a danish and an obligatory bowl of Grape-Nuts to balance it out, Cassie tucked her Bible under her arm and settled into a lawn chair. Fog hung on all sides, and the sight triggered a memory: she, Dabney, and Bruce sneaking through the pine grove, pretending it was the moors of England and that the three of them were ridding the world of "gargoyles"—fog-covered bushes and boulders. They'd done it countless times, even up until high school. What a shame Bruce wasn't arriving a day earlier! Their walk together might have been a trek through her fondest memories as well.

The image of the pine grove stuck with her as she opened her Bible, and she closed the pages again. Why not have her quiet time in the woods? She knew just the place. A quick drive, a quick walk, and she'd fill her mind with the peace of the fog-drenched forest as insulation against the day's inevitable chaos. The winding main road would be too dangerous, but she could leave her car at the cemetery and hike from there.

Cassie went back into the house to throw on her leather hiking boots, an ivory merino cardigan, and a pair of chestnut-twill tab pants, then headed for her car. She was going to hop the hedge and ask Rhoda to come with her, but then she remembered the hour. Sane people would be sleeping.

Starting the engine and slipping a Bible tape into the deck, Cassie eased out of her driveway. Fog drifted over the road like low-drifting clouds. Perfect. If only she weren't going alone.

Catching herself missing Bruce again, Cassie shut out the feeling by concentrating on her Bible tape. "God is our refuge and strength, an ever-present help in trouble. Therefore we will not fear, though the earth give way and the mountains fall into the heart of the sea." Comforting words, though she rarely thought of God as a refuge. Didn't he expect her to charge into battle, not sit it out? His strength was to fight with, his help to win with, wasn't it?

Wasn't it?

Be still. What if the verse meant more than a time-out from life's hectic pace. What if being still was a way of living?

Interesting thought. Someday she'd puzzle it out.

Foggy mist floated in suspension, stirring along with Bruce as his movements displaced the air. He stepped past ferns and towering birches, trillium, and brooks that sang with recent rains. The ridge trail had become overgrown in the decade since he'd hiked it; apparently the residents of Copper Bluff didn't brave the mosquitoes often enough to keep it well trodden as he and Dabney and Cassie had. Many days they had met at some appointed spot: near what Cassie dubbed Mosquito Falls, or at their underground clubhouse, or if it was foggy, in the virgin white-pine grove.

He was nearing the grove now, passing hemlocks that stood like scraggly frosted skeletons. If not for the heat radiating from the shrouded sun, Bruce could have imagined that the evergreens carried a dusting of snow. Pencil-thin traces of winter's five-foot drifts clung from the shadowed earth under the north side of the ridge. Leaves and twigs pressed flat from the weight of the melted snow packs released rich scents of foliage and earth with each step he took. Ovenbirds cried *teach-er, teach-er,* joining the muted songs of other warblers, all choristers hidden by fog.

As Bruce turned a bend he saw the clearing, a bright spot in the midst of gray. He made for it, breathing the thick, moist air and thinking of his impending meeting with Cassie. He considered the fog God's gift to him for returning early. Upon waking, scouting out a picnic spot for Cassie had been uppermost in his mind. He'd decide upon the exact location after his reconnaissance. Then, after work, he'd bring Cassie there to tell her about his accident…and its results.

That thought sent a shock through his nerves. As he walked, he prayed and pieced together what he'd say. He watched the sun's strong rays cut away the fog. By the time he reached the clearing's tall grass, light had caught the edge of a protruding rock rise. Fog crowded the clearing's outskirts, but in the middle it thinned and rose up in a column, reflecting the sunlight like brilliant, magical smoke from an invisible fire.

The spot was one of his favorites because it was also one of Cassie's. He'd often found her clasping her knees while perched on a mossy boulder that had fallen from the rise onto a ten-foot ledge. There, she was hidden by overhanging brush; she could see without being seen until the trail veered close beneath her.

Edging the clearing's far side were pale blue and pink blooms, the last of spring's hepaticas, and Bruce left the trail to move toward them. A bouquet of one of Cassie's favorite wildflowers might persuade her to come on a walk with him, if nothing else would.

The hepaticas were nearly within grasp. Bruce bent down.

"Flowers last longer if you don't pick them. Any florist worth his salt should know that."

"Cassie?" Turning instinctively toward the boulder, Bruce peered through the wisps of fog.

"I thought you weren't coming until tomorrow." Fog obscured her features, but as she emerged from the shadows, he could see a tranquil smile on her lips. It warmed him more than the climbing sun.

"I got in late last night. Planned to surprise you." He didn't add that he couldn't wait any longer. Settling his affairs in New York had taken three very full days. It called for remarkable restraint not to rush over and find her when Dabney had driven him into Copper Bluff at midnight. It called for even more now. He wanted to sprint across the clearing and clamber up on the rock beside her. "What are you doing here, Cass?"

He stepped close enough to glimpse her widening smile. "I saw the fog."

"And you had to go for a hike." He nodded. "Me, too. I was hoping to find a place for our picnic." Dread at what he'd have to tell her made his mind go blank. "The fog's almost gone," he uttered, unable to think of anything to say except the obvious.

"Almost." She hadn't moved so much as a hair. Like the mist, she seemed suspended. Sunlight and shadow splashed across her form, each struggling for domination. But Cassie stood motionless.

"Are you coming down?" Bruce asked at last, sorry to disturb the silence and the picture she made. He had to tell her what he'd told no one before, and he'd never find a better setting. "I don't have anything for a picnic now, but we could go on a walk," he said, checking his watch. "We've got an hour before work."

As she climbed down, Bruce felt his heart constricting. If she responded as he anticipated, their relationship from then on would be platonic. *A nice word for dead end,* he thought bitterly. *God, why did you allow—* He cut off the prayer and watched Cassie jump the rest of the way to the ground. God had allowed his accident to happen, but Bruce had asked for it by being too proud to let someone else drive him home. Drunken idiot. Thank God he'd hurt only himself.

"Ready, Cassie?" It was a casual question, one that hardly prepared her for what was coming. He gave her a trembling smile and reached for her hand.

"I'm ready."

C assie mutilated the fern frond in her hands, tearing off green serrated leaves and dropping them into her lap. Bruce talked on, his voice a low drone. The fog had lifted. But her heart sank lower with each of his words.

He finished speaking and waited, expressionless, for her reaction. Sitting beside her on the fallen maple tree trunk, dressed in a sage henley and khakis, he was the picture of masculinity. His well-defined forearms rested on strong, muscular legs; his body was tensed, ready for action. She had a flashback of his running the bases, cracking a homer, launching a caught fly ball to the infield. This strong man, with his powerful frame and athletic ability, was sterile?

"You're certain? There's no way you can father children?"

"Not without a miracle." He was pale but answered matter-of-factly, as if he didn't care or didn't realize what his revelation was doing to her.

"Why are you telling me this now?" She choked back other irrational questions that bruised her heart. *Why did you let me love you? Why did you let me hope?*

"How would you have felt if I'd waited any longer, Cass? It's bad enough now, isn't it?" Bruce reached for her hand. She was surprised by the heat of his grip and the tremor that came with his touch. She could still feel, then?

"I want honesty between us, Cass. No fouls, no errors. If we ever consider marriage, I can offer you financial security, complete loyalty and love, a sacred and satisfying physical relationship…but I can't offer you children, unless they're adopted."

"It doesn't seem possible. A car accident and…" Her voice trailed off into a whisper. "How?"

"You want me to get into the details? Because, believe me, I remember every word the doctors said."

She looked away from his haunted blue eyes. Make him relive it? He was suffering enough. "No. You've told me all I need to know." *Father, help me not to add to his pain.* She summoned her strength and weakly squeezed his hand.

The hopeful smile that crept to his lips sent another surge of distress through her, and she felt bitterness following close behind. He still thought they might have a future? Her chance at a normal life had been critically wounded the night Alan shouldered his way into her apartment and got her drunk. It was struck a near fatal blow when she lost Ian. And now it had died completely. She slipped her hand from Bruce's and pushed off the trunk to stand. "I'll have to hike back to my car quickly to make it to the center in time." She winced at the iciness in her voice.

"Are you okay?"

"Are you? I'll live, Bruce." But she wished she wouldn't. He'd been too drunk to be driving. His partying, like hers, had ruined their future together. "The future depends on us," she had said only weeks ago, wondering if he would perceive her double meaning. She'd been wrong. Their future had been determined six years ago, written in the same stone that was now crushing the life out of her heart.

She surfaced from self-pity enough to recognize that his loss outweighed hers. A one-in-a-million chance still existed that she might marry someday, have children. Perhaps. But not with him. *Not with him.* The words repeated in a faulty, labored rhythm. *Not with him. Not with him.* Like a heartbeat about to cease.

She glanced at him and thought she saw something flash in his eyes before he turned away. Disappointment? Impatience? Resentment? How exactly had he expected her to react? He'd had two years to get used to the news. She couldn't get over it in two minutes. She couldn't get over it period.

"I'll walk you to your car. You said it's at the cemetery, right? That's this way." He seemed to understand her thoughts. His voice was flat, and empty hands hung at his sides as he stood. Apparently this had been some sort of test. One she'd failed.

Anger was a ready ally, and it leaped to her rescue. "I'm capable of finding my car myself. Or do you doubt my ability to drive? I'm fine."

"You might be," he answered quietly. "But I'm not."

Cassie saw it again: a flash of pain in his eyes. Pain, not blame or answering anger. She felt ashamed but had no inkling of how to respond. What could she say? Or do?

Be a friend. The hushed answer spoke to her mind, to her dying heart. *Be still. Be a friend.*

She fought the suggestion. Prolong the pain? Why not just cut it off clean, be done with it, done with him? Forever.

"Mind giving me a ride?" Bruce continued in his hopeless tone. "Otherwise I think I'm going to be late my first day on the job." He started down the trail without looking back.

"You're not returning to New York?" She took several unsteady steps toward him, but his long strides were quickly outdistancing her. He obviously wanted to be alone. Why not accommodate him?

Be a friend, she heard again, stronger. A command, almost.

"No, I'm staying. I've got a job here," he answered over his shoulder. He had quit walking, but now he began again, faster.

The inner prompting forced her to speak. "Bruce—" she croaked, but couldn't go on. Be a friend? A mere friend? That would hurt far worse than breaking it off.

"Yes, Cassie?" He turned, his face a careful, neutral mask.

She sighed, but only partially submitted to the inner voice. "Wait up."

Acute awareness marked their relationship from then on, at least for Bruce. He felt a charged energy within himself as he watched Cassie and tried to guess her feelings. He had nothing more to hide, but somehow he sensed that she did. Every day he prayed she would trust him enough to unlock her heart.

Discovering she'd never been to the "Porkies," as the locals called the nearby Porcupine Mountain range, he met Cassie after church one day with a packed pickup and pasties in hand. She laughed and came up with excuses not to go, but at last yielded. The drive there was one blissful, uninterrupted conversation. When Bruce spotted clouds on the horizon, he prayed that the sunny weather and mood would hold, but before they had time to make the climb to the top of Summit Peak, rain struck, turning the hike into a slippery uphill wade.

And Cassie loved it.

The waterfalls were full and the trails empty. Rain deepened the forest scents and brightened the hues of leaf and earth. Though they couldn't see far from the observation tower, they shared an umbrella and looked out over the misty treetops to the gray horizon of Lake Superior. The moment was strangely intimate, as if they were the only two on earth, watching as God formed the rest of creation somewhere beyond the primordial haze.

From that day on, Bruce's goal was to enjoy at least several day trips with Cassie each month. Cassie gave him a good argument whenever he suggested they get away, but she always enjoyed herself once she'd left the town's cares far down the road. She needed the break, and for one day at a time, anyway, he could protect her from whatever force drove her so hard.

Tense moments at the center often dissolved into laughter as they recalled their various misadventures: the day they caught absolutely nothing during an afternoon of fishing at Lake Gogebic, the time they almost capsized their canoe on the Manistique River, the scuba diving trip to the *Mesquite* wreck in the Keweenaw Underwater Preserve, searching for greenstones on the beaches skirting Lake Superior, watching the maples cast a kaleidoscope reflection in the high-altitude waters of Lake of the Clouds. Bruce felt sure they were progressing toward a firm friendship, but Cassie still had moments, days, and weeks of retreat.

What was holding her back?

Bruce pondered the mystery as he took a white carnation from the display cooler and brought it to the back of the flower shop. Was she struggling yet with giving up natural children, or was it something more?

Lord, help me know how to reach her.

As Bruce prayed and pondered, he selected an aerosol can of pink paint. Twirling the carnation by its stem, he sprayed it lightly. He tipped another two dozen, then set the batch in the back cooler to dry. It was after midnight. Dabney and their new worker, Janis, could finish the order before the early afternoon ceremony. While Bruce himself generally helped with wedding setups, he couldn't bring himself to do another. Not when he longed so much for his own.

From the bucket of fern filler, he plucked several withering bunches and discarded them. Then he jotted down an order for

Dabney to make on Monday. Hopefully the alstromeria and Ecuadoran roses would hold out until then, though passersby had been coming into the shop lately and cleaning them out. Tourist trade increased daily, and Cassie was working longer hours than ever, pushing to keep the park proposal moving, pushing to attract more tourism so Copper Bluff would survive when Conglomerate shut its doors.

Was business the only thing keeping her from him? He was doing all he could to lighten her load: working overtime at the center, calling every business contact, and talking to any government official who would listen. He finally convinced Michigan U.S. Representative Jim Longstreet to personally ask the secretary of the interior to read the park proposal. In October, the secretary requested further reasons to justify the area's national interest.

That meant spending more hours with Cassie, researching the geology, history, culture, flora, and fauna surrounding Copper Bluff. Together, they documented the earth's oldest and largest lava flow, which had made possible the area's 97-percent-pure native copper; the unique aboriginal copper mines and pits; the area's rich cultural heritage and unparalleled corporate paternalism; the largest tract of old-growth Eastern white pine in Michigan; and the region's organic life, including orchids and rare warblers.

And then the plans for the park came to a standstill.

"It's not going to happen this term," Representative Longstreet told Bruce in early December. "And probably not in the next, either. You've got a long line to wait in. Acts don't pass overnight, you know."

Try telling that to Cassie, Bruce thought. "Is there anything we can do?"

"I'd recommend concentrating your efforts at the state level, building momentum. I'll keep the bill circulating, let you know if it can make it as a rider, but I think you've got at least a few years' wait."

Bad news wasn't something he wanted to keep from Cassie, but Bruce didn't tell her until just before the conference with Steve and the new park board. Her fire would do the most good then. She was something to see when she became impassioned about a cause.

She was something to see anytime.

One victory was already hers: she'd assured Copper Bluff of a future, whether or not the park ever materialized. By this time, Conglomerate had officially announced that it was closing in the spring. Although the town would lose some of its citizens, it had already gained a few new ones. In affiliation with the state's Department of Natural Resources, the Michigan Nature Association and Keweenaw County Historical Society entered into negotiations with Conglomerate to purchase the land and buildings that formed the smallest but most critical part of the proposed park acreage. Snowmobile, hiking, and cross-country ski trails being constructed on the land attracted businesses to accommodate Copper Bluff's new industry: tourism.

Accordingly, Bruce expanded his own business. Displaced dried-flower arrangements hung from the ceiling to make room for the selection of gourmet coffees and hot chocolate mixes lining the alcove walls nearest the cash register. The wooden counter now was a glass display case with truffles, bonbons, and cinnamon rolls made fresh each morning by Rhoda.

Judging from the way the pastries sold out an hour after opening, Bruce figured Copper Bluff could stand a local bakery. Maybe even a chalet-style bed-and-breakfast. With the village council doing all it could to encourage commerce, the only problem Bruce could foresee was finding employees. Until Conglomerate closed, they'd be scarcer than a triple play. He'd been lucky to find Janis.

Blessed, he corrected himself, *not lucky.* His new worker did seem like a godsend. New to the area, Janis had few friends, so she'd been spending extra time at the shop in order to learn the business. She and Rhoda were talking about stocking the shop with caramel rolls and glazed doughnuts besides the cinnamon rolls. That's what had started Bruce thinking about a bakery. He wasn't ready to spring it on the ladies yet. But when he did, he knew he'd have a cheerleader in Janis. Her spiritual gift was encouragement, no doubt about it. She'd already done his wounded ego a world of good.

Christmas was approaching when Bruce returned home from his latest lobbying trip to the state capital. Dabney had managed the shop in his absence, and upon Bruce's return, he was met by a breathtaking display window, complete with lights, holly, mistletoe, and poinsettias that framed a nativity scene created from dried flowers. The effect was rustic, pastoral, and—judging by sales—an effective draw as well as a great witness.

Bruce admired the window again as he fired up the old Ford. Foster's had a new look and was making profits his father hadn't dreamed possible. The last he'd heard from New York, the garages were booming as well, and one of his managers urged opening another. Financially, Bruce had never seen better days. But personally? He was lonely.

Fellowship with God and friendship with Dabney, Rhoda, Janis, and others at church still didn't satisfy a Cassie-sized emptiness in his heart. Now Bruce understood Adam's feelings when the first man stood in Eden and watched the parade of animals, realizing no mate would be found for him. As Bruce had read the story that morning, he'd felt with a sure sadness that God had made Cassie for him. Except...this wasn't Eden. It was Copper Bluff. And Cassie was more distant than ever.

Was it finally time to give up hope?

In the months since returning to Copper Bluff, he'd come to

grips with many past failures, but he still had far to go. His schedule didn't permit him the time he needed to grieve for his father fully; nor did it leave time to pray, read his Bible, or simply sit by the window and watch the snow fall. And he felt God calling him to be still.

He had to quit one of his jobs, and as much as he hated to face it, he was pretty sure which one it would be. No matter how many hours he worked alongside Cassie, she would still find more to do. It did no good to point out that the pace was wrecking her health and killing her spiritual life. Whatever kept her from him also kept her running. She alone could stop the race. He knew that from personal experience.

Bruce continued to drive down the deserted blacktop toward home, his lights on low beam to minimize the blinding effects of the snowflakes. He was living in his father's house now, and though the trip home took him in the opposite direction from Cassie's place, he felt a strong urge to wheel the pickup around and see her.

Holding his course, he flicked the lights on high beam, then low again. She'd think he was crazy, showing up in the middle of the night. What would he say? If they had trouble communicating during the day, a midnight visit wouldn't help. As much as he wanted to rush the process, they both needed time to work through the barriers separating them.

How much longer would it take? Months? Years? Forever?

Be still, a voice whispered to him. *Be still....*

Bruce sighed and nodded slowly. He'd thought humility was a hard lesson, but patience was harder still, and obedience the worst. If God was asking him to quit working with Cassie, she'd never understand. It would look like he was abandoning her as he had his father. He could only pray that when she filled his position at the center, she wouldn't also fill his place in her heart.

⌁ 10 ⌁

Apart from Mother's Day, Cassie found Christmas to be the hardest time of year to bear. It was so utterly a family holiday, with the focus squarely on children. Most carols and hymns centered on them, from the Babe in the manger to the child opening his gifts. The Twelve Days of Christmas? December was more like one month-long nightmare. She'd tried to keep herself too busy to think, but as she sat alone in her living room with even the tree lights turned off, watching the snow come down, despair hit her like an air blast from the mine. Cassie felt herself free-falling.

She got up from her hunter green divan and moved to the fireplace. A blaze would chase away the physical chill. As she touched a match to the paper and kindling, she wondered how Bruce was spending his evening. The fire shed enough light to illumine the clock above the mantle. One o'clock. The time dismayed her. In the swiftly approaching morning, the only thing she'd have to show for her wasted night would be circles under her eyes.

Was Bruce sleeping, unaware of her troubled spirit? Cassie settled back on the cushions and pulled her Battenberg lace comforter around her. There was no use in going to her bedroom. She had a better chance of sleeping on the divan, near the fire's glow, as she'd spent each Christmas season since losing Ian. If she ever did marry Bruce, would her Christmases be any different?

No children. The prospect was a howling winter wind through her soul.

So was the thought of living without Bruce. In the seven months since he'd returned to Copper Bluff, he'd amazed and humbled her by weathering all her moods, cheerfully sticking by to offer help and direction. In return, she dared hope that someday she might make him a wife he could be proud of. No matter how tired she was becoming, she had to keep laboring to make the park a reality. That achievement would redeem her in the eyes of the community and bring lifelong honor to both herself and Bruce. If she couldn't leave her own flesh and blood as a legacy, perhaps she could leave a national park.

Adoption…the idea was becoming more natural to her. Still, the thought of never again bearing children grieved her. Deeply. If she did marry Bruce, would she resent his infertility? Would regret and bitterness swallow up her love?

Cassie wasn't sure enough to answer, and until she could, she wanted to go no further. She and Bruce hadn't shared another kiss after the first two, but she was dangerously involved nevertheless. Cassie felt a strong bond with him, a kind of jealous possession that had made the last few months even harder.

Because of Janis. The woman was after Bruce.

It didn't matter what Rhoda said. Cassie had observed the way Janis quietly made herself indispensable to him. She'd tasted the glazed doughnuts Janis had made. She'd seen Foster's Christmas display window. She'd heard about Janis's volunteer overtime hours at the shop, and watched her watching Bruce in church from the choir loft. Janis was the epitome of the Proverbs 31 woman: industrious, dignified, an expert home-maker. She hadn't captured Bruce's heart yet, but she wanted it. And she might succeed, if Cassie didn't make up her mind soon.

Janis impressed everyone, including the pastor of Faith Chapel, who'd asked her to give her testimony to the singles Sunday school class. If Janis hadn't lied, the only sins she'd ever committed were of the garden variety. She said she struggled with covetousness. Who didn't? She badly wanted a husband and home. What about children, the forthright Rhoda had asked. If possible, Janis answered shyly. Did she intend to stay in Copper Bluff long, a recent widower wanted to know. Janis's eyes had flickered to Bruce before she answered: maybe. So far she loved Copper Bluff, and she loved her job. How convenient that Bruce had been there to hear.

A prick of guilt penetrated Cassie's thoughts, and she shifted uncomfortably. What if Janis wasn't scheming? What if she were simply a perfect match for Bruce?

And what if Cassie had no business standing in their way? Perhaps she could forget Bruce in time. Steve still claimed he wanted to marry her, though he had yet to produce a ring. His law practice and position assured him of respect, so his reputa-tion wouldn't suffer if he took Copper Bluff's only unwed mother in history for his wife. And if she did somehow marry Steve, they might have children. Their own.

Father, just tell me, Cassie prayed. *You know what's right. For all of us.*

She prayed an hour longer before her eyes closed, but the only answer she got was another enigmatic urging to "Be still," a behavior she hadn't yet mastered. Arranging, taking control—that was where she excelled. But to wait and let things run their course?

You'll have to teach me how, Father, were her last conscious thoughts. *Maybe someday I'll catch on.*

Though he hadn't finagled an invitation to Cassie's parents' place for Christmas, Bruce did get to go for New Year's. Her father was gruff, as she had warned, but the visit answered many of Bruce's questions. Doug Jenson hadn't forgiven his daughter for bearing a child out of wedlock. It was apparent in the way he spoke to her, the way he avoided her touch and the mention of anything to do with children. Cassie's mother did her best to bring the two together, but the gentle pushes simply drove the wedge between father and daughter even deeper.

Cassie was in no mood to talk at the end of the night, so Bruce merely held her to his chest, breathing the warm scent of her hair, feeling its silken strands between his fingers. Though her nearness quickened his senses, he concentrated on letting his love surround her. The electric thrill of their first touches had matured into a soul-deep tenderness, and it took all of his resolve to release her. Would the time ever come when they would no longer be separated by distance or hidden emotions? The question ate at him, gnawing away at his reserve of patience. Cassie didn't need more pressure, Bruce knew, but keeping his own desires and needs in check was a constant struggle.

Winter favored Copper Bluff with nearly two hundred inches of snow. Despite the heavy tourism, Bruce made sure he and Cassie took the time to go tobogganing, cross-country skiing, and snowmobiling. They did some alpine skiing at Iron Mountain, had better luck ice fishing at Lake Gogebic, and strapped on snowshoes to visit the pine grove. At Marquette's Winter Festival, they tested out a luge run and watched a sled-dog race. They observed a ski-flying competition in Ironwood, checked out Michigan Tech students' snow sculptures in Houghton, and helped Lake Superior University students burn a snowman in effigy to celebrate winter's end.

Whether they were under the stars, the white vapor of their breath behind them; or warmed by the glistening sun; or under a glowering winter sky, every moment with Cassie made Bruce more sure of his love and need of her. These moments also made him realize that somebody had to be the first to jump off the giddy merry-go-round they rode.

By February, he'd reduced his hours at the center and reinvested that time into getting to know his God—with the result that by March he was sure he had to quit altogether. He postponed it as long as possible. Then in April he took Cassie out for a lake-trout dinner at Eagle Harbor's refurbished Lighthouse Lodge and told her, as carefully as he could, that it was time for the pinch-hitter to lay down his bat and walk away from the plate for good.

She reacted without sarcasm, without visible signs of surprise, even. She quietly studied the candle burning on their table, then looked out the lighthouse windows to the buoy marking the harbor's reefs. The red light blinked rhythmically in the darkness, as though keeping time with the waves. "You don't care about the park anymore?"

"I care." He reached for her hand and wondered if it was the last time she'd allow him to do so. "But my relationship with God has to come first. You come next, and business is last. I can't keep up Foster's and my work at the center and keep my priorities in line. So I have to quit."

"I see." She picked up her fork and put a flake of trout in her mouth.

"Cassie? Are you angry?"

She shook her head and swallowed. "Just at myself. I've been misjudging you again, Bruce. I thought the park meant the same to you as it once did to me."

"Did? Have your feelings changed?"

"I used to consider the park, I don't know—a monument, I suppose."

"To what?"

"I'm ashamed to answer, actually. To me. A monument to me." She squeezed a lemon quarter over her filet. "I'm beginning to realize what a conceited notion that was. I may not even insist they name it after me anymore." The words were spoken tongue-in-cheek, but her eyes were serious.

"No?"

"Copper Bluff National Park sounds better. Or perhaps Keweenaw National Park, for the county. What do you think?"

I think I love you. But Bruce kept himself from saying it. Though he'd heard her opinions on current politics and social issues, and shared her strongest beliefs, he had never again asked how she felt about him. He sensed her love, but he also sensed that she wasn't quite secure enough to admit it. And he loved her enough to wait.

"I'm half serious, Bruce," Cassie continued, her gaze steady, her brown eyes dark in the candlelight. "I've been so arrogant. But it's finally sinking in that I don't have to prove or somehow redeem myself. Only Jesus pays for sins. My part is…just letting him."

"Being still and knowing that he is God?"

She smiled. "Exactly. I memorized that verse last year. It keeps coming up, reminding me that I still have something to learn from it."

"I think I know what you mean." It was time to test the waters. Reaching into his pocket, Bruce pulled out a polished copper bracelet.

"That's not—" Cassie peered closer at the burnished jewelry's intricate woven design. "It is. Our marriage bracelet." She ran a fingertip over the gleaming metal. "Thank you, Bruce."

Did she understand the bracelet's significance or just consider it an interesting childhood trinket? He pushed away his disappointment, comforted by her evident delight. Maybe in time she'd understand.

"You won't quit until Conglomerate closes, will you, Bruce?" she asked, glancing at him suddenly.

"Not unless you find someone first."

"Good." She studied the bracelet on her wrist. "Maybe we can work something else out by then, too."

He looked at her sharply, but she'd turned her attention to finishing the lake trout, and he could get nothing more out of her.

Winter did a slow, stretching warm-up into spring. Come May, waterfalls gushed in the Porkies; in Copper Bluff, streams widened, and snow packs from the forest trails melted. At the end of a long hike one day, Bruce found himself approaching the edge of the village cemetery.

Bristly blades of grass poked out from his father's grave mound. After Bruce had stood before both his parents' headstones, he visited a site about a hundred yards away, in the shadow of a tall white pine.

Ian Jenson. The letters carved into the piece of copper were small, like that small body Cassie had buried. Losing a father and mother was hard enough, but a child? Grief and regret must have exploded Cassie's heart when she put to rest the little one who was supposed to outlive her.

A son. She'd had a son.

How Bruce wished he could.

Not that a daughter was any less priceless. Or an adopted child any less valuable. But a son. Maybe the old man in him fed his desire for a son of his own flesh, his and Cassie's. He knew it was impossible, perhaps even wrong, but he wanted it anyway. He always had.

Bruce toed the dirt, caught himself, and reached to put the sod back into place. He shoved his earth-stained hands into his pockets, touching the velvety box he had carried around for weeks in case the moment should come when he might slip its contents onto Cassie's finger. He and Cassie had talked of having a family in a what-if kind of way, haltingly and painfully at first. Having a family necessarily implied a wedding, prospects that sent a tingle through him. Maybe they weren't ready for marriage yet, but they had made the play-offs. In recent weeks, Cassie had even come to the defense of adoption during a controversial Sunday singles class.

Steve had said that making each child a wanted child was the way to end the abortion crisis, but Cassie disagreed. "Making room in your heart for a child, wanted or unwanted, your own or someone else's, is the ultimate pro-life act. Most women don't choose abortion. They're pressured into it by a boyfriend or husband who's emotionally or financially unprepared, a parent who wants to hide the shame. If children were valued as children, no matter how, when, why, or by whom they were conceived, there would be no abortion. Ever."

Hers had been the last words on the subject, and Bruce's eyes weren't the only ones blurry when she finished.

Tears smeared his vision now as he looked at Ian's headstone. A wanted child? Probably not at first. But a loved child at last. A very loved child.

Bruce turned as a familiar hand nestled into the crook of his arm. "I've been looking all over, but I didn't think I'd find you here."

"Cass?" He choked, and pulled her to him, swallowing and blinking hard to shut off the flow of emotion.

"What's wrong? What have you been thinking?"

"That I love you." The words were out before he could stop them. "And that I'd love to have a son."

She made no reply except to lay her cheek on his chest.

"Cass, maybe this isn't the greatest setting, but—" He pulled the jewelry box from his pocket and opened it to reveal an engraved gold band of entwined roses with a diamond at each flower's center, seven gems in all. "I've been waiting long enough."

She stared at the box, and tears washed away the words she was struggling to say.

"What's wrong?" Nausea made inroads on his hope.

She held him tightly, but she didn't answer.

"Cass?"

She was trying to regain control of herself. Trying and failing. He held her, but he couldn't let her escape into silence this time. "Cass, please tell me."

"You…want to give this to me? Still? But what—what about Janis?"

"Janis Tate? My employee?" He peered into her face to see if she was serious.

"I think she loves you." Cassie lowered her head as if waiting for a blow. "She's perfect, Bruce. You know how much trouble I'd give you. And…I'm no virgin. No matter how much I wish I was."

"Cass—"

"It was my own fault. I unlocked the door. I let it happen. Sometimes yet I think I glimpse Alan, skulking behind some building or tree, waiting until I'm alone to badger me into getting an abortion. When he began threatening me, I came home. My father told me I should go right back and try to get Alan to marry me because no one else ever would. Deep down, I've always thought he might be right. How could anyone truly want to marry me?"

The missing piece. Now she'd told him everything, and they could move together toward healing. Bruce nudged Cassie's chin upward and kissed the wet corners of her eyes. "Cass, I love you. Only you. I want to marry you. God's love covers all our mistakes, and I believe he meant us for each other. But you'll have to give up...so much. Can you do it, Cass?" His eyes dragged over the verdigris-edged headstone, the tiny raised mound. "With me you'll never have another Ian."

Now it was she who forced their eyes to meet, as she gently turned his face toward hers. "I never would anyway," she answered softly, crying no more. "I've thought a lot about adoption. In some ways, it might be better than having our own. And it would still be something God would arrange. Still a miracle."

Had he heard her right? Numbly, Bruce took the ring and reached for her hand. "Cassie, will you marry me?"

"Ye—" her voice caught as he placed the band on her finger.

"That was a yes, wasn't it?" he asked anxiously.

"Yes. Yes, yes!"

"For better, for worse?" He had to be sure.

"Forever." She smiled, and a single tear slid down her cheek. One tear. For Ian.

"I love you, Cass. I always will." He sealed his promise with a kiss that expressed his love, his years of waiting, his hopes for the future. Their future. Their incredible future together.

When the embrace ended, she whispered shakily, "Think we can do that again?"

"Again and again. And much more—after we're married." He kept his mouth close to her lips, savoring the aftershocks. "Just say when you want the wedding to be."

"I've always liked early spring."

"Next year?" He groaned.

"Next week, if we can get the local florist in gear. He should have time if we make it before Mother's Day."

"That's my Cassie." He moved to kiss her, and stopped short.

"Something wrong?"

"Not a thing. You're marrying me." Joy bubbled up from his soul. He laughed and pulled back to search her face, reading and rereading the love written on it. "They still happen, you know."

"What happen?"

"Miracles." He drew her to him and snuggled in close. "Let's not ever forget."

Epilogue

By the time the Keweenaw National Historical Park was established by Congress, Bruce and Cassandra Foster had shared in four miracles as they adopted four children: their oldest boy from Peru, their youngest from Brazil, and their middle two daughters from China.

And their fifth miracle, their firstborn...was a son.

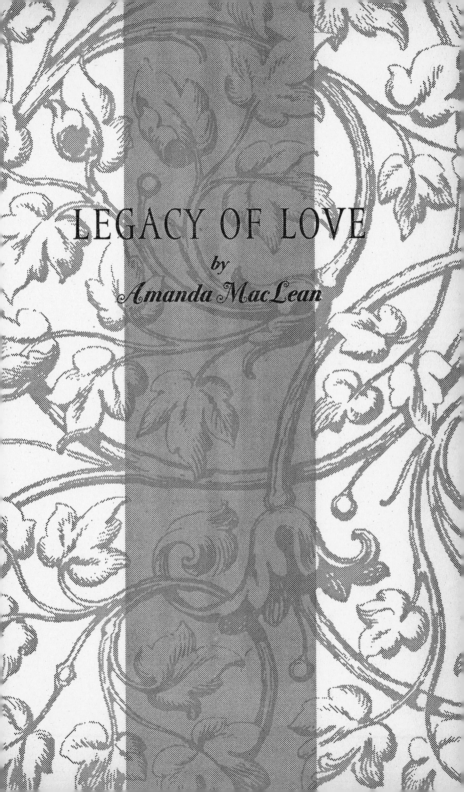

LEGACY OF LOVE

by

Amanda MacLean

1

If the registered letter had arrived any other day, Annie Westbrook would have ripped open the envelope and devoured its contents. But today she signed for its receipt, quickly noted the return address of the Potter and Finch law office in downtown San Francisco, then jammed the unopened post into her jeans pocket.

What she had to tell Gregory tonight made everything else, including the important-looking letter, pale in significance.

Humming to herself, Annie sailed around the condo's tiny kitchen, grabbing fresh chives from her windowsill herb garden and dried spices from the cupboard to make *giambonetti di pollo alle verdure brasate osteria San Matteo*. She planned for the mid-week candlelight supper to be a surprise for Gregory. Normally, on busy weekday evenings they did no more than throw a frozen entree into the microwave. Only on weekends did they have time to experiment with new recipes from *Gourmet* magazine.

But today was different.

Annie grinned as she pulled a bunch of parsley from the

veggie drawer in the refrigerator. Oh, yes. This was a day to celebrate! She held the clump of bouquet-like herbs heavenward and danced around the middle of the floor.

Soon, she had all the ingredients lining the counter. Still humming, Annie began to snip, chop, mix, and sauté. Then she popped the chicken dish into the oven and went on to slice ripe avocados for salad, finishing with a drizzle of sesame vinaigrette atop the pale green fruit.

Standing back, she surveyed the results of her artistry. She and Gregory viewed a wonderful meal that way—pure art, pleasant for the palate as well as the eye. Everything looked perfect.

Annie turned to the table at the far end of the kitchen, near a window that faced a neighboring high-rise apartment complex. She adjusted the blinds to block the view of the ugly building. Now only her three bird feeders, one for songbirds and two others for hummingbirds, were visible outside the glass.

She scooped Gregory's research papers and her own birding books from the table, then reset it with a linen cloth, her grandmother's silver and china, cloth napkins tucked into pewter rings, and a vase filled with fresh roses in the center. Annie had just set a couple of candles in antique holders on either side of the flowers when she heard Gregory's car pull into the carport. She lit the tapers and flipped off the kitchen lights on her way to meet him at the front door.

Annie hastily checked her reflection in the entry mirror, smoothing her sleek, honey blonde hair just as Gregory's footsteps sounded outside.

When she opened the door, her husband smiled into her eyes. She gazed up at him, her breath catching. She'd known Gregory since college and had been married to him for seven years. Still, her husband's very presence caused her heart to thud.

He grinned. "You're looking especially radiant tonight, Mrs. Westbrook." He touched a strand of her hair then tucked it behind her ear.

Annie couldn't help grinning back, her joyful news so overwhelming she wondered whether she could wait until dinner to tell him.

Gregory planted a warm kiss on her lips. "Wow," he murmured, gazing into her eyes. "You make this weary professor *very* glad he's home." He glanced over her shoulder toward the kitchen and raised his brows when he caught sight of the candlelit table. "Something smells delicious. And a table set with candles?" He looked in wonder at Annie. "Someone from school must have called you." Before she could comment, he continued, "And what a reason to celebrate!"

"Celebrate—?" She opened her eyes wide. He couldn't possibly know her news, but before she could say so, his face lit up like an excited schoolboy.

"Come, I think you'd better sit down," he said.

She nodded. But he was the one who needed to sit, she thought wryly. They moved to the small living room and settled onto the sofa in front of the fireplace.

Gregory took her hand. "Do you remember the box of old letters I bought at the old Rutherford place?"

She nodded. "The ones you picked up at the auction a couple months ago?"

"For a song." He grinned. "I've had the box in my office at school. I didn't have time to go through them until today." He shook his head slowly in wonder. Then he stood and retrieved his briefcase from where he'd left it by the front door. He opened it up and rifled through the contents. Finally, he turned back to her and strode across the room.

He held out some yellowed papers to her. "Look through these, honey." His face was alight with expectation. He swiped at his brown hair, pushing it from his forehead.

Annie took the brittle pages from him, first scanning the date, then the signature on the last page. She gasped audibly. "Greg…" she whispered in awe, understanding the significance. "Jedediah Smith? The mountain man?"

He nodded wordlessly, his excitement showing on his face.

"You said that only a few of his journals have been found." She paused. "And virtually no letters." She knew this only because for years Gregory had talked about writing a book about explorer and trapper Jedediah Smith, a young man who had blazed new trails into much of the West in the early part of the nineteenth century.

He nodded excitedly. "He was an educated man and wrote incessantly—that was noted by many others who observed it. But most of his work was destroyed in a fire after he died. Very little remains."

Annie looked down at the letter in her hands, touching it almost reverently. "How many are there?"

"Three complete letters. Very lengthy. Seven to ten pages each." Gregory threw back his head and laughed in joy. "Annie, do you know what this means?"

"Your book," she said. "It means you have new information for your book. You can begin it now."

He couldn't stop grinning. "And credibility, Annie. Publishers will look at my work with interest. Tremendous interest. Now the college won't dare turn down my request for a sabbatical." He picked up the letters. "With these in my possession—how can they say no?"

"Sabbatical?"

"Oh, honey, I know this comes as a surprise. But we've talked about it before. Dreamed about it. Taking a year off, retracing Jedediah's steps on the trails he blazed west." He picked up Annie's hand again and looked deep into her eyes.

"Of course, we'd still need money to live on. I'll have to go on half pay during the sabbatical. But now that I've got the letters, maybe I can get an advance from a publisher."

Gregory pushed himself up from the couch and moved the fire screen to stoke the fire. The flames licked upward for a moment. Then he turned back to Annie. "Just think, honey. A year from now we may be on the road! Just as we've always planned."

Annie gave him a small smile. Gregory's own smile faded. He studied her face thoughtfully, carefully. "There's something wrong, isn't there?" he asked softly. "I can see it in your face."

She swallowed hard, then let out a deep sigh.

"It's Birds of a Feather, isn't it? We'd be away during the fall migration."

Annie chuckled quietly and shook her head. Gregory knew the delight she took in her bird-watching enterprise. Her background was ornithology, specializing in bird behavior, particularly along the Pacific flyway of migrating birds. She had begun a small group, Birds of a Feather, for bird lovers, and led bird-watching tours around nearby marshes, foothills, and canyons. It was a volunteer effort; the members counted and reported on species in a certain area several times a year for the American Ornithologists Union. Although she loved the group of eccentric people and was committed to their efforts, she could certainly leave it for a short time.

No, much less than a year from now there would be another reason that would make it difficult for her to accompany her husband.

He regarded her intently. "What is it, Annie?"

"No one from school called to tell me about the letters."

Gregory frowned. "Then how did you know?"

"I didn't."

He glanced toward the kitchen, the candlelit table, then

191

looked back to Annie with a quizzical expression. "You didn't?"

She shook her head and took another deep breath. "You're the one who needs to sit down, Greg."

He crossed the few feet between them and settled onto the sofa beside her, his eyes never leaving her face. "What is it, honey? Are you all right?"

"I've never been better. Or maybe I should say *we've* never been better."

"We?"

She laughed softly again. For most of their married years she'd been waiting for the moment when she could finally tell Gregory they were going to have a baby. They had tried for so long. Only recently had they given up hope, thinking that maybe God meant for them to remain childless.

"We," she repeated, arching a brow. "My suspicions were confirmed by the doctor today." She watched her husband's face as the dawning came.

"Doctor?" There was a moment of stunned silence. "You don't mean 'we' as in…" He seemed to lose his voice.

Annie nodded, smiling. "Darling," she whispered, "we're going to have a baby!"

"A baby…" He looked into her eyes with wonder. "A baby?" he repeated. "Annie, are you all right? I've been rattling on about mountain men and trappers and sabbaticals, and you're sitting here holding in the news of a miracle. A real miracle." His gaze caressed her face.

"Yes, I'm all right. A bit tired, perhaps, but the joy makes up for it." She touched his face gently. "And I wanted to hear your news. The letters—"

He reached for her hand and turning it over, kissed her palm. "What letters?" he finally said with a grin. Then he pulled her into his arms. "Oh, sweetheart," he whispered, "you've just made me the happiest man in the world."

Annie snuggled against his shoulder, but she couldn't help wondering about his joyous plans of taking the sabbatical, writing, and traveling. The college would pay him only half a year's salary for an entire year away. And there was the expense of traveling.

And, of course, the expense of the coming baby.

No matter how happy they were right now, part of Annie was saddened knowing that Gregory's dream seemed unachievable. It broke her heart, knowing how important the trip was. She only hoped it wouldn't break his.

After supper, intent on babying her, Gregory filled the bathtub with fragrant bubbles, then ordered Annie to relax and soak while he loaded the dishwasher and cleaned the kitchen.

Weary and grateful, Annie gave him a kiss on the cheek and headed for the tub.

She'd already tossed her jeans into the hamper and stepped into the water when she remembered the registered letter—still crammed in her pocket, in the hamper. But as she lazily settled into the bubbles, closing her eyes and leaning back against the inflated pillow, Annie decided she'd wait until morning to read it.

After all, it probably had to do with Birds of a Feather. The group was always stepping on corporate toes—protesting the building of something or other in endangered-species habitats. It wouldn't be the first warning letter she'd received. Or the last.

She slid further under the bubbling water, closing her eyes in reverie. Suddenly, she sat up with a start. Potter and Finch weren't corporate lawyers. And the letter wasn't addressed to Birds of a Feather.

Her eyes widened. She remembered hearing that they specialized in estate and inheritance law.

What could they possibly want with Annie Westbrook?

Dripping wet, she stood, grabbed her terry robe, and padded back to the hamper.

With trembling fingers, Annie opened the letter and began to read.

∿ 2 ∿

Gregory unlocked his office door at the college, placed his briefcase on his desk, then opened his file cabinet and rifled through the folders until he came to the lecture notes for his next class, History of the American West.

He settled heavily into his chair, propped up the sheets of paper, and began to read. But his mind was anywhere but on Texas cattle drives and the Goodnight-Loving Trail.

For nearly half an hour he tried to concentrate. Finally, giving up in exasperation, he headed for the faculty lounge to grab a cup of coffee. A short time later, he returned to his office, mug in hand, ready to give his work another try.

Again he sank into his chair and stared at his notes. The words swam in front of him. He chuckled softly. It was no use. He could only think of Annie and the baby.

He was going to be a father!

He wanted to shout it from the rooftops. Would it be a boy or a girl? Maybe he'd have his mother's eyes, the color of dusky emeralds. Or perhaps she would look like him, with dark curly hair.

It seemed like forever that he and Annie had prayed for a baby. Now, after seven years, their prayers had been answered.

Gregory's joy was deep and profound. *A child.* The fruit of his and Annie's love for each other. A small piece of eternity that God was giving them to bear and to raise. He found it difficult to take in.

Suddenly, he sat up straighter. His child to raise?

He drew in a quick breath. He was responsible for this child's well-being...from now until adulthood. Until then, Greg and Annie would provide the nurturing—emotional, spiritual, physical—that their little girl or boy needed.

Gregory took a sip of coffee, trying to calm his pounding heart. How could he do it? It was one thing for him and his wife to work together providing a loving and stable home for themselves. But now, this precious little life would be dependent on them—on him—for everything.

He set his mug on the desk, thinking about the condo that he and Annie had rented for the last few years. It had no nursery. Or any space to make one. He didn't even know if children were allowed in the complex.

Annie and their coming baby deserved better. Somehow, he would see that they got it. With that thought in mind, Gregory settled back in his chair, propped his feet on his desk, and picked up his lecture notes once more.

He'd just started to read when his gaze moved to his still open briefcase. Tucked in a protective manila envelope, the Jedediah Smith letters lay atop a stack of papers and file folders.

He knew their value to him as a historian, but now he considered them with new wonder. What might their value be to a serious collector of Western Americana or to a museum, for that matter?

Could they possibly bring in enough for a down payment on a house? He pictured a place in the city near their jobs but with yard enough to fill with playing children.

He and Annie loved San Francisco, with its museums, concert halls, and gourmet restaurants. And they had a church home here, an integral part of their lives and friendships.

They had talked of someday buying an old Victorian to restore, putting down permanent roots in the city they both loved. He grinned slowly as a plan began to form. Maybe now was the time.

He would begin making inquiries immediately. It didn't matter if he had to drive the length of the state himself, showing the letters to every collector and museum curator he could find. As soon as they were authenticated, he would sell them and begin the house search.

Wasn't it just like God to provide exactly what he and Annie and the baby needed, even before they were aware of the need?

Gregory took another swallow of coffee, gathered his notes and papers for class, then reached across the desk to lower the briefcase cover. Before he flicked the clasp shut, he straightened the Smith envelope and slid it into a secure leather pocket, thinking how the letters now held even greater value to him than before.

By the time he locked the office door and headed to class, he'd made one more decision: all of this would be a surprise for Annie. He was sure she'd try to discourage him, knowing how important the letters were for his work.

Yes, he decided, this would be his surprise.

Annie sat in the plush Potter and Finch offices, awaiting her appointment. She pulled the letter from her purse, rereading the words for at least the tenth time since the night before. She scanned through the legalese of the first three paragraphs, then let her gaze settle on the final few sentences:

As the sole executor and beneficiary of the estate, please immediately contact the law offices of Potter and Finch for an appointment to expedite the issues listed above pertaining to the last will and testament of Sheridan Anne Jade.

Annie smiled as she thought of her grandmother's maiden sister. She'd been named for her, although even as a child, she'd preferred Annie to Sheridan. She remembered her great-aunt's telling her about the ancestor for whom they'd both been named, Sheridan O'Brian Jade. She'd come from Ireland, and it was said she'd traveled to California's gold-rush country in the 1850s, looking for her missing twin brother, Shamus. She'd found her brother, and a handsome husband in the bargain. It was a romantic story that the older folks in Annie's family enjoyed telling and retelling through the years.

Annie couldn't count the number of times she'd heard the tale before her grandparents died and her aunts and uncles and cousins moved from the area. Even her own parents now lived a half a world away, in Africa, working as staff members of a humanitarian agency.

Only Aunt Sheridan had remained, living in a little house in a place called Everlasting, the same home that Annie's great-great-grandfather Marcus O'Brian had built for his beautiful Irish wife, the first Sheridan.

And now—Annie glanced again at the letter in disbelief—the house and all the acreage around it belonged to her.

"Mrs. Westbrook?" The chic but pleasant-looking receptionist glanced in Annie's direction.

"Yes?"

"Mr. Potter is ready to see you now."

"Thank you." Annie gathered her handbag and followed the young woman into the law office's polished-mahogany-and-leather inner sanctum.

Already seated at the far end of a large desk, Charles Potter stood and shook her hand. He had a mane of silver hair, but his face remained unfurrowed by time except for some laugh lines around his eyes. "Please, sit down," he invited with a nod.

Annie sank into a soft, high-backed leather chair near him, folding her hands in her lap.

Charles Potter smiled as he reseated himself. "I don't know if you were aware that my friendship with your great-aunt went back some years."

Annie shook her head. "No, I'm sorry, I didn't know," she said, then paused. "I hadn't been out to see Aunt Sheridan for quite some time," she added with some embarrassment. It was one of those things she always planned to do in the future, but with Everlasting more than a two-hour drive from San Francisco, she hadn't gotten around to it. And except for time pressures and busyness, there was really no excuse.

"Your aunt did not die a lonely old woman," Potter said, as if reading her thoughts. "Quite the contrary. She was as full of spirit and laughter on the last day of her life as when I met her decades ago. And she didn't lack friends." He chuckled. "Far from it. She was active in the community and in her church. Always fighting a cause of some sort or another, especially when it came to preserving Everlasting Diggins in all its gold-rush glory. Twenty-five years ago it was actually Sheridan's idea to get the state government to turn Everlasting into a state historical park."

"I was only five at the time, but I remember the celebration when the state finally approved the application. She invited the whole family for a party at her house, a big barbecue in the yard for aunts, uncles, and passels of cousins."

"Sheridan was also actively involved in wildlife preservation." Potter smiled. "And no lumber company in the West dared fell a giant redwood without knowing at some point they'd face the wrath of one Sheridan Anne Jade." He laughed softly. "That's where I came into the picture. She hired me to help her fight the entire logging industry. It wasn't really my area of practice," he explained. "But Sheridan became good friends with my wife, and I didn't have much choice in the matter." He smiled again, caught up in memories.

"It became a labor of love. We didn't win many battles. But believe me, when they saw the fire in that little white-haired lady's eye, they did sit up and take notice."

"I wish I'd taken the time to know her better," Annie said wistfully.

"I think she understood. I also think that's why she left you everything."

"What do you mean?"

"I suspect she hoped that when you traveled to Everlasting to take possession of her house, you'd feel the spirit of the place." He let out a deep sigh. "She loved that little place and used to speak of the love it held. She often told me about the generations of loving words uttered within its walls. One time she said she wished the walls could talk. She longed to hear the voices of the children who'd been raised there."

He paused, looking at Annie with a smile. "You'll soon see. One doorjamb in the kitchen has never been painted over. The measurements of growing children date back to the 1860s. Sheridan and Marcus Jade's children are the first recorded. They had their own, of course, as well as two children they'd adopted. Duncan and Evangelia, I believe their names were. You can trace their heights through the years from the marks."

Suddenly, Annie couldn't wait to see the old place, even if she did plan to sell it. "How soon can I go there?"

Charles Potter chuckled. "I think you're more like your aunt than you know. She was never one to hesitate in any circumstance."

He looked through some papers on the desk, then back to

Annie. "I'll go over all the legal documents in a few minutes, but in short, all of your aunt's possessions now belong to you. Even including the house and its contents, your inheritance is modest, except for the land, of course, which includes some ten acres just outside Everlasting."

Annie let out an appreciative sigh.

"I don't know how much you remember about the place, but there's a pond, some marshlands, and beautiful rolling hills covered with live oaks."

"Do you have any idea what it all might be worth?"

Potter gave her a sharp look. "You're not thinking of selling it?"

"Our lives are very much entrenched in San Francisco. We love it here. Besides, it's too far to commute. And I wouldn't want the cottage to go to ruin. I'm afraid it would if someone isn't living there, caring for it."

He nodded sympathetically. "I understand. As far as its value..." He hesitated, a frown pleating his forehead. "The real-estate market's flat right now—especially in the foothills area. He quoted her a figure, looking apologetic. "And there's no legal stipulation in the will that you can't do exactly as you like with the inheritance. I do encourage you, though, to go out there and take a look at the contents of the house before you put it on the market, if that's your intent. Your aunt left you some beautiful antiques."

Potter pulled more papers from the stack and began the tedious task of explaining the details of Annie's inheritance.

But as he droned on, Annie's mind raced ahead to the sale of the property. She hadn't told Gregory about the letter last night because she'd had an inkling of what she might do with her inheritance. Now she was certain.

She smiled to herself. If she could sell it for a price close to what Charles Potter mentioned, it would more than pay for

Gregory's sabbatical and the research time he needed to write his book. Now that he had in his possession the Jedediah Smith letters, his credibility as a historian would be enhanced, and his dream of writing that book could become a reality.

Annie sat forward, forcing herself to focus her attention on the legal documents. But all she could think about was the light she'd see in Gregory's eyes when she finally told him about her surprise.

~ 3 ~

An hour later, Annie swung her custom-decorated Birds of a Feather van into the carport at the condo. She was puzzled to see that Gregory hadn't yet arrived home from school.

She hurried up the stairs and checked the answering machine. The light was blinking rapidly, showing three messages had been recorded. While she changed into her jeans, she listened to the first.

It was from Pearl Flynn, who volunteered in the Birds of a Feather office, haphazardly kept the books, and manned the decades-old Olivetti manual typewriter. Even on their field excursions, she wore bright caftans, which more often than not were covered with prints of wildfowl plumage of every description. Pearl sported brilliant red hair springing out from beneath an ever present plastic visor. She had confided to Annie that her natural hair had only a little help from a bottle, though sometimes Annie noticed it tended more toward a deep purple shade than the auburn Pearl wanted.

"Hello, sweetie!" Pearl chirped on the tape in her raspy voice. "Looking forward to the Birds' trip tomorrow. I've arranged for the sack lunches and drinks for seven people.

Even picked up a new cooler. Styrofoam from the corner mini-market. Though you know how easily the last one cracked. Leave it to Woodrow to drop it." She sighed loudly. "Well, we'll just hope he hangs on to this one." She paused. "Oh, and don't forget to gas up the van. Gonna be a long jaunt. I've told everyone to be here by eight in the morning, with lists and birding books and binocs in hand. That's all, honey. Ta-ta."

The second message was from Woodrow Hornberger, a courtly widower in his early seventies. Although officially retired from his job as a building contractor, he was busier than most working people. He spent summers building houses in Mississippi with Habitat for Humanity, volunteered the rest of the year as a consultant for nonprofit agencies helping the poor around the world, and—in his free time—pursued his hobby of amateur bird-watching. He'd been part of Birds of a Feather for the past three years.

Woodrow's patience knew no bounds, except when it came to Pearl Flynn. He was the woman's polar opposite: while he was genteel and dignified, speaking softly and earnestly, Pearl burst into lives, rooms, and conversations like a flame-haired dervish. In short, she drove the normally amiable Woodrow to exasperated distraction.

Annie listened to Woodrow's message as she laced up her hightop sneakers.

"Hello, Annie," he said. "I've just checked tomorrow's weather in the Sierra foothills. Should be a grand day for us all. Temperatures in the seventies. I also stopped by the American Ornithologists Union and picked up a few regional checklists using common names for classification."

Annie grinned. She knew Woodrow was too polite to say so, but he'd picked up the lists for Pearl. Most of the group enjoyed the challenge of using the Latin scientific names to identify birds, but Pearl merely rolled her eyes and stuck to the common names. She sometimes even made up a few of her own.

"Anyway, dear," Woodrow went on, "while I was there, I heard there've been some sightings of the Bohemian waxwing. They normally don't venture this far south. Would be a wonder to see one." Before hanging up he went on to describe a few more species they might see tomorrow and said he'd picked up a map of the region.

Finally, the tone sounded for the third message. It was from Gregory. Annie smiled and stepped closer to the answering machine.

"Hi, honey," he said. "I'm sorry I'm going to be late tonight. I need to drive to Sacramento to see someone about the Smith letters, so it's going to be late by the time I get home. Sorry for the short notice, but the expert I want to see is heading to England by the end of the week, and this was his only available appointment." He let out a deep sigh. "I'm sorry, sweetie. I miss you." With that, the message cut off.

Annie frowned, disappointed that they couldn't spend the evening together. Although she had to admit to herself that she was uncharacteristically tired from her day, something her doctor had warned her would happen during her first trimester.

She rummaged through the refrigerator for some juice, then headed to the living room. After lighting a crackling fire—glad that Gregory had set some fresh logs in the fireplace—she curled up on the sofa with a deep sigh.

On her way home from the attorney's offices, she'd stopped to purchase some books, and she pulled them out of the shopping bag lying on the floor next to the sofa. She glanced at the first, *A Guide for Naming Your Baby,* then set it aside to wait to share the fun with Gregory. She picked up the second, *Nutrition and Exercise for Expectant Mothers,* leafed through it, then also set it aside for later.

Finally, she dug out the small paperback she'd found in the used-book bin and glanced at the title with a smile: *The History of Everlasting Diggins*.

With a satisfied sigh, she leaned back and opened the cover. Just inside was a simple map of the area. She couldn't help but notice that Birds of a Feather would be traveling very near Everlasting Diggins tomorrow.

Annie smiled as a new thought occurred to her. There was a pond on her new property, in all likelihood a haven for birds. A small detour might be just the thing. Just the thing indeed.

When Gregory arrived home, the condo was dark except for the glowing lamplight that spilled over the sofa. Annie lay curled up on it with an afghan over her. Several books were scattered on the floor.

"Sweetheart," he murmured softly, giving her a kiss. She opened sleepy eyes and smiled up at him. Gregory's heart caught. She'd never been as radiantly beautiful as she was now, especially in this half-awake, rosy-cheeked state. He touched her nose with its dusting of freckles, then with the backs of his fingers, he caressed her cheek gently.

"Hi, honey," she murmured, sitting up. "I'm glad you're home. I missed you." She stretched her slender limbs, feline-like, and brushed her honey blonde hair away from her face. "I tried to wait up for you."

He grinned. "You're sleeping for two now, remember? You should've gone on to bed."

She chuckled. "I don't know about sleeping for two, but I sure feel like I'm eating for two. I fixed myself a good dinner earlier, but I'm hungry again. Have you eaten?"

Gregory nodded. "I grabbed something on the way home. But let me fix something for you."

"That would be nice. I'd love a piece of toast and some warm milk."

"Coming right up." Gregory started for the kitchen, then stopped, his eye caught by the cover of one of the books. He stooped to retrieve it and glanced at the title. "Hmm, *The History of Everlasting Diggins,* huh?" He grinned at his wife. "I guess I'm not the only one interested in California history." He leafed through a few pages, noting the map of California's gold-rush country during the 1850s. "Some of your ancestors lived there at one time, didn't they? I remember you telling me about someone involved in the gold rush."

Annie nodded, and Gregory thought he glimpsed a shadow of uneasiness cross her face. "Marcus Jade and his wife, Sheridan, lived there, but I don't think he ever mined for gold. He was a newspaperman originally from San Francisco. He owned a newspaper here called the *Grizzlyclaw Gazette.*"

Gregory grinned as he handed the book to Annie. "Sounds like a colorful character. No wonder you bought the book. Did you find any references to the Jades?"

"No," she said quickly. "No, I didn't. But the book is still very interesting."

Gregory was puzzled as he headed for the kitchen to fix Annie's toast and milk. He wondered why his wife seemed so anxious to drop the topic of Everlasting and her ancestors.

"Honey," Annie suddenly called to him from the living room. "I almost forgot to ask, how did things go in Sacramento?"

He sighed as he placed the mug of milk in the microwave. "It went well," he called to her through the doorway. "Nothing definitive, but he did say the letters appear to be authentic." He didn't tell her the expert was planning to contact the Bancroft Museum at University of California Berkeley for further testing— and to see about interest in buying the letters.

"Now, let's have a look at that baby-name book," he

announced, changing the subject, as he carried the tray of milk and toast to Annie.

She looked up at him sweetly as she took the mug. "Yes, let's."

Annie turned the van into the parking lot early the following morning. The Birds of a Feather members were waiting for her. Pearl was there, clipboard in hand, visor on head; Woodrow, hunched over his map; Flora, a city librarian, and her sister Theda, a beautician; and Wyatt, full-time fireman and part-time search-and-rescue volunteer. The only person she didn't see was Gabe Parker, a novelist. His last book had made the New York Times best-seller list, and now that he was in demand for media interviews, he always seemed to be running late. They'd had to wait for him on more than one occasion.

Annie smiled hello as she slid from the seat and closed the van's door behind her. "Everyone ready?"

Pearl let out a clearly audible and irritated sigh. "*We* are," she said pointedly. "But it appears that Gabe Parker isn't."

"Now, now. He'll be here soon," Woodrow said mildly. "It's not yet eight o'clock."

Annie strode over to look at Woodrow's map. "I'm thinking of swinging past Everlasting," she said, pointing to an area just off Highway 49. "I've just found out about a piece of property there—off the beaten path, I believe—with some marshlands and a pond. Might be some good birding. I'd like to take a look, if you all don't mind."

The others gathered around, discussing the foothill area and agreeing that the Everlasting jaunt might be an interesting side trip.

Just then, Gabe Parker sped up in his little green convertible sports car, braking with a loud squeal. He climbed out over the top instead of opening the door, grinning as he approached the other group members. "Well, folks," he pronounced, hanging the strap of his binocular case over his neck. "What are we waiting for? Let's go find some grebes."

As Annie backed out of the parking lot, the discussion turned serious. Woodrow started telling about an oil spill he'd heard about the day before, just off the central California coast. They talked about volunteering for the seabird rescue effort as Annie headed across the Bay Bridge. A short while later, they moved through the dry foothills of the East Bay and into the San Joaquin Valley.

It took just over two hours to reach the first sign announcing Everlasting Diggins. Annie turned the van north on Highway 49, and the terrain changed to rolling hills covered with pale gold grasses and dotted with live oaks and scrub pines.

Beside her, Woodrow consulted the map she'd copied from the *The History of Everlasting Diggins,* looking for landmarks. Finally, he spotted a carved wooden sign reading "Jade Pond," with an arrow pointing east. Annie eased the van onto a rutted, winding dirt road that headed straight up into the foothills.

Slowing, she shifted the van into low gear, wondering at her heart's sudden thudding as the road climbed into the forest. It was almost as if the place held even greater significance than she'd anticipated. She was crossing the same ground that her ancestors had trod a century and a half before. The thought of it filled her with awe.

She had been driving along the dusty road for several minutes when they came to an outcropping of boulders and obsidian, affording a breathtaking view of Everlasting. She pressed on the brakes and pulled to one side. The group clambered from the van and walked to the overview. When they spoke to each other, it was in awestruck voices. Below them, the town of

Everlasting lay bathed in the morning sunlight. Brick houses, shops, theaters, and liveries—everything in the small mining town—had been kept much as it was in the 1850s through the preservation efforts of the state.

Annie smiled at the sight. Smoke circled heavenward from several chimneys, and a few people in period costumes could be seen strolling along the sun-dappled cobbled streets. A blacksmith was already hard at work, and the sounds of his hammer and anvil carried toward them on the wind, mixed with the faint music of a harmonica and a banjo in the background.

"So this is Everlasting," Annie murmured. Her gaze took in the purple blue skies above the jagged Sierras, the thick pine forests covering the foothills, and a bubbling stream leading down the mountain. She breathed in the musty fragrance of the brush and late-blooming wildflowers.

Around her, the others were lifting their binoculars and searching for birds, listening now for songs and chirps instead of the sounds carrying from Everlasting. But Annie couldn't pull her gaze from the small town.

A few minutes later, the group again climbed into the van, and Annie pulled back onto the rutted, dirt road, heading farther into the forested foothills. They laced through some pines and oaks and endured a series of frightening hairpin turns leading down the mountain before the road straightened abruptly.

Suddenly, a pale green meadow stretched out before them, a thick forest on one side, a large pond the color of sparkling sapphires on the other. As Annie drove closer to the water, an air of excitement rose in the van.

"I see a grebe!" whispered Gabe Parker. "I knew it. I knew we'd spot some today. Look, there's a dozen at least. Toward the far end of the pond! Wow."

"And up on that manzanita branch. A double-crested cormorant," breathed Theda. "It's magnificent."

"I see a merganser. Common, I think," her sister Flora said in awe. "Listen, I can hear its calls."

"Hey!" cried Pearl. "A buffalo-head duck!"

"Bufflehead," Woodrow corrected evenly. "A bufflehead."

"I'm surprised you didn't give me its Latin name," Pearl said, shrugging a shoulder nonchalantly.

"If you insist. It's called *Bucephala albeola* of the *Anatidae* family," Woodrow muttered, again lifting his binoculars. Then his tone lightened. "I do see a cedar waxwing, Gabe. Look, there in the oak at the far end of the pond."

Annie put her own field glasses to her eyes, at first concentrating on the magnificently plumed merganser floating gracefully across the pond. Then she lifted her gaze beyond the water to the two-story cottage almost hidden in the foliage. She adjusted the focus, then looked again.

It had to be the house Marcus Jade had built for his bride, Sheridan. From this distance, it looked to be in disrepair. Still, her heart raced in excitement.

"All right," she said to everyone. "Load up. Let's get closer to this magnificent bird sanctuary." And to the cottage, she added to herself with a smile. She couldn't bear to wait a moment longer to step across the threshold and see what treasures lay inside.

~ 4 ~

Annie parked the van beneath a canopy of live oaks not far from Aunt Sheridan's house. At this end of the pond the waters lapped gently against cattails and tall grasses, creating perfect marshlike conditions for migrating birds and ducks on the Pacific flyway.

Everyone piled out of the vehicle and looked around to find a place to take up a silent vigil among the cover of trees and brush. After agreeing to meet back at the van at midday for lunch, they slipped quietly away. Along with binoculars and birdcalls, each carried a clipboard with a regional checklist of birds—rare and common—listing identification colors, plumage, song, and field marks. Some also carried their life lists, hoping to see a bird they'd never spotted before.

Annie, knowing the seriousness of today's endeavor, watched as they took cover. Not only did they record each new discovery, they also competed for numbers. Woodrow came in first with some four hundred different birds. His dream was to see as many of North America's eight hundred species as possible in his lifetime. And Pearl, whom it was suspected had no qualms about embellishing her life list, came in second at three hundred fifty-seven.

As soon as the others had taken their places, Annie turned toward the cottage. She carried the key, given to her by Aunt Sheridan's attorney, in her sweatshirt pocket.

A weathered picket fence was nearly hidden by the overgrown grass, and the gate's rusty hinges creaked as she opened it and let herself through.

She paused, looking up at the house and shading her eyes from the brilliant sun. Although the whitewashed wood had faded to gray and the shutters hung lopsided from the windows, the house still held its original charm. She didn't know much about nineteenth-century architecture, but she thought she recognized the style as Queen Anne cottage, with the fish-scale shingles and small round turret on the second floor. A wide porch wrapped around nearly the entire house, but its spindled banister had mostly decayed, and great lengths of it had been removed. It was obvious that during her great aunt's last years, there hadn't been money for repairs. Annie felt a pang of conscience that she hadn't been out even once to help.

Annie walked across the yard and up the rickety stairs to the front door. Then, taking a deep breath, she placed the key in the lock and turned it. The door opened easily, and Annie blinked in the dimly lighted interior.

A wide smile crossed her face as she stepped into the front entry. She glanced around for a moment, then headed to the large room on her right, a small parlor. Hurriedly, she opened the drapes and turned to survey the contents.

It must have been the room that Aunt Sheridan had used the most. Several books, her eyeglasses, and a knitting basket were piled on top of a small table near a cushioned rocker. Most of the furniture was made of pine or oak, local woods, making Annie wonder if Marcus Jade had made them himself. She lovingly touched each piece, feeling a wave of unexpected emotion.

Then she turned and faced the window and gazed out at its perfect view of the cattail marshes and sparkling pond. She sighed, leaning briefly against the windowsill, taking in the graceful flight of the birds across the water, the sounds of their songs and calls, the whisper of the wind in the nearby pines, even the burnished glint of sunlight on the autumn grass.

It seemed that Sheridan and Marcus had planned the cottage's location and view to be part of the structure itself. She marveled at the thought and, looking up, imagined that the upstairs master bedroom probably also faced the pond.

She hurried from the room and up the stairs to see for herself. Grinning, she ran across the bedroom to the French doors, flung them open, and after testing the strength of the balcony's wood-plank surface, stepped outside.

Annie blinked back her tears. It was exactly how she would have designed it. The view seemed to stretch into eternity. In the foreground, the pond's ripples danced in the sunlight, and in the distance, the snowcapped peaks of the Sierra Nevada mountains rose into the heavens.

With a deep sigh, she imagined Sheridan and Marcus standing here on the balcony in the moonlight, their arms circling each other. And she could see Sheridan by herself, probably watching her children play in the yard or waving good-bye to her husband as he rode off to his newspaper office in Everlasting Diggins.

Reluctantly, she closed the doors and turned back to the bedroom. But the things in here were every bit as interesting as the view outdoors. Again, the furniture looked handmade, the rough-hewn oak softened by the intricately carved designs. A four-poster bed, its mattress high enough to require a stool to climb upon, stood at one end of the room, a small fireplace at the other. A faded trunk, atop an oval braided rug, had been placed at the foot of the bed.

Annie knelt beside the chest and lifted the top, expecting to find extra quilts and linens. Instead, it was filled with books and photographs, bundles of letters and journals, and in one corner, baby clothes, yellowed with age.

She reached out one hand carefully, almost afraid to touch the delicate fabric. Slowly, she pulled out a lacy crocheted bonnet, tiny enough to fit a newborn infant. A matching sweatercoat lay beneath it, and Annie lifted it carefully from the trunk. She smoothed it on her lap, then lifted it to her cheek for just a moment, wondering which of her ancestors had made it…or worn it.

Next she reached for a faded hatbox, untied its ribbon, and pulled off the lid. It was filled with photographs, some the old-fashioned tintypes made on thin metal plates. She lifted one in an oval picture frame. A young woman, about Annie's age, with cascading dark curls and a heart-shaped face, smiled back at her.

Annie caught her breath, then held the photograph up to the light spilling in through the French doors. Except for the dark hair, it was as if she were looking at herself. Turning over the frame, she lifted out the tintype and found an inscription in feminine handwriting on the back: *Sheridan O'Brian Jade, October 21, 1860.*

Annie stared at the photograph for several minutes; then as she reached inside the trunk again, a small leather-bound book with a tooled design of wildflowers on the cover caught her attention.

Intrigued, Annie lifted it and carefully turned to the first page. Again, she saw what she supposed was Sheridan O'Brian Jade's elegant handwriting: *My Journal*, it read, *The Year of Our Lord 1862.* Annie's gaze flicked down to the first entry: January 1, 1862. She began to read.

Aye, but my Lord is a worker of miracles! Today I felt the babe move inside me. Like butterfly wings a-fluttering, so light it was. I hold my hand on the place, awaiting another small movement. Aye! There it comes again.

I carry life inside me, a wee bit of Marcus and me. 'Tis a secret joy, this feeling that I am somehow God's partner in this wee one's creation, and I marvel again at the wonder of it! My heart is as filled with joy as my eyes are with tears.

If only my sweet husband could be here, my happiness would be complete. There is still no word from him, and sometimes my heart is numb with worry. 'Tis both an affliction and a blessing, his job. And this time, with the threats against his life, I am thinking 'tis worse than even an affliction!

Marcus has been gone two weeks now, and my heart cries out in fear. If not for Duncan and Evangelia and the precious life I carry inside, I wonder how I could go on. Lord, help me be brave for all my wee babes!

Annie clutched the small leather book to her heart. She might have to sell the cottage and all its acreage, but never would she part with this link to her family's past. She closed the trunk with a lingering, caressing touch and stood, tucking the journal into her purse.

She was just heading back down the stairs when she heard the front door open.

"Annie?" a voice called out. It was Woodrow. "Annie, are you all right?" he called again.

"Yes, I'm fine," she said, hurrying down the remaining steps. She turned the corner to where he stood in the parlor. She grinned. "Just taking a quick inspection of my inheritance," she explained.

"This is yours?" He looked around appreciatively, a slow

smile appearing on his face. "Ah, now I understand why you headed us in this direction."

"It is quite a bird sanctuary, you have to admit," she countered. "Actually, I just found out about this place yesterday. I couldn't wait to have a look."

Woodrow closely inspected the doorjamb he was standing next to, rubbing his hand down one side. "Solid," he pronounced, his contractor mind-set taking over. "They don't make them like this anymore."

"Actually, I'm going to sell it," she told him, trying to ignore his look of surprise. "And I'll need some work done on it before I can put it on the market." She felt a twinge of regret as she spoke the words. "Could I entice you to come out of retirement to help me out?"

"Sell it?" He shook his head slowly. "It seems so perfect...the pond, the woods beyond. This house needs work, but it'll be a beauty once it's repaired, painted." He frowned at her. "You just found out about it, and already you want to sell it?"

She nodded quickly. "Yes. It's too far for a commute for either Gregory or me. I'm hoping to find someone who'll keep it just as it is and love it for its rich heritage."

Woodrow looked unconvinced, but he nodded. "I'd be glad to help you out, honey. What is it you're thinking of doing to the old place?"

The two of them toured the rest of the house, Woodrow inspecting sinks and cupboards, doors and flooring, all the while making notes on his clipboard. As they moved from room to room, Annie explained how she wanted to use the proceeds of the sale as a gift for Gregory. She also told Woodrow about the coming baby.

It was just past midday when they walked out to the porch to watch for the Birds of a Feather members now making their way back to the van for lunch.

"What do you estimate it will cost?" Annie finally asked as they walked toward the gate.

Woodrow held the gate open for Annie. "I think I can do most of the work myself." He grinned. "It's not much different than the work I do for Habitat."

"I can't pay for much more than the materials right now," she admitted. "Can you wait until after the sale for the rest?"

He chuckled. "Annie, you give tirelessly to Birds of a Feather. You've got a volunteer's heart—just as I do. Let me do this for you. No cost, other than materials."

"I'll tell you what," Annie said just as they reached the van. "I'll come out and help. I'm pretty good with a paintbrush."

Pearl stepped up, purple red hair gleaming in the sunlight, white plastic visor resting on her forehead. "What in the world would you be needin' a paintbrush for, Annie-girl?" She looked back toward the house. "And what were you doing—?"

"Now, Pearl," Woodrow interrupted. "That's Annie's business."

By now, Flora, Theda, Wyatt, and Gabe had joined them. All eyes, expectant and curious, were on Annie.

She laughed. "It's all right, Woodrow. I'll explain." And she proceeded to tell the others about the inheritance, the surprise she planned for Gregory, and the coming baby.

When she finished, there were hugs of congratulations about the baby, and expressions of delight about her property, as well as her gift to her husband.

"I think we all ought to pitch in!" Pearl said. "I'm pretty handy with a hammer and nails. Been known to saw up a storm from time to time. Woodrow, dear, you can just point me to the board you want put in place, and it'll be done."

Annie, nearly overwhelmed by her response, tried to protest. But the others joined Pearl, exclaiming that after all the time Annie had given to them and the group, they wanted to do something for her, Gregory, and the baby.

Finally, she agreed. A few minutes later, Pearl, with help from the others, handed out sandwiches, chips, and soft drinks from the cooler. Then everyone settled onto nearby rocks and folding chairs.

Before discussing the birds they'd spotted during the morning, Woodrow spoke in detail of the repairs on the house and the need to work fast because of winter approaching. The other members spoke of the time they could give. Some said one or two days a week. Woodrow offered three, and Pearl said she could volunteer four, to which Woodrow rolled his eyes.

Finally, it was agreed that Woodrow would order the materials to be delivered one week later, and the group would plan another combined field trip and work day.

The group went on to discuss grebes, mergansers, and cormorants, but Annie, seated so that she faced the cottage, couldn't take her gaze or her mind from the house. Even without the needed repairs, it seemed to glow with a humble beauty in the afternoon sun.

A feeling of sadness touched her deeply, bringing an unexpected mist to her eyes. She reached into her purse for a tissue, and her fingers briefly brushed against the soft, worn leather of the journal. She sighed. The cottage, the pond, the majestic beauty of the land paled in comparison with the priceless gift of Sheridan's journal. She couldn't wait to explore the treasures that would be hers in getting to know this young woman who, like Annie, was expecting her first baby.

Annie thought of Sheridan's joy about feeling her baby's first kick. It would be weeks before Annie would feel the first signs of life, but already she felt the miracle Sheridan wrote about, the partnership with God in the creation of a child.

Then she remembered Sheridan's worry about Marcus. She tried to recall if she'd heard any stories that had been passed down through the generations about her great-great-grandfather, his adventures, or near brushes with death. Had he died a young man? She couldn't remember. Shivering, she felt a twist of fear in her heart for what Sheridan must have experienced during her long wait.

Suddenly, Annie couldn't wait to get home to Gregory and to the feel of his strong arms encircling her.

⤚ 5 ⤙

It was late afternoon, just after his last class had been dismissed, when Gregory headed to the Bancroft Museum for his appointment with Carlton Thurston, the curator. Although it had been three weeks already since his meeting with Dr. Hyde, the expert in Sacramento, this was the soonest Thurston could see him.

When Gregory arrived in the reception office, a round, gray-haired woman looked up at him through her wire-rimmed glasses.

"I'm here to see Dr. Thurston," Gregory explained. "I've got a four o'clock appointment."

"I'm sorry. He just called to say he's been detained," she said with a sympathetic smile. "He said you're welcome to wait, but he'd certainly understand if you want to set up another appointment."

"Do you know how long he'll be?" Gregory didn't want to be late getting home again tonight. It seemed to have happened too often lately, with all his appointments regarding the letter.

He wanted to take care of Annie, let her rest while he fixed dinner and straightened up around the condo. She had mentioned very little about morning sickness or fatigue, but he could see a new tiredness in her face. And he wanted to do everything he could to help her through the pregnancy.

A delay getting in to see Dr. Thurston meant he'd hit rush-hour traffic getting back through the city, and he'd indeed be late again. On the other hand, it might be weeks before another appointment could be set up.

"Dr. Thurston didn't know how long he'd be," the receptionist said, raising an eyebrow as if prompting him for a decision.

"I'll wait," he said, looking at his watch. He'd give the curator an hour or so. He had the Jedediah Smith letters with him, and it was too important a meeting to postpone.

"Help yourself to some coffee. It's in the lounge around the corner," the woman said before turning back to her computer.

"Thanks," Gregory answered, but the woman was already concentrating on a complicated-looking spreadsheet.

Gregory waited for an hour and twenty minutes before Dr. Thurston finally arrived. The balding man was apologetic as he shook Gregory's hand and invited him into his office.

When Gregory had taken a seat, Dr. Thurston leaned toward him from the opposite side of his massive desk. "Now tell me about the letters," he said. "When Dr. Hyde called to set up the appointment, he said something about some letters you have in your possession. Jedediah Smith, I believe it was."

Gregory nodded. "I bought a stack of old papers and letters at an estate sale some time ago. Didn't take a look at them until just recently." He smiled. "I couldn't believe what I found." He shook his head slowly. "Would you like to see them?"

"You've got them with you?"

"Oh, yes."

"Yes, let me have a look." He pulled off his eyeglasses and

222

cleaned them with his handkerchief while Gregory opened the briefcase.

A moment later, he handed the first letter to Thurston. The curator examined a single sheet of the paper closely, holding it up to the light. Then he began reading the missive, nodding slowly from time to time. Finally he peered up at Gregory through his glasses.

"The writing style certainly looks like Smith's. I'd have to go into the archives for samples of his handwriting, but it does appear to be true to what I remember seeing." He pulled off his eyeglasses, folded them, and set them aside. "You do realize how easily forgeries can be made, Mr. Westbrook. There are some talented people out there. You ever hear about Mark Hoffman?"

Gregory nodded. Hoffman had made millions forging documents, then selling them to the highest bidder. "Why would a forger take a chance and plant something like this in an estate sale? It might lie unnoticed for years."

"That's true," Thurston conceded. "But nonetheless, your letters must be tested for authenticity."

"I agree," Gregory said with a nod. "Actually, that's one of the reasons I came to you. Can you—or someone at the Bancroft—perform the necessary tests?"

"Of course. It will take about a month. Perhaps more." He again picked up the letter to scrutinize. "Something like this doesn't come along often. It's going to be a pleasure to work on this project. In fact, I think I'll oversee it personally." He smiled at Gregory. "I should tell you that Jed Smith is one of my favorite historical figures. He's an unsung hero of the nineteenth century."

"Mine, too. In fact, I'm planning to write a definitive history about Smith. Someday I'd like to retrace his steps, travel the trails he maps out in his journals and letters."

They exchanged anecdotes about Jed Smith for several minutes, laughing with sudden camaraderie at their mutual admiration for the mountain man-trapper-explorer.

Then Carlton Thurston leaned back in his chair. "These letters are probably more valuable to you than to the average historian. I'm always delighted when someone wanting to publish makes such a significant find."

Gregory nodded. "Perhaps."

Thurston considered him intently. "You said you've got more than one reason for this visit. What's the other?"

"As soon as we authenticate the letters, I want to sell them."

"Sell them?" Thurston suddenly sat forward. "That's right. I do remember Hyde mentioning you might put them up for sale." He hesitated. "But I thought you just said—"

Gregory interrupted quickly. "That I plan to write about Smith? I did. But I don't need the letters in my possession to do that."

"But just to have them in your possession would be advantageous for your publishing plans." Then he paused, frowning. "I'm sorry, it's really none of my business, of course. I'm just surprised, that's all."

Gregory smiled, though a bit sadly. "I could be magnanimous and tell you that I feel the public has a right to them, that the letters should be in a museum. But that's not the case. There are other concerns, more urgent and personal, that take precedence."

Carlton Thurston nodded slightly and said no more about Gregory's decision. "I can ask around about them," he said. "The Bancroft itself might be interested. Probably the Huntington Library in southern California. Perhaps even some of the state universities or colleges, for their collections. I'll put out the word as soon as we know about the test results."

"Thank you," Gregory said, feeling strangely bereft. He pulled the remaining letters from his briefcase and handed them to Thurston.

"Walk with me to the vault, and we'll get the paperwork started on your agreement to the tests and our responsibility for their safety. Then I'll show you the lab where the tests will be performed. In fact, if you'd like to stop by during some of them, you're perfectly welcome. It's quite interesting."

The two men walked together across the main floor of the museum and down a long side wing. Minutes later they entered a room filled floor to ceiling with massive, thick-walled vaults. As Gregory saw the letters locked away, he couldn't help feeling sorrowful, knowing that they would never again be in his possession. Swallowing, he tried to push all thoughts of regret from his mind, dwelling only on his love for Annie and the joy his gift would bring her.

Annie pulled the van into the carport just as the autumn sun was sinking into the horizon. With a disappointed sigh, she realized that Gregory's car was missing from its usual parking spot next to hers. She trudged wearily up the stairs and into their little condo. It had been a long day out at the property. She'd painted the new porch banister, and her back ached from the bending and kneeling.

As she pulled off her jacket in their bedroom, she caught her reflection in the mirrored closet door. She turned sideways to check her profile, the tiny bulge already showing below her waistline. Her jeans didn't zip quite as easily as they used to, and she worried they'd begun looking too tight.

She moved closer to the mirror, scrutinizing her face, wondering if she looked as tired as she felt.

Gregory was late getting home from school so often now. Was he avoiding her? What if Gregory was one of those men who found pregnant women unattractive? And if he already considered her so, what would he think by the time she entered her third trimester? She nibbled at her bottom lip and looked at her changing figure in the mirror again.

She'd never doubted her husband's love for her. But she knew that some men handled the dramatic changes during pregnancy better than others.

Why else would Gregory be staying away from her? He'd breezily explained many times that his absences had to do with authenticating the letters. But why did he always seem to change the subject when she pressed him for details?

Annie sat down to untie her sneakers and reached for her worn and comfortable bedroom slippers. Then she headed into the master bath, splashed cool water on her face, and pulled a brush through her hair.

After she'd eaten a peanut butter sandwich and raw carrot sticks, washing them down with a tall glass of milk, Annie felt immensely better. As had become her pattern, she settled into the cushioned sofa in front of the fire and pulled out Sheridan's journal. Finding the place where she'd left off, she began to read.

February 11, 1862

Oh, how my heart aches with worry for Marcus. Since I learned that Carter Bainbridge was released from prison, my worries have increased tenfold. When Marcus left, he said he was going to investigate the whereabouts of an old nemesis. Had I known it was the same man who tried to kill us both— and sweet Lia and Duncan too—nearly seven years ago, I would have begged my husband not to go. How my heart breaks with the thought of Marcus's being anywhere near the man!

I have tried hard to dwell on Grandma'am's words about God's care. How clearly I remember them in my mind, but so often I forget to take them to heart. I am going to write them

*now, then read them each morning and hold them close all
day…as close to my heart as the wee one I carry inside.*

*I remember so clearly Grandma'am telling me: "When
you cannot see your next step, child, then it is time to look
heavenward and ask for God's help. It is his strong arm of
grace that will keep you steady even when you cannot see
ahead.*

*"Sometimes God allows trying and confusing times just so
we will look to him. Then he scoops us up—just as your papa
did when you were but a wee babe lifting your arms to be
held. But God wants us to ask for his help, sweet Sheridan, he
does. He wants us simply to raise our arms like a wee child
and ask."*

*Aye, dear Father, I ask for your help right now, and I am
lifting my arms on behalf of us all. As it says in Deuteronomy
33:12, hold us all in safety near your heart.*

Annie let out a deep sigh as she read Sheridan's words; then
she reached for her Bible and opened to Sheridan's verse in the
book of Deuteronomy.

It was new to her, and she read it with a dawning sense of
peace and joy. It was as if Sheridan had penned her words of
nearly a century and a half ago, just for her great-great-grand-
daughter to read.

Annie could scarcely take in the impact. A family's legacy,
contained in the beautiful words of Scripture, had been passed
down through the generations. Down to even the precious seed
of life Annie carried inside.

She breathed a prayer of thanksgiving for Sheridan's words.
God was carrying her near his heart…as she was carrying her
child near hers.

What a wonder! For the first time in weeks, Annie felt at
peace.

~ 6 ~

I just saw a spotted owl!" Pearl proclaimed loudly, trotting toward the others at the cottage.

The sun was high in a crystal blue sky, with just a hint of winter's chill in the mild breeze. The group rested on or near the porch, taking a rest from the morning's labor, and finished the submarine sandwiches Flora had packed. Woodrow, without comment about the owl, popped the top from a soda, then leaned against one of the posts flanking the bottom steps.

It had now been four weeks since they'd begun the project. Annie looked at the group affectionately. They had literally transformed the cottage. In another two weeks, it would be finished and ready to put on the market.

"It was a spotted owl. I swear it!" Pearl called out again, letting herself in the new gate. "You all missed out by not coming with me." She settled onto the steps by Woodrow with a heavy sigh and adjusted her visor.

"They're rare this far inland, Pearl," Woodrow finally muttered. "They're seen as far south as Mexico, but I don't think I've heard of any around these parts."

"Not to mention they're on the endangered-species list," Theda said.

"And they're nocturnal. This is midday," added Wyatt with a wink to Flora, who was sitting near him. "Highly unlikely you saw an owl at all."

"You can think what you like," Pearl countered with a frown, "but I know what I saw. If any of you skeptics want to come, I'd be glad to show you."

Annie stood with a small groan, rubbed the small of her back, and stretched. A walk would do her some good. "I'll go with you," she said to Pearl.

Pearl gave her an answering grin. "The rest of you will be sorry." She raised a penciled red brow. "Mark my words."

Moments later, Annie and Pearl walked around the pond to the woodlands just beyond. Pearl, leading the way, retraced her footsteps along a deer path winding deep into the pines. The sky nearly disappeared in the thick grove. A wonderful, rich fragrance of earth and leaves lifted from the path as they walked deeper into the forest.

Finally, Pearl stopped, finger to her lips. "Listen!" she mouthed.

Annie held her breath; then a slow grin spread across her face. She nodded to Pearl. In the distance, among other birds' chirping and chattering, the distinct song of the spotted owl could be heard, a series of three or four hesitant, almost dog-like, barks and cries.

Annie motioned Pearl to continue on, and silently they moved through the forest, following the cries.

As they walked, the brush became even denser and darker. The owl stopped its crying for a while, and Annie and Pearl stopped, listening intently for the creature's music to begin again. Finally, it did, and the two smiled triumphantly at each other. The owl's cries came from directly overhead.

Annie looked up until she saw the round, dark-eyed face and spotted brown plumage nearly hidden in the boughs of a large live oak. Almost afraid to breath, she lifted her field glasses, adjusted the focus, then zeroed in on the creature again.

Her heart caught with delight. Pearl had been right! It was definitely a spotted owl. The first she'd ever seen.

She studied the little owl intently. It was a juvenile, judging from its small size. Perhaps that's why it had appeared in the daylight, dusky as it was, rather than the black of night. Babies often did get their days and nights mixed up, she thought with a wry smile.

Annie and Pearl watched quietly as the owl sang its barking cry; then suddenly, it silently lifted from the branch and disappeared deeper into the forest.

"I told you," Pearl declared when it had gone.

"So you did," Annie said with another grin, giving the older woman a hug. "Now, let's go give the others a bad time about what they missed!"

That afternoon, as Annie wallpapered one of the bathrooms, she thought about the sighting. If there was one spotted owl, that meant that there were more. Especially since this one was so young. It also meant that her woodlands may have become a sanctuary for the endangered bird.

It was getting harder to think about selling the house. Even without her love for the surrounding acreage, each day she worked on the place, her touches became more evident, from the shades of paint she'd chosen to the period wallpaper going up on the walls.

The holiday season was approaching, and she had already purchased dozens of strands of tiny white lights to decorate the outside, and garlands to hang in scallops across the porch banister. They would complete the final touches when the painting and landscaping were complete.

She'd heard that Christmas was a good time for a house to go on the market. The warmth of the season, the decorations, all served to appeal to potential buyers. But Annie also knew the effect the house, with all its Christmas charm, would have on her.

"Annie!" Flora called up from downstairs, interrupting her melancholy thoughts. "Annie! Someone's here to see you."

"I'll be right down," she called back, glad she'd just finished trimming the final strip of paper. She checked her watch. Three o'clock. The realtor she'd called earlier was right on time.

"Hello," she said, sticking out her hand in greeting as she stepped into the parlor from the entry. "I'm Annie Westbrook."

A pretty middle-aged woman with a white blonde pixie haircut strode toward her. "Hi, I'm Dana," she said pleasantly. "This is a beautiful place."

"Thank you," Annie said with a nod. "Let me show you around." She led Dana from room to room, stopping as the realtor measured with a tape and made notes on her clipboard.

"You've got how many bedrooms?" Dana asked as they headed upstairs.

"There's the one off the front parlor, though it could be used as an office or den. And we've got three upstairs. I'll show you the master bedroom first." After they reached the top landing, she led Dana into the bedroom, now flooded with light from the late afternoon sun. The lustrous oak floor gleamed from its recent application of stain and varnish. Annie crossed the room to open the French doors.

Dana let out an appreciative sigh and headed toward the balcony. "This alone should sell the house," she declared. "What a romantic place!"

Annie nodded. "Yes, it is."

Dana took once last glance at the view and turned back to Annie. "I see that you've put a lot of effort into the house." She looked solemn. "But I need to tell you that if you're looking to sell quickly, I think you've wasted your time."

Annie frowned. "What do you mean?"

"You've made this into a wonderful place for some young family, perhaps a retired couple. But you need to understand, it's a ways off the beaten path. There's not even a paved road leading here. The buyer you're looking for has to be unique. That means your market is very limited."

"You said I wasted my time—?"

"Developers are your largest market, Annie."

Annie shook her head vehemently. "I'll not even consider it. These are special acres of land, with wildlife and bird sanctuaries. It's right on the Pacific flyway. If anyone turned this into a housing tract, thousands of birds would be affected."

The realtor nodded seriously. "But the truth is," she continued, "if you want to sell right away, you may have to consider it."

"I won't."

"You realize that if you do put the place on the market and a developer makes an offer equal to your asking price, and you refuse to sell—"

Annie interrupted, finishing the sentence for her. "I'll be in breach of contract. Yes, I realize that. But I'm willing to take my chances."

Dana suddenly gave her a satisfied smile. "I just wanted to make sure that you understood."

"I do," Annie said. "How about if we put a top-dollar price on it? I want to make sure developers don't think it's a steal. And I'll help you write up the ad, targeting just the right person."

Dana grinned. "This will be a challenge, Annie, but I promise you I'll do everything I can to find someone who appreciates the heritage of this place and the care of its wildlife."

Annie led Dana back down the stairs to the carved pine table in the dining room. They settled into their chairs and examined the paperwork that legally placed Sheridan and Marcus's house up for sale, agreeing on the date exactly two weeks from now.

As Annie signed the documents, she tried to push all thoughts from her mind except the gift she'd soon be able to give to Gregory.

That same evening, Gregory bustled about the condo's little kitchen, an apron looped over his neck and tied around his waist. Bright yellow, the fabric was splashed with bold black letters: CAUTION! MAN AT WORK. It had been a gift last Christmas from Annie.

At the center of the table he'd placed a vase of long-stemmed red roses with an accompanying card for Annie; then he'd set their places with her grandmother's china and silver.

He checked the recipe—salmon with grilled citrus and mango—again, then pulled the fresh salmon from the refrigerator to marinate in lemon juice and fresh ginger. Opening the patio door, he stepped outside to the condo's small balcony to start the gas barbecue grill.

When that was done, he returned to the kitchen to make Annie's favorite drink: fresh cranberries blended with raw sugar, lemon, nutmeg, cinnamon, and crushed ice. He set up the blender, tossed in the ingredients, then poured the pureed mixture into a crystal goblet, awaiting Annie's homecoming.

But Annie didn't arrive.

By six-thirty, Gregory was still waiting patiently, thinking she'd been held up in traffic. He tried to remember where she'd said she was going this morning, but he'd forgotten to ask, he thought guiltily. They both had been too busy recently, almost too busy to talk. That was partly what prompted him to fix a romantic dinner for his wife.

The truth was, he missed her. Desperately. He was so intent on finding a buyer for Smith's letters that even his relationship with Annie seemed to be cooling.

He looked at his watch. Six-forty-five. He paced the living room, then returned to the kitchen and switched off the grill. He called the Birds of a Feather office but got a recording. Noticing that the cranberry cocktails had started to melt, he placed the goblets in the freezer and went back to his worried pacing.

Finally, just past seven o'clock, he heard Annie's van pull into the carport. She had just reached the top of the stairs when Gregory opened the door.

"Honey, I've been so worried," he said with a frown. "Couldn't you have called?"

Annie seemed surprised by his reaction and regarded him with a frown. "You've been late dozens of evenings recently, Gregory. And you're upset because I'm late once?"

"Dozens—?" he said, arching a brow to silently make a point of her exaggeration.

Annie stepped into the condo, brushed past him, and headed for the bedroom. He followed her, watching as she pulled off her parka and reached for a hanger.

Then she turned, her gaze on him. He loved the way she looked right now, cheeks aglow and eyes luminous with some secret joy, glossy hair brushed back haphazardly.

Suddenly she gave him a small smile. "Here we are, finally together for an evening, and we're arguing." She lifted her shoulder in a shrug.

"It's just that I didn't know where you were. If you'd gone bird watching out in the wilderness someplace, maybe had car trouble..." His voice trailed off.

Annie stepped closer and gently touched his cheek. "I'm glad you were concerned," she whispered.

He stepped back slightly. "Sweetheart, what a thing to say! Of course I'm concerned. You and that little one you carry are more important to me than anything in the world."

Her eyes suddenly brightened with tears. "You've been gone so much lately," she said. "I thought maybe…" Annie's voice faltered, and he noticed that her glance flicked to her image in the wardrobe mirror.

Gregory reached for her hand and turned it palm up, his fingers examining its smoothness. He kissed it, then lifted his eyes to meet hers. Annie felt her heart lurch with the tenderness she saw in their depths.

"Oh, Annie," he whispered, pressing her close. "I love you more than life itself." He seemed to read her innermost doubts with his gaze. "You've never been more beautiful than you are right now."

"Really?" she breathed in wonder. "I worried that because of the pregnancy…" She frowned, nibbling on her bottom lip. "Some men have difficulty dealing with all the, ah, changes. And it seems that right after I told you about it, you, well, disappeared. I realize you've been busy with the Smith letters, but down deep, I've been worried about us."

"I know," Gregory admitted. "I've worried, too. I've missed our closeness. We're soul mates. We've always been."

"And always will be," she added with a deep sigh.

Gregory pulled Annie closer and covered her mouth with his. The touch of his lips took her breath away and sent little tingles rushing up and down her spine. She circled his neck with her arms, feeling the warm comfort of his embrace, and returned his kiss with a passion matching his.

Then, pulling back slightly, she looked into his eyes. "You know, even after seven years of marriage, Mr. Westbrook, your kisses make my heart pound."

He chuckled, touching her cheek with the backs of his fingers. "And, Mrs. Westbrook, you have no idea of the depths of my feelings for you!"

Suddenly, Annie focused on his silly, bright yellow apron and tilted her face toward his. "Man at work, huh?" She laughed softly. "Does this mean there's something wonderful waiting for me in the kitchen?"

"It depends on your mood, dear heart," he murmured, playfully nibbling her ear lobe. "Your pleasure."

"I think you can guess the answer to that, darling," she breathed as he pulled her closer.

Gregory swept her up and into his arms, as if she were light as a feather, to carry her across the room—just as the answering machine clicked on.

Startled, he set her down as they listened to the message being recorded.

"Annie, dear," Pearl said in her loud, raspy voice. "I don't want to give your secret away in case you-know-who is listening. But I've been talking to someone who knows someone else who might be interested in, well, you-know-what. Oops! Maybe I shouldn't mention anything about that on the phone either." There was the sound of a loud exhale. "Well, Annie, give me a call, and I'll explain it all when we talk. Ta-ta."

A shadow crossed Gregory's face, and he stepped away from Annie. "Your secret?" he said, his frown deepening. "Annie, what is she talking about?"

~ 7 ~

The following morning as Gregory headed for school, he mulled over Annie's phone message from Pearl the night before. Although she'd quickly said something about the operative word being *surprise*, not *secret*, Annie would tell him nothing more. But he knew from her flustered expression and the high color on her cheeks that she'd been terribly disturbed by the telephone call. Not to mention that their romantic interlude had been spoiled. Even the gourmet meal had been eaten in silence.

He swung into the faculty parking lot, switched off the ignition, and stepped out of the car. There were too many secrets between them. How he wanted to share his plans with Annie! If he didn't know her so well, he'd tell her everything right now. But his wife had a heart as big as San Francisco Bay. She wouldn't let him give up something as important as the letters for her sake. No, he had to wait.

He sighed as he unlocked his office door and flipped on the overhead light. Settling into his chair, he lifted his phone to check his voice-mail messages.

The first, from Roland Harper, a realtor downtown, confirmed his appointment for later in the afternoon.

The second, from Carlton Thurston at the Bancroft, made him sit up and take notice. "Gregory, I've just heard from Columbia College, out near Everlasting, that they're looking for a keynote speaker for the annual banquet of the California Historical Society, being held this year at the college. Seems the original speaker has taken ill. I hope you don't mind, but I gave them your name. When I mentioned your area of expertise, particularly Jed Smith, they became quite interested. I hope you hear from them."

There was a brief pause, then Dr. Thurston went on. "Regarding the letters. You might want to schedule some time in our lab during the next few days. We'll be doing the final tests. Let's talk later. Thanks."

The third message was from the chair of Columbia's Social Science Department, a Dr. Theodore Taft, asking if Gregory could get back to him about the speaking engagement, apologizing for the short notice, but also letting him know how interested they were in talking with him.

Grinning, Gregory dialed the number, connecting him directly with the chair's office.

"Ah, yes, Mr. Westbrook, it's good to hear from you," Dr. Taft said pleasantly. "The first Friday in December is the night of the banquet meeting. It's rather formal, and, of course, your wife is invited. In fact, we normally don't offer this, but because it is such short notice, in addition to the stipend, we'd like to offer you and your wife a weekend in Everlasting.

"Columbia College offers our students a culinary arts and hotel management program. We run a small historic inn called the City Hotel. We'd love to have you as our guests."

"What was the date again?" Gregory asked, leafing through his desk calendar.

The department chair told him, and Gregory confirmed that the weekend was open.

Dr. Taft gave him the details of the program's agenda, the length of time he'd be given for his talk, then added another word about the City Hotel. "It's quite a romantic place," he said. "I'm going to reserve one of the two balcony suites for you."

"Thank you," Gregory said, already imagining the delight on Annie's face when he told her. Before signing off, he took some notes as Dr. Taft gave him further details about the Historical Society and their annual conference.

Gregory had just enough time before his U.S. history class to telephone Annie with the news. But the phone rang four times before the answering machine clicked on. Obviously, Annie had already left with Birds of a Feather.

Disappointed, Gregory laid down the receiver, then gathered his notes and hurried out his office door.

That afternoon he met Roland Harper, a dignified graying man, at the realtor's office. They sat together a brief time while Gregory gave Roland a description of the properties he wanted to see: a Victorian, perhaps with some fixing up to be done; view of the water, if possible; a small yard, very necessary, he emphasized; and close to the city because of his and Annie's commutes.

Harper took notes as Gregory spoke, then asked politely about the price range. After Gregory told him, the realtor turned to his computer and scrolled through some screens.

He turned back to Gregory. "You'll get more for your money if you wouldn't mind a bit of a commute."

Gregory considered his words for a moment, but he didn't want to be sitting in rush-hour traffic on the freeway when he could be home with Annie and the baby. "No," he said definitely. "It must be close to the city."

"Let me see," mused Harper, turning again to his computer. "Yes, I've got some possibilities." He hit a few keys, and a few minutes later, Gregory was scrutinizing the printout.

"Here are a couple I'd like to take a look at." Gregory pointed to some listings. "Maybe this one, too."

"Ah, yes. This one's particularly nice. Great location, but it does need some fixing up," said the realtor. "Want to go have a look?"

"Sure, let's go."

Half an hour later, Harper, with Gregory seated opposite him, pulled his Lincoln into the driveway of a large two-story Victorian. But before Gregory even opened the passenger door, he told the realtor the house wasn't right. The neighborhood was run down and didn't look safe for children.

Harper nodded. "Don't worry," he said. "A lot of what you'll go through is simply trial and error." He consulted his list, then backed out of the driveway and headed to another house.

The second was no better, but by the time they reached the third, Gregory's hopes rose. He grinned as they strolled up the walk. Harper unlocked the front door. But when Gregory stepped inside, he knew the house was wrong. It was dark, with heavy wood paneling and too few windows. Even after the realtor flipped on the lights, the house felt empty and cold and dark. Annie would hate it, and in truth, so would he.

He shook his head. "I'm sorry," he said. "We don't even need to go upstairs. This isn't it."

"No problem," the realtor said patiently.

"It's getting late," Gregory said, disappointed that his first day of looking hadn't at least offered some options. "Why don't we continue this another day?"

They headed back to the real-estate office where Gregory had left his car earlier. Harper said he'd watch for new listings and call Gregory if he saw anything that might meet his criteria.

As Gregory stepped from the car, he reminded the realtor not to call him at home. "It's a surprise for my wife," he explained.

"I understand," Harper said, but he was busy writing on his clipboard, and Gregory wondered if he'd really heard him.

"Call me only at the college," Gregory repeated.

"Yes, yes, of course," Harper said, still writing. "Of course."

"Darling!" Gregory proclaimed, bursting through the condo door awhile later. "You'll never guess what's happened!"

Annie looked up from the sofa where she'd been reading. She seemed startled and quickly slid the book she'd been reading under the knit throw on her lap.

"I—I didn't hear your car," she said uncertainly, lifting her face for a kiss. Again he noticed the high color of her cheeks.

"I couldn't wait to tell you my news." He grinned. "So I parked on the street. If you're not too tired, I thought we'd go out to dinner to celebrate."

"Must be something pretty wonderful," she said, smiling into his eyes, the earlier tentativeness gone.

He tossed his briefcase onto a chair and sat down beside his wife. "Sweetheart, I got a call from Columbia College—out in the gold country by Everlasting."

She nodded.

"I've been asked to be a keynote speaker at the California Historical Society annual conference. They're planning to make us their guests for the weekend at a romantic old inn run by the school."

"That's wonderful, honey. When is it?"

"Exactly two weeks from this weekend. They apologized for the short notice, but the original speaker couldn't make it. I don't mind at all being second choice. It's still an honor to be asked by that organization."

Her face fell. For a moment she didn't speak. "I—I don't think I can make it, Gregory."

"You can't make it?"

"You should have asked me before committing. I've got some things to check on, but no, I don't think so."

"Honey, don't you see the importance of this? Not just to me and my career. But we need some time away. A romantic weekend together."

She studied him for a time, then sadly turned away. "I'm sorry," she whispered, then stood and went into the kitchen to start dinner.

Annie was troubled and tried to collect her thoughts as she pulled out a bowl of leftover soup from the refrigerator.

She'd met with Dana, her realtor, again that afternoon. Dana had showed her a copy of the invitations—already mailed—to the open house for the cottage. It was the same weekend as the conference. Although sellers normally didn't attend their own open houses, Annie planned to be there to scrutinize potential buyers and explain the importance of preserving the wildlife and waterfowl. She couldn't miss it, and with the hundreds, even thousands, of flyers in the mail, it was too late to change.

But she thought of Gregory, sitting in by the fireplace, alone. She let out a deep sigh. Was anything more important than sharing his joy, sharing a romantic weekend with him in, of all places, Everlasting?

Not even her gift of love was worth that. She'd have to figure out a way to be two places at once, but she had two weeks to plan it, and several people, Woodrow and Pearl among them, that she could count on for help.

Annie placed the soup bowl back in the refrigerator and headed again into the living room. She bent over the back of the sofa, kissing Gregory on the neck.

"Sweetie," she murmured, "I don't want to miss out on our weekend...on your talk. I'll work out something. I'm sorry I was too quick to say no." She kissed him again. "Can you forgive me?"

When he didn't answer, she looked down at the book he was holding in his hands, the book she'd been reading when he arrived.

It was Sheridan's journal.

8

Holding the unopened journal in his hand, Gregory looked up at Annie, an eyebrow lifted in question.

Annie hurried from where she'd been standing at the back of the sofa and settled beside him. She reached for his hand. "Honey, I'm sorry about my hesitation earlier. I'll rearrange my schedule. Nothing is more important than the two of us being together."

Instead of answering, though, Gregory glanced at the leather-bound journal then back to his wife. "What is this, Annie?"

Annie let out a deep sigh and reached for the small book, gently flipping it open to the first entry. Then, meeting Gregory's eyes, she asked quietly, "Did you look inside?"

He nodded. "Yes. I saw that it was written by Sheridan O'Brian Jade in 1862."

"My great-great-grandmother."

"I know." He paused, a frown pleating his forehead. "I couldn't help but notice how you hid it from sight earlier. I don't understand. Why didn't you want me to see it?"

Annie took a deep breath. "I received some things from my Great-aunt Sheridan's estate recently. I found a number of items that I knew would be of special interest to you." She hesitated briefly, searching for the right words. "I was saving the journal for you until everything else was ready."

"Ready?" Gregory asked, but much to Annie's relief, didn't pursue the question. He looked relieved. "This diary is wonderful, Annie." He reached for the book, then held it reverently, lightly touching the leather binding.

"We seem to have a knack for historical writings finding their way into our hands."

Leafing through a few pages, he didn't respond. "May I read some of it now—or would you rather I wait for the rest of what you've got planned?"

Annie laughed lightly. "No need to wait. In fact, I've gotten so excited about Sheridan's words that I was having a difficult time waiting to show you."

"I've got an idea," Gregory said suddenly, leaning forward. "How about dinner right here in front of the fire. Then we can read the diary together. Let's order—"

"Pizza!" Annie finished with a grin. "I like your idea, Mr. Westbrook. Just my kind of evening."

"*Our* kind of evening," he corrected. He headed for the telephone, then swung around toward her. "Shall I order thin-crust vegetarian gourmet or thick-and-spicy, loaded with everything terrible for us?"

"I think thick-and-spicy sounds divine," she said, settling into the sofa with a sigh. "Just what I've been craving."

"At least it's not pickles and ice cream," he said with a wink.

An hour later, the pizza had been consumed. Gregory tossed a few more logs on the fire, then settled onto the sofa.

Snuggling close to her husband, Annie leafed through the journal, giving him an overview of what she'd already read. She explained about Sheridan's worries about Marcus, how he'd disappeared while investigating a criminal who'd once put the young couple in grave danger. Then she showed him several of the earlier entries that had been so special to her.

Gregory turned to where Annie had left the ribbon marker. He glanced through the entry, smiling. "Listen to this one, honey," he said in wonder.

March 3, 1862

Aye, but life is confusing sometimes!

My dear Marcus rode in from Sacramento yesterday. When I saw him riding down the road on the far side of the pond, I cried out and ran all the way to meet him.

I frightened the poor birds that were floating peacefully on the water, and by the time I reached Marcus, they'd taken to the heavens, singing and crying, wings shining in the sun. 'Twas a sight, me hugging and kissing my husband as if tomorrow might never come, with the snow geese descending like a sign of God's spirit all around us.

Then Marcus stood back and considered me up and down, and I took his hand and placed it on the spot where I could feel his baby kick. His beautiful eyes filled with tears, and then he said, "I think, dear Sherrie, we may be expecting more than one. Either that, or our baby's going to be filled with more vim and vigor than Lia and Duncan put together."

"Aye! My sweet love, can you imagine such a thing as twins?" said I, though secretly I had pondered the same in my heart.

But back to the confusing times. I know my sweet husband is trying to protect me from danger, perhaps, or from worse. He is telling me so little of where he's been. It makes me feel he's crossed some bridge I have not yet reached. How much better to be crossing that bridge together, no matter what the danger!

"Her writing is so real I feel I know her," Gregory said almost reverently.

"I know," Annie agreed. "I've felt this sense of kinship with Sheridan that's hard to explain. It's as if she's not just someone who lived long ago, but rather, a living, breathing, expectant young woman like me. Her thoughts about marriage and children and God are as relevant now as when she wrote them."

They thumbed through another few pages, reading as they went, laughing softly at times at the young Irishwoman's observations about life, sometimes wiping their tears as she wrote of her disappointments and sorrows.

"Listen to this!" Gregory said a few minutes later. He grinned into Annie's eyes. "Wait till you hear this one."

April 15, 1862

God is so good to me, knowing my every thought, my hopes, my dreams and desires, the way he does! And how he has blessed me with a husband whose love never fails to delight me! I am the most blessed of women!

Sweet Marcus has planned a stay in town for just the two of us. 'Tis at the Empress Hotel, in the room with the balcony where he first declared his love.

'Tis been seven years since that night he climbed the tree outside my window. Scared to death of heights, so he told me later. But still he climbed that tall elm to stand with me in the moonlight. Oh, sweet remembrance! He spoke of his love, and so dear and sweet and powerful were his words, I will never forget my heart's pounding just hearing them.

We are going back to that special room with the balcony. Marcus tells me that if the weather holds, 'twill be another moonlit night!

"You don't suppose," Annie said, "it's the same place as the restored inn where we'll be staying?"

Gregory grinned slowly. "You know, I was considering the same thing. I'll try to find out if the City Hotel was ever called the Empress. Wouldn't that be something?" He paused in thought. "Dr. Taft did mention something about a balcony room."

They read a few more pages; then Annie stopped Gregory and lifted the journal closer.

"Oh, dear," she said with a small laugh. "I hope this doesn't happen to us."

May 1, 1862
Aye, 'tis me again, Lord, a-pounding on the Glory's gates
with another worry. We are heading tomorrow into
Everlasting for our little bit of time alone. I have not yet told
Marcus, and I think I shall not (Oh, dear heavens, 'tis me
now with another secret!), but I am having the first signs of
our baby's coming birth. Our wee one is not due until June,
and I hope above all hope that my signs are wrong. So often, I
have heard, with a first babe the signs are false.
'Tis shameful all my talk about what Marcus will not tell
me, and here I am holding this secret close to my heart. For I
fear my dear husband will confine me to bed and send for the
doctor all too soon.
My dearest hope is to go with him to our special place.
'Tis my heart's dearest longing!

Gregory laughed with Annie. "Shall we read on to see what happened? Do you remember hearing anything about your great-grandmother's arrival in a hotel room?"

"No, I don't." She paused, smiling up at him. "But why don't we wait until later to read more?" She snuggled closer.

Gregory closed the journal, circling his right arm around his wife. With his left hand, he lifted her chin gently and kissed her lips. "I love you, Annie," he murmured. "Are you thinking what I'm thinking?"

Annie kissed him back. "I'm thinking how much I love you, Gregory," she breathed.

"And…?" he asked, tracing her cheek with his fingertips.

"How God has blessed me with a husband whose love never fails to delight me!" she said, quoting Sheridan. "I am the most blessed of women."

"Not half as blessed as I am, Annie!" He smiled into her eyes and flicked off the lamp beside the sofa, leaving only the orange glow of embers still crackling in the fireplace. Then bending over her once more, he kissed her deeply.

The following afternoon, Gregory was ushered by the receptionist into Carlton Thurston's office at the Bancroft.

"Gregory, good to see you again." Dr. Thurston stood and shook his hand.

"Dr. Thurston."

"Please, call me Carlton," the older man said, nodding to a leather chair in front of the desk.

"Carlton, I got your message," Gregory said, sinking into the chair. "I'd be very interested in seeing some of the tests in action. Thanks for inviting me."

"There are a couple of things I wanted to discuss with you before we go over to the lab," Carlton began. "The first"— he pulled out a California history magazine called *The Californians* and laid it on the desk— "is this. One of my colleagues brought this to my attention."

Gregory reached for the magazine. It was open to an article he'd written a year or so earlier on California's gold rush.

"You didn't mention that you've been published. I read this.

It's well thought out. Good documentation. Expertly done. I doubt that you'll have any problem finding a publisher for a book on Jedediah Smith."

Gregory felt himself flush slightly from the praise. "Well, thank you," he managed. "It was part of a series of six."

"I pulled some of the others out of our library. And after reading through several, including your credentials in the bio, I thought about something that Ted mentioned when we talked earlier this week."

"Ted?" Gregory inquired.

"Ted Taft out at Columbia College."

"Oh, yes."

"When he called for a speaker recommendation, he also mentioned that he's got an open position in his history department. Asked if I knew of anyone who might be interested."

"What is the position?" Gregory asked to be polite. He was perfectly happy with his present job.

"History of the American West and California history. Seems they want to develop a pilot program in conjunction with the California Historical Society and with the English Department."

That was an unusual partnering. "What is the pilot program about?"

"Of course, Dr. Taft has all the details, but just to give you a quick overview," he said, smiling, "seems they want to start a small publishing house."

"That's never been done before in a community college."

Carlton nodded. "We've got some good presses through the University of New Mexico, University of Oklahoma...just to name two."

"They're some of the foremost publishers of historical books, journals, and papers," Gregory agreed.

"As I said, this is a pilot program, to see if the same thing might work at the community-college level."

"And the available position has to do with overseeing the project?"

"It would be a joint-chair position. Teaching, of course, but also running the new program in partnership with a professor in the English Department."

"It's an exciting prospect, but I'm quite happy here in San Francisco. It would be difficult to give up tenure." He paused, thinking of Annie. "And I doubt that I could talk my wife into moving."

"I understand. I just thought I'd mention it."

"I appreciate your thinking of me. It does sound exciting."

"Well, if you change your mind, why don't you give Ted a call before the conference. Let him know we talked."

"Thank you. I'll consider it."

"Now, onto a more difficult subject." Carlton leaned back in his chair.

"What's that?"

"Well, first the good news. Thus far, the tests on the letters are coming out just as we expected. By the end of the week, we'll be able to confirm that the letters were, in fact, penned by Jedediah Smith."

Gregory broke into a wide grin. "That's wonderful." Then he paused. "What's the bad news?"

Carlton drew in a deep breath. "I know you were hoping for a good price for the letters. I've talked with several collectors, with the experts at the Huntington Library in Pasadena, as well as our experts here."

"And?"

The older man shook his head. "I'm afraid their general consensus is a rather low number." He quoted a figure.

Gregory shook his head slowly. "I thought they'd be worth much more than that."

"I've been doubtful from the beginning, but I wanted to

251

pursue this for you. If you do want to move forward with the sale, the Bancroft is prepared to make you an offer as soon as the final tests are complete. The sale could be finalized by the end of next week."

Gregory's heart sank. The figure quoted wasn't nearly enough for the down payment on the kind of house he wanted for Annie and the baby. Now he'd only be able to afford something in an unsafe neighborhood or far out of the city with a long commute.

"Let me get back to you," he said finally. "I appreciate the offer, but it's much lower than I had anticipated."

"I realize that, and I wish I could offer more." Carlton shrugged, although not impolitely.

After a few minutes of discussion, the two men left the office for the lab. But as they walked across the museum's polished floor, Gregory's heart was heavy with disappointment.

～ 9 ～

One week later, Annie gingerly climbed the ladder that Woodrow had set up on the porch. Despite everyone's protest, she wanted to hang the first strand of the pine garland along the roofline above the porch. The garland was wrapped with tiny white lights, and she'd purchased enough to hang in scallops along the full length of the house and to circle the porch and stairway banisters,

Finally, she hooked the last section of her strand in place, and the group applauded. Woodrow said very firmly that he would finish the rest. The little audience breathed a collective sigh of relief as Annie stepped down from the last rung of the ladder.

The entire gang from Birds of a Feather had gathered for this the final day of work on the cottage. As Woodrow and Wyatt continued hanging the garland, Annie walked back to the front gate to watch.

Everything was ready. The final coat of paint—white with gray trim—had been applied to the house the week before, narrowly missing the season's first dusting of snow.

She gazed at the cottage, smiling at the results of their hard labor. The house radiated a genteel warmth inside and out. Lace curtains graced the windows upstairs and down, and in the wide bay parlor window, the tiny white lights on a Christmas tree sparkled and glowed. The tree had been a surprise from the group, decorated on a day when Annie had been absent.

At Dana's urging, Annie had agreed to leave all the furniture in place while the house was on the market. She had even planted tulip and daffodil bulbs for springtime color, in the event the house hadn't sold by then.

But now, as she watched Woodrow and Wyatt string the garland, then turned her gaze to the pond and the woodlands beyond, she thought how she'd soon have to lock the door for the last time and give the key to the new owner. Very likely, by the time the tulips' bright blossoms pushed through the earth, someone else would tend them, revelling in their beauty.

How she would miss coming here! Even more than the connection she felt with her family's roots, she felt a kinship with the peaceful beauty of the pond and its surrounding forested hills and mountains.

Just then a snow goose rose into the sky, and Annie caught her breath as its wings glinted silver in the sunlight. Several others followed from out of the marshes, rising and swooping and calling. Annie remembered Sheridan's words about the day Marcus had finally come home, and she pictured them running into each other's arms.

Annie turned to walk back to the porch, then stopped abruptly. Her hand flew to her stomach, and she waited, almost afraid to move, to breathe.

Then a smile of recognition slowly spread across her face, and she felt it again: the dance of butterfly wings in her womb, her baby's first flutter of life. She thought of Sheridan's words: "'Tis a secret joy, this feeling that I am somehow God's partner in this wee one's creation!"

Quick tears moistened her eyes. *I am that indeed! Thank you, Lord, for this precious miracle of life!*

That afternoon, Gregory, leaning back in his office chair, reached for the telephone after the first ring.

"Yes, this is Gregory Westbrook," he said.

"Hello, Gregory. This is Theodore Taft—out at Columbia."

"Hello, Dr. Taft. It's good to hear from you."

"Please, no need for formalities. Call me Ted. I called to let you know that your reservations are confirmed at the City Hotel for Friday and Saturday nights. Before we hang up, remind me to give you directions."

"We're looking forward to the weekend. By the way, Ted, do you know if the hotel was ever known by a different name?"

"Oh, yes. It's actually had several. Why?"

"My wife Annie's great-great-grandparents lived in Everlasting Diggins in the mid-nineteenth century. Annie recently found her ancestor's journal, describing a stay in the Empress Hotel. We wondered if it might be the same."

"Yes, it is the same place." Ted Taft sounded impressed. "Of course, it's been added onto, torn apart, rebuilt, restored, you name it, many times through the decades. But, yes, basically, it's the same place."

"That's wonderful. Annie will be so pleased," Gregory said.

"The two of you must have a knack for finding historical writings," Ted said with a chuckle.

"My wife said the same thing." Gregory paused. "You're obviously referring to the Jedediah Smith letters, but I wasn't aware you knew of them."

"Oh, yes. In fact, Dr. Thurston called me to check on our interest in buying them for our library's collection. I told him we don't have the funding for such a purchase, but we discussed the find at length. There's a lot of interest in Smith in our neck of the woods. The national headquarters for the Jedediah Smith Society isn't far from here."

Gregory grinned. "I wasn't aware there was such an organization."

"You know, if you decide not to sell your letters, would you consider publishing them?"

"Dr. Thurston told me about your new venture—the small press Columbia's starting. Is that where you'd like to see them published?"

"With a companion book on his life, of course." Ted chuckled.

"The sale is a must, Ted, although I appreciate the offer," Gregory said. "But how did you know about my book?"

"Actually, Dr. Thurston called me after the two of you spoke. He told me about your publishing plans. He said you'd be the perfect choice to head up our pilot program."

"He did?" Gregory sat forward. "What else did he say?"

"That we'd have to do some tall convincing to move you out of your present position."

Gregory laughed. "We do love San Francisco. Both Annie and I have lived here all our lives. Also, as I told Dr. Thurston, tenure isn't something I can easily give up."

There was a pause, then Ted spoke again. "Don't discount it, Gregory, until we've had a chance to talk further. I'd like to meet with you for a few minutes after your talk Friday evening, introduce you to some of the members of our department."

"I'd like that," Gregory said.

"In the meantime, we're counting on you and Annie falling in love with Columbia. The two of you need to get out into the countryside. Look at some houses. It's a great place to raise a family."

"I don't think I can move Annie out of the city." Gregory chuckled. "But it's worth a try." He also knew that without selling the letters, he couldn't buy a house in Everlasting…or anywhere. And he wondered if Columbia College would be as interested in publishing his book—or in offering him the new position—if he didn't have the letters.

They spoke again about the new publishing venture before saying good-bye. Gregory looked forward to meeting Ted in person. Dr. Taft had such a great mixture of humor, finesse, and intelligence. The kind of department chair he'd enjoy working with, he thought, then quickly pushed the thought from his mind.

That night over dinner, after Annie shared the joy of the baby's first movement, Gregory told her what he'd found out about the Empress Hotel. "Seems it's one and the same," he said with a smile.

"Wouldn't it be something if we stayed in Marcus and Sheridan's room?" Annie said in wonder as she fished for a piece of tomato in her salad.

"Ted did say, though, honey, that most of the hotel isn't original. It's been restored." He set aside his salad bowl then served them each a helping of vegetarian lasagna.

Annie grinned. "I don't care. As long as I see a big elm outside our balcony, I'll be satisfied. And stand with you in the same moonlight that Sheridan described," she added with a wink. "Talk about romantic!"

Gregory chuckled and reached for her hand. "I agree, Mrs. Westbrook. You do know I'm already planning to reenact Marcus's climbing of the elm!"

Annie laughed. "You wouldn't dare, Mr. Professor. Though I'd love to see it!" She tried a bite of Gregory's pasta dish. "Mmm, good," she murmured.

Gregory paused, studying her thoughtfully. "I'm going to try to get away from school early Friday. I'd like for us to get to Everlasting by midmorning, take a drive around the countryside. After all, I've never been there, and I'd like to get to know the area better. See some of the historical sights."

Annie nodded but didn't speak. She concentrated on buttering a piece of hot sourdough bread.

"What time can you leave, honey?" he asked as he took a bite of pasta.

She hesitated. "I have some commitments. Remember, I mentioned them last week? I've got to do some running around Friday. I'll drive up separately in the van. Meet you at the hotel in time for the banquet." She stood abruptly to refill their glasses with sparkling cider, but not before she saw the shadow that crossed Gregory's face.

⤸ 10 ⤶

Friday dawned bright and clear. An early December breeze reddened her cheeks as Annie packed the van and prepared to leave for the cottage. She planned to join Dana by ten o'clock for the first day of the open house, and by late afternoon, she'd head to the hotel for her evening with Gregory. The Birds of a Feather members planned to drive up separately to help fill in for the time she needed to spend away from the cottage.

Annie pulled out of the condo driveway, her heart light with the prospect of seeing the house again, especially on a glorious day like today. She thought about the gift she'd soon be able to give Gregory. He hadn't said much lately about the letters—or about the sabbatical—but she knew his dream remained in his heart. She couldn't wait to place the check in his hands that would make it possible.

A little more than two hours later, she turned off Highway 49 and headed down the rutted road, around the pond, then parked the van by the cottage.

She saw Dana lift the lace curtain, peer through the window, then hurry to the porch to greet her. "Hurry out of the chill, dear," the realtor called as Annie closed the van's door. "I've got some good news."

Annie hurried up the front steps and into the entry, sliding off her coat and hooking it on the antique hall tree. "We've got some prospects?"

"We've had a number of calls about the property at the office. Several who sound very interested."

"That's wonderful," Annie said. Somehow she couldn't dredge up much enthusiasm. "No developers, I hope."

"There was one. I tried to discourage him. He may stop by later. Didn't sound like the type to take no for an answer." Dana paused, then went on in a reassuring tone. "The rest were families looking for a place that can accommodate lots of children." Then she smiled. "One family has already driven by twice. The Andersens. They've got four children and another on the way. They're crazy about the house. The husband has already consulted an architect about adding on some bedrooms. Now, that's interested, in my book," she added triumphantly.

"Add on?" Annie croaked. "They're going to change the house?"

"And build a garage out front."

"In front? Oh, no. That'll ruin the look of it." Annie shook her head.

Dana looked sympathetic. "I know how you must feel, Annie, especially after all you've done to the place. But you can't control what people do to the property once you sign the final·papers." She paused. "But you'll be happy to know they did say they're animal lovers. They raise German shepherds."

"Dogs?" Annie whispered raggedly, trying not to picture them chasing her beloved snow geese. "Oh, no."

Dana moved over to the bay window, reached around the Christmas tree, and peered out at the lane leading to the house. "Oh, here comes someone now. And there are two cars behind

260

the first," she declared. "Oh, dear, and I don't even have the cinnamon potpourri on yet."

"I'll start it," Annie said, suddenly glad to hide in the kitchen. "You meet them, and I'll fill in any information they need, if necessary."

Dana nodded as she quickly stooped to plug in the Christmas-tree lights. Then she bustled to the front door.

Minutes later, Annie heard the voices of several adults as they started a tour of the house, followed by the sounds of some giggling children. She stepped into the entry to see two middle-aged couples and a young family. She watched as Dana gave them a tour. On their way out, Annie was introduced and given an opportunity to tell a little bit about the property's history.

As she spoke, she noticed that no one seemed the slightest bit interested. She ended her little talk with a word about the wildlife refuge, especially the importance of the pond as an integral part of the Pacific flyway.

"Any trout in that pond?" a middle-aged man asked. He winked at his wife. "Just think, honey, we could have fresh fish for dinner every night." Annie tried not to show her irritation.

The first group finally left, and she heaved a sigh of relief. An hour later, the Birds of a Feather members drove up in Pearl's lavender '67 Buick. They piled out of the car and hurried into the house, greeting Annie as if they were as much a part of the sale as she. Gratefully, she hugged them all.

A hour after that, a minivan drove into sight. A man and a woman and four children poured out, standing and smiling at the house as if they'd seen it before. A frisky shepherd pup raced around the children, barking and wagging its tail.

"Ah, these must be the Andersens," Dana said, standing to greet them. She adjusted her pixie hair in the hall mirror and opened the door. They spent two hours touring and inspecting the house. Then, as the children played in the yard with the dog, the couple measured each room carefully and discussed where they could add on a new bedroom wing.

Pearl exchanged a glance with Woodrow, and the others were uncharacteristically subdued as they listened.

"They're gonna take it," Pearl said in a disappointed whisper. "I think you've found your buyer."

As his family headed back to the minivan, Mr. Andersen made an appointment to return the next morning at nine o'clock with the architect. Ignoring Pearl's frown, Annie agreed, figuring the offer would be presented at that time.

Just past four o'clock, after she and Dana locked the cottage, Annie climbed into the van for her drive into town to meet Gregory. The Birds of a Feather members piled into Pearl's big Buick, and Annie gave them a wave as she turned down the long rutted road to the main highway.

When she reached a small crest beyond the pond, she glanced back. Tiny white lights, laced among the pine garlands, outlined the house, now basking in the late afternoon glow of the slanting sunlight. Annie smiled. It was Christmas-card perfect. She let out a deep sigh, hoping the new owners would cherish it as much as she did.

At precisely four-thirty, Gregory, following directions a realtor had given him over the phone, turned onto the rutted road leading to Jade Pond. He bounced along until he saw the pond, first noticing the abundance of birds among the willows and marshes, then turned to gaze at the two-story Queen Anne cottage a short distance away.

He drove closer, then stopped the car and got out, stepped up the front stairs and knocked. Frowning, he pulled the ad from his pocket and reread it.

CHERISHED HOME BUILT IN 1860, RECENTLY RESTORED. OWNED BY SAME FAMILY FOR FIVE GENERATIONS. OPEN HOUSE FRIDAY, SATURDAY, AND SUNDAY. PROPERTY INCLUDES BIRD AND WILDLIFE SANCTUARY FOR NATURE LOVERS.

The open house times hadn't been listed, and Gregory had hoped to find someone home to show him the house. But, obviously, he was too late.

He walked around the property, checking the condition of the house, then moving back to the porch, he stood looking out to the pond and woodlands beyond.

Snow geese soared on the breeze, swooped, then landed again on the water, and Gregory thought about Sheridan Jade's description of the pond on her property, the birds that reminded her of God's spirit.

Annie would love this place! If it reminded him of Sheridan and Marcus's home, he could only imagine how Annie would feel about it.

He stuck his hands in his pocket and strolled out to the pond, then turned and looked again at the house. He pictured the yard filled with children, Annie strolling among her beloved birds and wildlife.

The Christmas lights glowed in the settling dusk, and the house seemed to come to life. He walked slowly back to the car, thinking how best to approach Annie with a move from San Francisco to this remote place. By the time he reached his car, he'd decided.

Before he mentioned anything about the job offer or his thoughts about relocating, he would bring Annie to this place. Once she'd seen it, then perhaps he could talk her into moving.

~~~~~

Just as the setting sun was slanting across the town of Everlasting, Annie pulled the Birds of a Feather van into the parking lot behind the City Hotel. She looked around for Gregory's car but didn't see it.

Thinking he might have been detained in San Francisco, she grabbed her overnight case and garment bag and headed around to the front of the hotel to register for them both.

Stepping to the front desk, she asked about their room.

"Oh, your husband's already arrived, Mrs. Westbrook," the clerk said, smiling her welcome. "But I believe he said he was going to do some sightseeing."

"Sightseeing?"

The clerk chuckled. "You know, with this being a state park, we have historical gold-rush sights all over the countryside."

A few minutes later, Annie crossed the parlor and climbed the stairs. With each step, she admired the highly polished burled antiques, the rich fabrics of the settees and chairs, the soft glow of the delicate lamps.

She opened the door to their room and stopped in astonishment. It was as if she'd stepped back in time.

Quickly she laid down her luggage and strode to the French doors. She threw them open and hurried onto the balcony. It faced Everlasting's brick-cobbled main street and all its tiny shops, perfectly preserved in their gold-rush days state.

Annie drew in a deep breath, leaning against the ornate iron rail. Feeling the need for a bit of rest, she settled into one of the scrolled iron chairs on the balcony. A light breeze ruffled the elm leaves. A few scrub jays chattered among its branches, and she smiled, feeling comfortable, feeling peacefully at home.

Annie closed her eyes. A short time later, a strange noise awoke her from her doze.

She heard the noise, a soft whistle, again, and peered over the balcony.

Gregory grinned up at her, just as Marcus had gazed up at Sheridan nearly a century and a half ago.

Without a word, he grinned and headed for one of the massive elms lining the street in front of the inn.

Annie caught her hand to her mouth to stifle a giggle. Her husband—the dignified, scholarly professor—was about to carry out his threat. "Surely you're not going to climb that," she whispered down to him.

But Gregory, in jeans and tennis shoes, had already swung one leg over the bottom branch and was hoisting himself up to another. He finally reached a large limb close to where Annie stood waiting.

His eyes twinkled. She reached for his hand as he jumped from the tree onto the balcony.

Laughing softly, he pulled her into his arms.

As Annie snuggled close, she felt the thud of his heart and smiled into his eyes. This might not be the same balcony that Marcus climbed to declare his love to Sheridan, but Annie didn't care.

All that mattered was looking into her husband's gaze, reveling in the love she saw there, and absorbing the words he murmured in her ear.

"Mrs. Westbrook," he breathed. "I believe I've come home."

~ *11* ~

Annie sat at an antique pine dressing table, applying a touch of lipstick and mascara as she readied for their evening at the Historical Society dinner.

Already dressed in his suit pants and shirt, Gregory lounged against the massive walnut headboard of the bed, leafing through Sheridan's journal.

"Listen to this, honey," he said with a smile. "There's one here written by Marcus."

Annie turned to face her husband. "Marcus?"

"Yes—the night the babies arrived."

"You said babies...as in more than one?"

He laughed again, his eyes still moving over the page. "Yes. Sheridan had twins."

"She didn't have them here, did she? In the last entry she was hoping she wouldn't go into labor before they had their romantic weekend."

"Well, they must not have made it, because he writes as if they're at their home. Listen to this."

May 2, 1862

   I knew there would be great and abiding joy in father-hood. And that was when I expected one child, not two. Now

I have discovered that in this, as in so many ways, God blesses us more abundantly than we can imagine.

At 2:07 this morning, Sheridan woke me and said that her time had come. I rode into town for the doctor, leaving Evangelia with Sheridan during the hour I was away.

When I returned with Doc, Lia and Duncan were frantic with worry. Our first child was about to enter the world, and my Sheridan, with her usual brave spirit, was trying her best not to frighten the children, though as Doc confirmed later, the babe was "crowning."

I had barely begun pacing the parlor when I looked up to see Doc coming to tell me the news. I was the proud father of twins, he said, a girl and a boy. I nearly burst my buttons with pride, and had it not been still the dark of night, I believe I would have ridden through the streets of Everlasting, shouting the very news of it!

We have named them Mary Elizabeth Sheridan and Shamus Mark O'Brian. Though because they are such tiny mites, we plan to call them Mary Beth and Mark.

"That's beautiful," Annie said with a sigh. "Just being in Everlasting makes me feel so close to them."

"I know," said Gregory, watching her intently. Then he smiled. "Well, we know now that twins run in the family. Has your doctor said anything to you about the possibility?"

Annie laughed. "I asked, but he assured me that there's no sign of a multiple birth." After running a brush through her hair once more, Annie stood and reached for her coat.

Gregory let out a low whistle. "Wow! You look absolutely radiant tonight, Mrs. Westbrook." His eyes took in her ankle-length black velvet dress. "Radiant, sophisticated, and beautiful. I'm so proud you're here with me." He held her coat so that she could slip her arms into it.

"I'm glad I'm here," Annie said simply, thinking how close she came to declining the invitation.

Gregory's talk to the Historical Society went better than he could have anticipated. He told the group about the Jedediah Smith letters and went into detail about the new information they provided about Smith's travels in the West. Afterward, several of the Society members gathered around him, asking more questions about the authenticity testing, the Bancroft, and his publishing plans.

Annie, still seated at the head table, was busy talking to Ted Taft's wife, Diane. And Ted, after congratulating Gregory on a job well done, pulled him aside to meet the other members of his department.

"Have you thought any more about the position?" Ted asked when the others had stepped away.

Gregory frowned. "I can't throw my hat in the ring until I convince my wife there's life outside San Francisco."

Ted grinned. "It's said that all it takes is a weekend in Everlasting to make it, well, everlasting."

"Sounds like the Chamber of Commerce." Gregory laughed.

"You're right." Then Ted's smiled faded. "Seriously, though, I can't hold this position, even though I'd like to see you at the top of our list of applicants, Gregory. It's already generated a lot of interest. I've been besieged with calls since the news has gotten out."

"I understand."

"If you want to be considered, I really need to know right away."

The two men shook hands, and lost in thought, Gregory headed across the room to collect Annie.

～ ～ ～ ～ ～

The following morning, Annie and Gregory sat on the balcony with a tray of coffee and fresh-baked blueberry muffins, compliments of the inn.

"A perfect day to explore the countryside," Gregory said, buttering a muffin.

Annie took a sip of coffee. "I've got an appointment at nine, but other than that, my day belongs to you."

"An appointment, Annie?" He frowned. "On a Saturday?"

Annie swallowed hard and nodded. Then she touched his jaw affectionately. "I'm sorry, honey. I'll be able to explain it all later. I wish I could tell you now, but it would spoil my surprise."

His gaze lingered on her face. "There are too many secrets between us, Annie. I've kept some things from you during the past few weeks. And I don't want to let them go any longer. We've got to have some serious discussions."

She frowned, knowing she needed to leave soon for her appointment with the Andersens. "When I get back, we'll tell each other everything. I promise. The day ahead will be only for us."

Annie thought of her gift of love. She'd planned to wait until the check was in her hand, but escrow might take weeks. *No, she decided, I'll tell him today. Just as soon as the papers are signed.*

Gregory nodded slowly. "All right. But Annie—" He caught her hand as she stood, studying her face thoughtfully for a moment. But he didn't finish what he'd planned to say.

Annie stooped and kissed him lightly on the lips. "I promise," she said softly, then stepped into the room to dress for her appointment with the Andersens.

The Andersens, architect in tow, arrived on time, just after Annie unlocked the cottage door. Dana drove in just behind them and showed them through the house once more as Annie waited at the large dining table.

The architect discussed the remodeling plans, offering several options. He told the Andersens he could draw up the blueprints and have them ready by the time escrow closed. Then he departed, and the Andersens and Dana moved to the living room to talk.

An hour passed, and Annie paced from the dining room to the kitchen, waiting for the offer she knew was being discussed.

Finally, Mr. Andersen stepped into the dining room, Dana following behind. "My wife and I have discussed the offer," he said.

"Please, sit down," Annie said with a smile.

He settled into one of the high-backed chairs, his wife on one side, Dana on the other. The realtor pulled out the documents and laid them on the table. "Mr. and Mrs. Andersen have already spoken to me about their offer. As you know, I'll be representing both parties."

Annie nodded.

"And I'd like to go through the details, if you'd like."

"All right," Annie said, taking a deep breath. Dana handed a copy of the document to her, then, line by line, began to explain the terms.

Several minutes later, Annie stared at the bottom line that demanded her signature. The offer was very close to her asking price, and there was no excuse to refuse it.

But she couldn't bring herself to lift her pen to the paper. "Can you give me a minute?" she said, swallowing hard.

"Of course," Dana said, and the Andersens agreed. "You take all the time you need, dear."

Annie excused herself and walked outside to the porch. Blinking back her tears, she stared out at Jade Pond, listening to the calls of the snow geese, the cormorants, the buffleheaded ducks.

She wanted to walk once more by the pond, knowing it belonged to her for just these few last minutes. So she moved down the stairs, let herself through the picket gate, and headed down the road to the pond.

She'd nearly reached the marshes when she heard the distant sound of a car approaching. It didn't surprise her, for after all, the open house was still being advertised. Her back to the road, Annie drew in several shaky breaths and concentrated only on the wild, tranquil beauty of the place.

She'd nearly forgotten about the vehicle until she heard it stop, followed several seconds later by the slam of a door.

She turned, shielding her eyes from the sun.

"Annie?" Gregory called, approaching her.

"Gregory! What are you doing here?"

Suddenly, he was standing in front of her, gazing into her face. "You're crying, Annie," he said softly.

"Yes," she managed. "And I shouldn't be."

He moved his gaze to the cottage, then back to Annie. "This belongs to you, doesn't it?"

Annie caught her breath. "How did you know?"

Gregory let out a deep sigh. "It's a bit of a long story, one I wanted to tell you this morning. I've been out looking for property here."

"You have?"

He nodded. "I came across this yesterday." He showed her the ad. "I drove out here, saw the pond, even thought about how it fit Sheridan's description. But it wasn't until this morning, when you left for your appointment, that I began to wonder if this might be part of your inheritance." He paused.

"When I found the journal, you said there were other items...."
He shook his head slowly. "I began to put two and two together."

She frowned, nibbling on her bottom lip.

"I asked one of the docents in Everlasting about the original Jade property. He sent me out here—then I knew for sure." He touched her face tenderly. "What I don't understand, Annie, is why you didn't want to tell me about it."

Annie let out a deep breath. "I'd planned it all so carefully. Wanted it to be a surprise, Gregory. It was to be for you...my gift of love."

"The house?"

"The proceeds from the house."

"I don't understand."

"I'm selling it, Gregory. The buyers are waiting for me inside the house right now." She felt fresh tears rush to her eyes. "It's my gift to you so that you can take your sabbatical, write your book. We can travel together over Jedediah's old trails."

He caught both her hands urgently. "Have you signed anything yet, Annie?"

She tilted her head. "No."

"Do you love this place as much as I do?"

Her tears were now spilling down her cheeks, and she couldn't get the words out, so she merely nodded.

"Then don't sell it, Annie!"

"But your letters, the book..." she began, then started again. "We can't live here—" Gregory interrupted her with a kiss.

"I've put the letters up for sale to buy you and the baby a house. Only I couldn't find anything decent in San Francisco. Then Dr. Taft offered me a position in his department, but I thought you wouldn't want to move...." Finally, Gregory stopped and began to chuckle. Then he threw his head back and laughed out loud.

Startled, the snow geese squawked and beat their wings into

the air, taking off and circling the pond. The rest of the birds and ducks followed. Soon the air was filled with their calls and the glint of their wings in the sunlight.

"Do you realize what we almost accomplished?" Gregory asked, pulling Annie into his arms.

She smiled up at him and nodded. "I do," she said softly. "We very nearly gave each other gifts of great sacrifice." She paused, chuckling softly and shaking her head in wonder. "But unfortunately, each of our gifts would have canceled out the other."

"But the love, Annie," he added, "was our true gift. Sacrificial love." And he kissed her again, deeply.

With Gregory's arm still circling her, they turned to gaze at the cottage. Annie pictured it filled with generations of love and laughter and hope. Now her family—hers and Gregory's—would fill it to overflowing with the same, a legacy for the precious life she carried.

After a moment, she grinned up at her husband. "Do you want to tell the Andersens, or shall I?"

He chuckled as they began to walk toward their new home. "Let's do it together."

Epilogue

Annie stood on the master-bedroom balcony, looking out at the pond with its abundance of spring birds who had come to feed in the rich, cattailed marshes.

Near the woodlands, the wild lilacs bloomed in a frothy profusion of lavender and white. Closer to the cottage, in the small plot of vegetables and herbs that Gregory had recently planted, sprouts of the rosemary, sweet basil, thyme, squash, and tomato plants had pushed through the earth and begun to lift their tender green blades heavenward. Someday, Annie thought wryly, they would be ready for the gourmet dinners that she and Gregory no longer had time to prepare.

She breathed in the sweet perfume of the spring afternoon, taking joy in a sky so blue it seemed purple, and in the breeze pushing great piles of lazy clouds above the distant Sierra Nevadas.

Pearl's big Buick would soon rattle down the rutted road, winding along the edge of the pond toward the cottage. Annie smiled at the thought of seeing her friends again. Woodrow had arranged for the rental of night-vision binoculars, and the group planned a late night trek through the woodlands to count spotted owls. That is, everyone in the group except Annie.

Annie returned to the bedroom and settled into the high-backed chair in front of the walnut secretary Gregory had found in the attic. After rolling up the top, she reached into one of the small drawers for her journal. She smoothed back the cover, opened the small leather book to the first page, picked up her pen, and began to write.

When I think of the legacy bequeathed me, it's not the beautiful countryside or Sheridan and Marcus's house that I consider. No, it's something far more precious than those possessions, wonderful as they are: it's their legacy of love that holds the greatest value of all.

Today, I begin a record for my children. I want my family to know about the chain of love that's been passed down through the generations.

In 1862, Sheridan recorded her grandma'am's words about God's strong arm of grace keeping us steady even when times are puzzling or obscure. She said that he scoops us up to carry close to his heart. And I picture us all—those who lived before us in this very house, those who live here now— resting in his arms, close to his heart.

In Deuteronomy 33:12, God says, "Let the beloved of the Lord rest secure in him, for he shields him all day long, and the one the Lord loves rests between his shoulders."

As Sheridan would say, "Aye, but I am the most blessed of women!" Now that I'm a mother…when I hold a wee babe near my heart…I understand that kind of deep and everlasting love. And mine is only a portion of that deep and abiding love of our heavenly Father's.

A tiny cry suddenly filled the silence of the room. Annie put down her journal and pen and moved to the cradle near the bed. She smiled into a set of eyes the color of heaven, then bending low, scooped two-week-old Mary Beth into her arms.

A few minutes later, her husband tiptoed into the room. Nestled over one shoulder was another tiny blanketed figure.

Grinning in triumph, Gregory breathed, "Shhh," as he moved close to Annie. "I finally got this little guy to sleep," he said. "Only took an hour of rocking this time."

"Shamus takes after his daddy," Annie whispered as she settled into a nearby rocker with Mary Beth, who'd stopped her fussing. "He's too curious about life to waste it sleeping."

Still holding Shamus Mark in his arms, Gregory settled onto the edge of the four-poster bed across from Annie. He reached over and touched Mary Beth's hand. Her tiny fingers curled around his much larger one.

Gregory's gaze met Annie's, and he smiled. She blinked back the sudden mist in her eyes. "We are so blessed," she whispered.

Through the open French doors drifted the calls and cries of the last of the snow geese yet to travel north on the Pacific flyway. And a few minutes later, when they were startled by the rumbling, rattling old Birds of a Feather Buick, the geese took to the air.

Annie and Gregory clasped their hands together and watched as the snow geese soared once again, wings glinting in the late afternoon sun.

Read the love story of Sheridan O'Brian and Marcus Jade in Amanda MacLean's *Everlasting*.

PALISADES...PURE ROMANCE

∼ PALISADES ∼

Reunion, Karen Ball

Refuge, Lisa Tawn Bergren

Torchlight, Lisa Tawn Bergren

Treasure, Lisa Tawn Bergren

Chosen, Lisa Tawn Bergren

Firestorm, Lisa Tawn Bergren

Wise Man's House, Melody Carlson

Arabian Winds, Linda Chaikin (Premier)

Cherish, Constance Colson

Chase the Dream, Constance Colson (Premier)

Angel Valley, Peggy Darty

Sundance, Peggy Darty

Love Song, Sharon Gillenwater

Antiques, Sharon Gillenwater

Song of the Highlands, Sharon Gillenwater (Premier)

Secrets, Robin Jones Gunn

Whispers, Robin Jones Gunn

Echoes, Robin Jones Gunn

Sunsets, Robin Jones Gunn

Coming Home, Barbara Jean Hicks

Snow Swan, Barbara Jean Hicks (April, 1997)

Irish Eyes, Annie Jones (April, 1997)

Glory, Marilyn Kok

Sierra, Shari MacDonald

Forget-Me-Not, Shari MacDonald

Diamonds, Shari MacDonald

Westward, Amanda MacLean

Stonehaven, Amanda MacLean

Everlasting, Amanda MacLean

Promise Me the Dawn, Amanda MacLean (Premier)
Kingdom Come, Amanda MacLean
Betrayed, Lorena McCourtney
Escape, Lorena McCourtney
Voyage, Elaine Schulte

A Christmas Joy, Darty, Gillenwater, MacLean
Mistletoe, Ball, Hicks, McCourtney
A Mother's Love, Bergren, Colson, MacLean

THE PALISADES LINE

*Ask for them at your local bookstore. If the title you seek is not in stock,
the store may order you a copy using the ISBN listed.*

Wise Man's House, Melody Carlson (March, 1997)
ISBN 1-57673-070-0
Kestra McKenzie, a young widow trying to make a new life for herself, thinks she
has found the solidity she longs for when she purchases her childhood dream
house—a stone mansion on the Oregon Coast. Just as renovations begin, a mysterious stranger moves into her caretaker's cottage—and into her heart.

Sunsets, Robin Jones Gunn
ISBN 1-57673-103-0
Alissa Benson loves her job as a travel agent. But when the agency has computer
problems, they call in expert Brad Phillips. Alissa can't wait for Brad to fix the
computers and leave—he's too blunt for her comfort. So she's more than a little
upset when she moves into a duplex and finds out he's her neighbor!

Snow Swan, Barbara Jean Hicks (April, 1997)
ISBN 1-57673-107-3
Life hasn't been easy for Toni Ferrier. As an unwed mother and a recovering alco-
holic, she doesn't feel worthy of anyone's love. Then she meets Clark
McConaughey, who helps her launch her business aboard the sternwheeler Snow
Swan. Sparks fly between them, but if Clark finds out the truth about Toni's past,
will he still love her?

Irish Eyes, Annie Jones (April, 1997)
ISBN 1-57673-108-1
When Julia Reed finds a young boy, who claims to be a leprechaun, camped out
under a billboard, she gets drawn into a century-old crime involving a real pot of
gold. Interpol agent Cameron O'Dea is trying to solve the crime. In the process,
he takes over the homeless shelter that Julia runs, camps out in her neighbor's RV,
and generally turns her life upside down!

Kingdom Come, Amanda MacLean
ISBN 1-57673-120-0
In 1902, feisty Ivy Rose Clayborne, M.D., returns to her hometown of Kingdom
Come to fight the coal mining company that is ravaging the land. She meets an
unexpected ally, a man who claims to be a drifter but in reality is Harrison
MacKenzie, grandson of the coal mining baron. Together they face the aftermath
of betrayal, the fight for justice…and the price of love.

A Mother's Love, Bergren, Colson, MacLean
ISBN 1-57673-106
Three popular Palisades authors bring you heartwarming stories about the joys and challenges of romance in the midst of motherhood.

By Lisa Bergren: A widower and his young daughter go to Southern California for vacation, and return with much more than they expected.

By Constance Colson: Cassie Jenson wants her old sweetheart to stay in her memories. But when he moves back to town, they find out that they could never forget each other.

By Amanda MacLean: A couple is expecting their first baby, and they hardly have enough time for each other. With the help of an old journal and a last-minute getaway, they work to rekindle their love.

❧

Also look for our new line:

PALISADES PREMIER
More Story. More Romance.

Arabian Winds, Linda Chaikin
ISBN 1-57673-3-105-7
In the first book of the Lions of the Desert trilogy, World War I is breaking upon the deserts of Arabia in 1917. Young nurse Allison Wescott arrives in British Cairo, torn between her love for a handsome officer and the doctor she has come to marry.

Song of the Highlands, Sharon Gillenwater
ISBN 1-57673-946-4
During the Napoleonic Wars, Kiernan is a piper, but he comes back to find out he's inherited a title. At his run-down estate, he meets the beautiful Mariah. During a trip to London, they face a kidnapping and an encounter with a French spy...and discover their love for each other.

Watch for more books in Sharon Gillenwater's Scottish series!